Crime Scene Singapore

Crime Scene: Singapore

The best of Singapore crime fiction

Richard Lord (Editor)

monsoon

monsoonbooks

First published in 2010
by Monsoon Books Pte Ltd
52 Telok Blangah Road
#03–05 Telok Blangah House
Singapore 098829
www.monsoonbooks.com.sg

ISBN: 978-981-08-5437-9

National Library Board, Singapore Cataloguing-in-Publication Data
Crime scene : Singapore : the best of Singapore crime fiction / Richard
Lord, editor. – Singapore : Monsoon Books, 2010.
p. cm.
ISBN-13 : 978-981-08-5437-9 (pbk.)

1. Crime – Singapore – Fiction. 2. Short stories, Singaporean (English)
I. Lord, Richard A. (Richard Alan)

PR9570.S52
S823 -- dc22   OCN655008112

Printed in Singapore

14 13 12 11 10   1 2 3 4 5

Contents

Introduction

There's an old German saying which, roughly translated, reminds us that 'there where you have a lot of light, you'll also find a lot of shadows'. That could well be the motto for this book, as the intrepid authors in this collection have chosen to poke through all the light in order to better probe the various shadows in Singapore life.

As the local law enforcement people here like to remind us, low crime does not mean no crime. Which is actually pretty good news for those of us putting this anthology together. Presented with the challenges of producing good crime fiction set in a society with little crime, nearly a dozen talented writers have released the full force of their imaginative powers to come up with absorbing narratives.

These authors persuasively show us that low crime may also mean interesting crime. Concealed there in the shadows of 'squeaky-clean Singapore' is the stuff of solid crime fiction and our writers make the most of it.

One can even argue that the fact that there isn't much crime in Singapore makes the crime that does occur that much more interesting and more tempting to deal with in fiction. Crime that occurs in a nation where the law is largely respected and adhered to tends to rock our sense of order more; it somehow seems a greater transgression and thus a more fertile field for writers of fiction.

Whatever the motive, the twelve stories making up this volume give us a broad view of the crime scene in the Lion City.

The collection opens with an engaging piece by famed author Stephen Leather. In *Inspector Zhang Gets his Wish*, Leather serves up a self-reflective piece of fiction that takes us step by step through the solution of a crime with a course in writing crime fiction thrown in as a bonus. And it's done humorously and deftly, showing us again why Leather is a master of the genre.

Another piece that plays with the conventions of the crime fiction genre is *A Sticky Situation*, an affectionate bit of persiflage that makes fun of outsider's attitudes about Singapore and its restrictions by probing a uniquely Singaporean type of crime.

Actually, many of the stories here feature crimes that are, if not uniquely Singaporean, at least typically Singaporean. For instance, Pranav S. Joshi's *The Corporate Wolf* shows us how business practices which strive to cut corners (a not uncommon practice here) can actually open a back door to some serious crime.

Lee Ee Leen's *Lead Balloon* is a convincing and alarming consideration of the ways in which school pressures can lead to crime. *Decree Absolute* (by the renowned local novelist Dawn Farnham) casts an ironic eye at a standard Singapore marriage with clearly recognisable strains that ends with a twisted, and ingenious, version of divorce, Singapore style.

A few of the stories in this volume even add a bit of social criticism into their well-knit plots. *The House on Tomb Lane*, for instance, looks at the abuse of maids by their employers, a not infrequent crime sometimes overlooked because its victims stay silent and unseen.

The Madman of Geylang also casts a critical eye at the situation of a foreign maid, in this case one who seeks to marry a poor Singaporean. The problems this pair encounter result in a cascade of sad consequences that are as upsetting as they are believable.

The First Time, by local radio personality Carolyn Camoens, is a treatment of another crime that is sadly not too uncommon, but is overlooked because its victims often seize silence as a shield. The skill and tact employed by Camoens in her handling of this story only makes its effect that much more chilling.

Another local personality, writer-educator-impresario Chris Mooney-Singh, gives us an engrossing piece which skilfully weaves together literary allusions from the past with conjecture on how social networking on the Internet might serve as an accomplice to a crime.

This volume's shortest piece, *Nostalgia*, is a poetic slice of speculative fiction by Ng Yi-Sheng, whose earlier book *Last Boy* won the coveted Singapore Literature Prize in 2008. The most atypical story in this collection, it is a haunting piece with strange echoes of things that have never happened but may be lurking just around the corner.

The longest story in the collection, *The Lost History of Shadows*, begins in 1930's Singapore and then traces how one horrific crime plays into a handful of follow-up crimes and then shows us how the crimes of the fathers are visited upon the sons and the grandsons. It also questions some of our comfortable notions of innocence and culpability.

As the collection opens with a story of a Singapore police investigator, it closes with the tale of a private investigator. In *Unnatural Causes*, a top private detective gets a reprieve from the near lethal tedium of his standard assignments when a beautiful woman strides into his office and offers him a most unusual, but very dangerous commission.

Crime fiction is in some ways our most existential form of fiction. Not only does it often (though not always) deal with life and death matters, but it brings us to question our sense of the world we live in and our own place in that world. When a crime shakes the comfortable reality we like to feel is so fixed, we start considering other prospects, be they good or bad. The writers in this anthology appreciate this fact and turn it to the advantage of their stories. In so doing, they assure us that even though Singapore may boast low crime rates, it can also now boast its production of strong crime fiction.

Richard Lord
Singapore

Inspector Zhang
Gets His Wish

Stephen Leather

Inspector Zhang walked out of the elevator and looked left and right. 'Which way, Sergeant?' he asked. He took out his handkerchief and polished his thick-lensed spectacles which had clouded over when he had walked from the cloying Singapore night into the blistering air-conditioning of the hotel.

Sergeant Lee was in her mid-twenties, with her hair tied up in a bun that made her look older than her twenty-four years. She had only been working with Inspector Zhang for two months and was still anxious to please. She frowned at her notebook, then looked at the two signs on the wall facing them. 'Room 634,' she said, and pointed to the left. 'This way, Sir.'

Inspector Zhang put his spectacles back on and walked slowly down the corridor. He was wearing his second-best grey suit and pale yellow silk tie with light blue squares on it that his wife had given him the previous Christmas, and his well-polished shoes glistened under the hallway nights. He had been at home when he had received the call and had dressed quickly, wanting to be first on the scene. It wasn't every day that a detective got to deal with a

17

murder case in low-crime Singapore.

They reached room 634 and Inspector Zhang knocked on the door. It was opened by a square-shouldered blonde woman who glared at him as if he was about to try to sell her life insurance. Inspector Zhang flashed his warrant card. 'I am Inspector Zhang of the Singapore Police Force,' he said. 'I am with the CID at New Bridge Road.' He nodded at his companion. 'This is Detective Sergeant Lee.'

The Sergeant took out her warrant card and showed it to the woman who nodded and opened the door wider. 'Please come in; we're trying not to alarm our guests,' she said.

Inspector Zhang and Sergeant Lee slipped into the room and the woman closed the door. There were four other people in the room—a tall Westerner and a stocky Indian wearing a black suit, a pretty young Chinese girl also in a black suit and a white-jacketed waiter. The waiter was standing next to a trolley covered with a white cloth.

The woman who had opened the door offered her hand to the Inspector. 'I am Geraldine Berghuis,' she said, 'I am the manager.' She was in her thirties with eyebrows plucked so finely that they were just thin lines above her piercing blue eyes. She was wearing an elegant green suit that looked as if it had been made to measure and there was a string of large pearls around her neck. She had several diamond rings on her fingers, but her wedding finger was bare. Inspector Zhang shook her hand. Miss Berghuis gestured at a tall, bald man in an expensive suit. 'This is Mr Christopher Mercier, our head of security.' Mr Mercier did not offer his hand, but nodded curtly.

The manager waved her hand at the Indian man and the Chinese woman. 'Mr Ramanan and Miss Xue were on the desk tonight,' she said. 'They are both assistant managers.'

They both nodded at Inspector Zhang and smiled nervously. Ramanan was in his early forties and the girl appeared to be half his age. They both wore silver name badges and had matching neatly-folded handkerchiefs in their top pockets. Inspector Zhang nodded back and then looked at the waiter. 'And you are?' Inspector Zhang asked.

'Mr CK Chau,' answered Miss Berghuis. 'He delivered Mr Wilkinson's room service order and discovered the body.' The waiter nodded in agreement.

Inspector Zhang looked around the room. 'I see no body,' he said.

Miss Berghuis pointed at a side door. 'Through there,' she said. 'This is one of our suites; we have a sitting room and a separate bedroom.'

'Please be so good as to show me the deceased,' said Inspector Zhang.

The manager took the two detectives through to a large bedroom. The curtains were drawn and the lights were on. Lying on the king-size bed with his feet hanging over the edge was a naked man. It was a Westerner, Inspector Zhang realised immediately, a big man with a mountainous stomach and a pool of blood that had soaked into the sheet around his head.

'Peter Wilkinson,' said Miss Berghuis. 'He is an American and one of our VIP guests. He stays at our hotel once a month. He owns a company which distributes plastic products in the United States and stays in Singapore en route to his factories in China.'

Inspector Zhang leant over the bed and peered at the body, nodding thoughtfully. He could see a puncture wound just under the chin and the chest was covered with blood. 'One wound,' he said. 'It appears to have ruptured a vein but not the carotid artery, or there would have been much more blood spurting.' He looked across at the Sergeant. 'Carotid blood spray is very distinctive,' he said. 'I think in this case, we have arterial bleeding. He would have taken a minute or so to bleed to death, whereas if the artery had been severed, death would have been almost instantaneous.'

The Sergeant nodded and scribbled in her notebook.

'Note the blood over the chest,' continued the Inspector. 'That could have only happened if he was upright so we can therefore deduce that he was standing up when he was stabbed and that he then fell or was pushed back onto the bed.' He walked around to look at the bedside table. On it was a wallet and a gold Rolex watch. Inspector Zhang took a ballpoint pen from his inside pocket and used it to flip open the wallet. Inside was a thick wad of notes and half a dozen credit cards, all gold or platinum. 'I think we can safely rule out robbery as a motive,' he said.

Sergeant Lee scribbled in her notebook.

Inspector Zhang walked back into the sitting room. Miss Berghuis and Sergeant Lee followed him.

'So, what time did you discover the body?' Inspector Zhang asked the waiter.

'About ten o'clock,' replied the manager, before the waiter could answer. 'Mr Chau called down to reception and we came straight up.'

'By we, you mean the front desk staff?'

'Myself, Mr Mercier, and Mr Ramanan and Miss Xue.'

Ramanan and Xue nodded at the Inspector but said nothing. Miss Xue looked over at the bedroom door fearfully, as if she expected the dead man to appear at any moment.

Inspector Zhang nodded thoughtfully. 'The corridor is covered by CCTV, of course?'

'Of course,' said the manager.

'Then I would first like to review the recording,' said the Inspector.

'Mr Mercier can take you down to our security room,' said Miss Berghuis.

'Excellent,' said Inspector Zhang. He looked across at his sergeant. 'Sergeant Lee, if you would stay here and take the details of everyone in the room, I will be back shortly. Make sure that nobody leaves and that the crime scene is not disturbed.'

'Shall I call in Forensics, Inspector Zhang?' asked the Sergeant.

'Later, Sergeant Lee. First things first.'

Inspector Zhang and Mercier left the suite and went down in the elevator to the ground floor. Mercier took the Inspector behind the front desk and into a small windowless room where there was a desk with a large computer monitor. On the wall behind the desk were another three large monitors, each showing the views from twenty different cameras around the hotel.

Mercier sat down and his expensively manicured fingers played over the keyboard. A view of the corridor on the sixth floor filled the main screen. 'What time do you want to look at?' asked Mercier.

'Do we know what time Mr Wilkinson went to his room?'

asked the Inspector.

'About half past eight, I think,' said Mercier.

'Start at 8.20 and run it on fast-forward if that's possible,' said Inspector Zhang.

Mercier tapped on the keyboard. The time code at the bottom of the screen showed 8.20 and then the seconds flicked by quickly. The elevator doors opened and a big man and a small Asian woman came out.

'That's him,' said Mercier. He pressed a button and the video slowed to its proper speed.

Wilkinson was wearing a dark suit with a Mao collar. His companion was a pretty Asian girl in her twenties with waist-length black hair, wearing a tight white mini-dress cut low to reveal large breasts. She was holding Wilkinson's hand and laughing at something he had said.

'Freeze that, please,' said Inspector Zhang as Wilkinson and the girl reached the door to the suite.

Mercier did as he was told and Inspector Zhang peered at the screen. He recognised the woman. 'Ah, the lovely Ms Lulu,' said Inspector Zhang.

'You know her?'

'She is an escort for one of the city's more expensive agencies, and when she isn't escorting, she can be found in one of the bars in Orchard Towers looking for customers.' The woman was wearing impossibly high heels, but she barely reached Wilkinson's shoulder.

'The Four Floors of Whores?' said Mercier. 'She's a prostitute?'

'Come now, Mr Mercier, as head of security in a five-star hotel, you must surely have your share of nocturnal visitors,' said

Inspector Zhang.

'We have a policy of not allowing visitors in guests' rooms after midnight,' said Mercier primly.

'And I'm sure that your guests adhere strictly to that policy,' said Inspector Zhang. He looked at the time code on the video. 'Ms Lulu is from Thailand, though she travels to Singapore using a variety of names. Now, from the time code we can see that Mr Wilkinson and Ms Lulu arrived at 8.30. Can you now please advance the video until the time she left the room.'

Mercier tapped a key and the video began to fast-forward. Guests moved back and forth up and down the corridor, hotel staff whizzed by, but the door stayed resolutely closed. Then at 9.30 on the dot, the door opened and Ms Lulu slipped out. Mercier slowed the video to real time and they watched as she tottered down the corridor in her stiletto heels.

'So we can assume that Mr Wilkinson paid her for one hour,' said Inspector Zhang. 'Now, when did Mr Wilkinson order room service?'

'I'm not sure,' said Mercier. 'We will have to talk to the waiter.'

'Then please fast-forward until the waiter arrives with the trolley.'

Mercier did as he was told. At five minutes before ten, the waiter appeared in the corridor, pushing a trolley. He knocked on the door, then knocked again.

'What is the hotel policy if the guest does not open his door?' asked Inspector Zhang.

'If the "Do Not Disturb" sign is on, then the member of staff will phone through to the room. If it isn't, then it's acceptable to use their key.'

The waiter knocked again, then used his key card to open the door. Inspector Zhang made a note of the time. It was 9.58.

'And at what time did the waiter call down to reception to say that he had found Mr Wilkinson dead on the bed?'

'Just before ten,' said Mercier. 'You'll have to ask Miss Berghuis. She'll know for sure.'

They watched the screen. After a minute or so, the waiter appeared at the doorway. He stood there, shaking, his arms folded, then he paced back and forth across the corridor. The time code showed 10.03 when Miss Berghuis appeared, followed by her staff. They hurried into the room.

Mercier pressed a button to freeze the screen and pointed at the time code. 'Three minutes past ten,' he said. 'No one went in or out of the room except for Mr Wilkinson and his guest. His guest left at 9.30 and the next time he was seen, he was dead.'

Inspector Zhang nodded thoughtfully as he put away his notebook. 'So, please, let us go back to the room. I have seen everything that I need to see.'

They went back to the sixth floor. Two uniformed police officers had arrived and were standing guard at the door to the suite. They nodded and moved aside to allow the Inspector and Mercier inside.

Sergeant Lee was scribbling in her notebook and she looked up as Inspector Zhang walked into the room. 'I have everyone's details, Sir,' she said.

'Excellent,' said the Inspector, striding towards the bedroom. 'Come with me please, Sergeant Lee. Everyone else please remain where you are. I shall return shortly.'

Sergeant Lee followed the Inspector into the bedroom and he closed the door behind them and then looked at her, barely able to control his excitement. 'Do you know what we have here, Sergeant Lee?'

The Sergeant looked at the body on the bed. 'A murder, Sir?'

Inspector Zhang sighed. 'Oh, it's much more than that, Sergeant. What we have here is a locked room mystery.'

The Sergeant shrugged but didn't say anything.

'Do you know how long I've waited for a locked room mystery, Sergeant Lee?'

She shrugged again. 'No, Sir.'

'My whole life,' said Inspector Zhang, answering his own question. 'We have so few unsolved murders in Singapore, and precious few mysteries.' He sighed. 'At times like this, I wish I had a deerstalker hat and a pipe.'

'This is a non-smoking room, Inspector,' said Sergeant Lee.

'I know that,' said Inspector Zhang. 'I'm simply saying that a pipe would add to the effect, as would a faithful bloodhound, tugging at its leash.'

'And hotels in Singapore do not allow pets, Sir,' said Sergeant Lee.

Inspector Zhang sighed mournfully. 'You're missing the point,' he said. 'The point is that we have a dead body in a room that was locked from the inside. A room that no one entered during the time that the victim was murdered. Sergeant Lee, we have a mystery that needs to be solved.'

'Shall I notify the Forensics Department, Inspector?' asked

Sergeant Lee.

'Forensics?' repeated Inspector Zhang. 'Have you no soul, Sergeant Lee? This is not a mystery to be solved by science.' He tapped the side of his head. 'Zis is a matter for ze little grey cells.' It wasn't a great Poirot impression, but Inspector Zhang thought it satisfactory. Sergeant Lee just found it confusing and she frowned like a baby about to burst into tears. 'Let me look around first, then we'll decide whether or not we need Forensics,' added Inspector Zhang, in his normal voice.

'Sir, that is not procedure,' said Sergeant Lee.

'Indeed it is not, but we shall inform them in due course. However, I would first like to examine the crime scene.' He turned to look at the body. 'So what do we have?' mused Inspector Zhang. 'We have a dead body on a bed. We have a wound, but no weapon. We have a room that was locked from the inside. We have sealed windows and no way in and out other than through a door into a corridor that is constantly monitored by CCTV.' He shivered. 'Oh, Sergeant Lee, do you not appreciate the beauty of this situation?'

'A man is dead, Inspector Zhang.'

'Yes, exactly. He is dead and somewhere, there is a killer and it is up to me to find that killer.' He looked over her and smiled like a benevolent uncle. 'For us to solve,' he said, correcting himself. 'You will be Watson to my Holmes, Lewis to my Morse.'

'Robin to your Batman?' suggested Sergeant Lee.

Inspector Zhang peered at her through his thick-lensed spectacles as he tried to work out if she was mocking him, but she was smiling without guile and so he nodded slowly. 'Yes, perhaps,' he said. 'But without the masks and capes. You know that Batman made his first appearance in *Detective Comics* way back in 1939?'

'I didn't know that, Sir' said the Sergeant, scribbling in her notebook.

'And that he is sometimes referred to as the World's Greatest Detective, which I always considered to be hyperbole.'

Sergeant Lee continued to scribble in her notebook. 'What are you writing, Sergeant Lee?' he asked.

She blushed. 'Nothing,' she said, and put her notebook away.

Inspector Zhang nodded slowly and walked slowly around the room. 'I assume you are not familiar with the work of John Dickson Carr?' he said.

Sergeant Lee shook her head.

'He was a great American writer who wrote dozens of detective stories and most of them were locked room mysteries. He created a hero called Dr Gideon Fell, and it was Dr Fell who solved the crimes.'

Sergeant Lee tapped the side of her head. 'By using ze little grey cells,' she said, in a halfway passable French accent.

Inspector Zhang smiled. 'Exactly,' he said. 'Now, in his book *The Hollow Man*, itself a locked room mystery, John Dickson Carr used Dr Fell to expound his seven explanations that lead to a locked room murder.' He nodded at his sergeant. 'You might want to make a note of them, Sergeant Lee,' he said. 'Now come with me.'

They went back into the sitting room. Miss Berghuis was sitting on the sofa next to Mercier. The waiter was standing close to the door, as if he was keen to get out of the suite as quickly as possible. The two assistant managers stood by the desk in the corner of the room, looking at each other nervously.

Inspector Zhang walked to the window and stood with his back to it. 'So, I have now examined the CCTV footage covering the corridor outside this room, and I have examined the crime scene.' Sergeant Lee fumbled for her notebook as Inspector Zhang continued. 'The CCTV footage shows that Mr Wilkinson arrived at his room with a guest at 8.30 and that his guest, a young woman who is known to the police, left exactly one hour later. What I need to know is when Mr Wilkinson ordered from room service.'

'That will be on the bill, Inspector,' said Miss Berghuis. She went over to the trolley and picked up a small leather folder and took out a slip of paper. She studied it, then nodded. 'The order was placed at 9.36,' she said.

'Excellent,' said the Inspector. 'So from that, we can assume that Mr Wilkinson was killed sometime between the placing of the order at 9.36 and the arrival of the order at 9.55.' He frowned. 'That does seem remarkably quick, Miss Berghuis.'

The manager smiled. 'Inspector, we are a five-star hotel. And Mr Wilkinson ordered only a club sandwich and a pot of coffee. Hardly a challenge for our chefs.'

'Very good,' said the Inspector, as Miss Berghuis went back to sit on the sofa. 'We can therefore rule out Mr Wilkinson's guest as the killer, as we know for sure that he was still alive at 9.36.'

Miss Xue nervously raised her hand. 'Actually, Inspector, we know that he was alive after that, because he spoke to his wife at about a quarter to ten,' she said.

'How so?' asked Inspector Zhang.

'She phoned at 9.45,' said Miss Xue. 'I was on the desk, and I was there when the call came through from America. Mrs Wilkinson was on the phone to her husband for almost five minutes.'

'Are you sure?' asked the Inspector.

'I am sure that it was his wife, and they spoke for several minutes,' she said. 'Whether it was for three, four or five minutes, I am not sure.'

Inspector Zhang nodded. 'Then we can assume that it was indeed Mr Wilkinson that she spoke to,' he said. 'I cannot believe that a wife could be fooled by an imposter. So we therefore know that Mr Wilkinson was alive just five minutes before the waiter arrived at his door. Yet we know for a fact that no one entered the room prior to the arrival of the waiter.' He drew himself up to his full height of five-feet, seven inches and looked in turn at the faces of everyone in the room. 'That means that what we have here is what we detectives refer to as a Locked Room Mystery.'

He paused for several seconds, nodding wisely before continuing. 'As I was explaining to my colleague earlier, there are basically seven explanations as to how a body can be found in a locked room. Explanations provided by the talented mystery writer John Dickson Carr. I think it would be helpful to run through them. The first possibility is that the murder is, in fact, not a murder, but a series of coincidences or accidents that give the impression that a crime has been committed. A man stumbles and hits his head on a piece of heavy furniture, for instance. Then we have a body, but no weapon and no killer.'

Inspector Zhang paused to make sure that he had everyone's attention before continuing. 'In this case, an accident is highly unlikely, considering the nature of the wound and the fact that the body is lying down. Plus the blood is only on the bed. If he accidentally stabbed himself on, for instance, the lamp on the bedside table, we would see blood on it. There is no blood anywhere but the bed, so it is safe to say that it is on the bed that he died.'

He turned to look out of the window and linked his fingers behind his back. His spine clicked as he straightened it, and he sighed. 'The second explanation is that it is indeed a murder, but a murder in which the victim is compelled to kill himself. Or herself. A mind-altering substance can be used, a gas or a pill, LSD for instance. Mr Carr suggested that a man might become so bewildered that he could strangle himself with his bare hands. But, of course, we know that is impossible.'

'You think he was drugged?' said Mercier. 'Or gassed? How could gas get into the room? We have central air-conditioning and the windows are sealed.'

'If he was drugged, the Forensics Department would know,' said Sergeant Lee. 'They could perform tests.'

'He did not stab himself to death,' said Inspector Zhang quickly. 'If he did, the weapon would be in his hands. Or on the bed. There is no knife, therefore he did not kill himself. And I see no evidence that the victim consumed food or drink in this room.'

He went over to the minibar and opened it. It was full. 'You see, nothing has been taken from the minibar, and there are no unopened bottles in the room.'

He looked over at the room service waiter. 'Mr Wilkinson was dead when you got here? He was dead on the bed and you saw the blood?' The waiter nodded.

'So he did not consume anything that the waiter brought into the room. We can rule out poison or drugs.' He went back to the window.

'It is the third explanation that creates some of the most fascinating fictional locked room mysteries,' he continued. 'That is where it is murder, and the killer uses some sort of mechanical device to carry out the killing. A gun concealed in a phone, for example. Or a knife that springs out of a suitcase. Or a pistol that fires when a clock is wound, or a weight that swings from the ceiling, a chair that exhales a deadly gas when your body warms it.' He waved a hand at the bedroom. 'In this case, we would be looking for some way of stabbing Mr Wilkinson and making the knife vanish.' He smiled at his sergeant. 'What do you think, Sergeant Lee? Do you think there is a mechanical device hidden in the bedroom?'

'It is unlikely,' she said quietly, as if she feared giving him the wrong answer.

'I agree,' said Inspector Zhang. 'It is a hotel room, like any other.' The Sergeant smiled with relief.

'It is a suite, one of our best,' said the manager.

Inspector Zhang nodded, acknowledging the point. 'But nothing in the room has been changed, am I correct? Everything is as it should be?'

'Other than the body on the bed, yes.'

'Then we shall move on to the fourth explanation. Suicide.'

'Suicide?' repeated the Sergeant. 'But if he stabbed himself, where is the weapon?'

'The point of the suicide is to make it look like a murder,' said Inspector Zhang. 'Either to throw suspicion on someone or to defraud an insurance company. I assume that a wealthy person such as Mr Wilkinson would have a lot of insurance. Perhaps he has an incurable condition. Cancer perhaps. So he kills himself in such a way that his wife can still claim the insurance.'

'Perhaps that's it,' said Mercier. 'Surely you check to see if he had any policies.'

'But where is the weapon he used?' asked the Sergeant. 'If Mr Wilkinson took his own life, where is the knife?'

'But that is the point exactly!' said Inspector Zhang. 'To make it appear to be a murder and not a suicide, the weapon must disappear. Mr Carr suggested a knife made of ice. The ice would then melt, leaving only water behind. Or a gun could be attached to a length of elastic which would then whip the gun up a chimney or out of a window.'

'There are no chimneys and, as Mr Mercier has already pointed out, the windows in our rooms are all sealed,' said the manager.

'And I think ice is unlikely as he would have had to carry it in from outside and the Singaporean climate does not lend itself to carrying ice around,' said Inspector Zhang. 'And if Mr Wilkinson wanted to make it look like he had been murdered, I don't think he would have positioned himself on the bed. The floor would be a more likely place. Plus, there is the matter of room service. He spent time with the fragrant Ms Lulu, then ordered a meal. Hardly the actions of a man who was about to take his own life.' He folded his arms.

'So, that leads me to the fifth type of scenario discussed by Mr Carr. A murder which derives from illusion or impersonation, where the victim is already dead, but the murderer makes it appear that he is still alive.'

'How would that work in this case, Inspector?' asked Miss

Berghuis, frowning.

'If, for instance, it was the prostitute who killed Mr Wilkinson and she then arranged for someone else to make the call to room service,' said Inspector Zhang. 'That would give her an alibi when, in fact, Mr Wilkinson was already dead when she left the room.'

'Do you think that's what happened?' asked Sergeant Lee.

'That's simply not possible,' said Miss Berghuis. 'When a call is made to our Room Service section, the number flashes up on the phone. An order would not be accepted if it came from outside the hotel.'

Inspector Zhang nodded thoughtfully. 'And, of course, he spoke to his wife after he had ordered from room service, so I do not think that Ms Lulu was the killer. So, that then brings us to number six on Mr Carr's list. One of the more complicated of his explanations for a locked room murder, and one of the most successful in works of fiction. In such a situation, we have a murder which, although committed by somebody outside the room, nevertheless appears to have been committed by someone inside the room.'

Mercier scratched his bald head. 'That doesn't make sense,' he said.

'Oh Mr Mercier, it makes perfect sense,' said Inspector Zhang. 'Take for instance the icicle dagger that Mr Carr spoke of. Suppose it could be fired through an open window or through a hole drilled into the door. Or a knife thrower in a room opposite the building who throws a knife through an open window but has it tied to a length of string so that he can pull the weapon back. It thus appears that the killer was inside the room when, in fact, he was outside all the time.'

33

'But the windows are sealed and there are no holes in the door, and, besides, the main door opens into the sitting room, so there is another door off that to the bedroom,' said the manager. 'The ice dagger would have to turn ninety degrees and pass through two doors.'

Inspector Zhang sighed. 'Madam, I am not suggesting for one moment that Mr Wilkinson was killed by a weapon made from ice.'

'Well, you are the one who keeps mentioning it,' said the manager, flashing him a withering look. 'And if the knife didn't melt, where is it?'

'Exactly!' said Inspector Zhang. 'You have put your finger on the crux of the conundrum. Where is the knife? If indeed, it was a knife.'

'Do you know?' asked Mercier. 'Why are you asking us if you know?'

'I was being rhetorical,' said Inspector Zhang. He took off his glasses and began to methodically polish them with his handkerchief. 'I am not sure where the murder weapon is, but I have my suspicions. However, let me first finish Mr Carr's list of explanations with the seventh, which is effectively the exact opposite of the fifth.'

Everyone frowned as they tried to remember what the inspector had said was the fifth method. They all looked around, shrugging at each other.

Sergeant Lee walked over to Inspector Zhang and whispered in his ear. 'Inspector Zhang, I need to talk to you,' she said.

'Sergeant Lee, I am in full flow here,' he said. 'Can't it wait?'

'No, Sir, it cannot.'

Inspector Zhang sighed with annoyance, then nodded at the

door to the bedroom. 'This had better be important,' he said.

They went through to the bedroom and stood at the foot of the bed. 'What is it, Sergeant Lee?' asked the Inspector. 'You seem concerned.'

'Sir, we really should be calling in the Forensics Department,' she said. She looked at her watch. 'It will soon be midnight.'

'Not yet,' said Inspector Zhang. 'I think we can solve this case without resorting to science.'

'But it's procedure, Sir. And we have to follow procedure.'

'Sergeant Lee, you know that I speak Japanese, don't you?'

She nodded. 'It came in very useful when we were working on the case of the sushi chef who ran amok in his restaurant,' she said.

'Exactly,' said Inspector Zhang. 'But do you know why I studied Japanese?'

The Sergeant shook her head.

'There is a famous Japanese writer called Soji Shimada who wrote thirteen locked room mysteries, only one of which—*The Tokyo Zodiac Murders*—was translated into English. I wanted to read his other stories, which is why I taught myself Japanese.'

'I understand, Inspector Zhang.'

'This is important to me, Sergeant Lee. This is a mystery that I can solve. I want to prove that to myself.' He smiled. 'And perhaps to prove to you that even in the third millennium, there is a need for real detectives.'

'Like Batman?'

'I was thinking more like Sherlock Holmes,' said Inspector Zhang. 'We have an opportunity here that we may never have again in our lives. In Singapore, we are lucky if we have a dozen murders a year.'

'Lucky, Sir?'

Inspector Zhang put up his hand. 'You are right; lucky is not the right word. I guess what I wanted to say is murders are rare in Singapore. As our island state is blessed with a population largely reluctant to break the law and a government which works very hard to maintain law and order, our crime rate is one of the lowest in the world.'

'Plus, we execute our murderers,' Sergeant Lee added. 'Which does act as something of a deterrent.'

'Exactly. So do you not see how special this case is, Sergeant Lee? Most detectives would give their eye teeth to work on a case such as this, yet all you want to do is to hand it over to the scientists.' He looked around as if he feared being overheard. 'And what if we have a serial killer, Sergeant Lee?'

'We have only one victim, ' said the Sergeant.

'That we know of,' said Inspector Zhang, fighting to stop his voice from trembling. 'What if there are more? What if we have on our hands a real live serial killer?' He shuddered. 'Can you imagine that, Sergeant Lee?'

The Sergeant nodded but didn't reply.

'You know that Singapore has only ever had one serial killer?' said the Inspector.

'Yes, Sir. Adrian Lim.'

'Exactly, Sergeant,' said the Inspector. Every detective on the island knew of the case, of course. It was taught at the academy. The Toa Payoh Ritual Murders. The killings had taken place in 1981, the year that Inspector Zhang had joined the Singapore Police Force.

Adrian Lim, who murdered two children as sacrifices to the Hindu goddess Kali. Lim and his two female accomplices were hanged in 1988.

'But he was caught by forensic evidence,' said Sergeant Lee. 'Police found a trail of blood leading to the flat.'

'Exactly,' said Inspector Zhang. 'Which is why I want to use deduction to solve this case. All the evidence we need is here, Sergeant Lee. All we have to do is to apply our deductive skills. Do you see that? Do you understand?'

The Sergeant nodded slowly. 'Yes, Sir, I understand.'

He patted her on the back. 'Excellent,' he said. 'Let me now finish my questioning,' he said. 'And you might give some thought as to what this case will be called, because I am sure that it will become the subject of much discussion , so it will need a name.'

'A name, Sir?'

'A title. "The Locked Hotel Room Murder", for instance. Or "The Vanished Knife". "Inspector Zhang And The Mystery Of The Disappearing Knife". What do you think?'

'I'm not sure, Sir,' said Sergeant Lee.

'Well give it some thought, Sergeant,' said Inspector Zhang, as he headed for the door.

Miss Berghuis was deep in conversation with her head of security when Inspector Zhang and Sergeant Lee walked back into the sitting room, but they stopped talking immediately and looked expectantly at the two detectives.

Inspector Zhang walked over to the window and turned to face the hotel staff. 'So, to continue, Mr Carr's seventh and final locked room scenario involves a situation where the victim is assumed to be dead before he or she actually is. That is the reverse of situation number five, of course where the victim is dead but presumed to be alive.'

'So that would mean that Mr Wilkinson wasn't actually dead when Mr Chau went into the room?' asked Miss Berghuis.

'He was,' said the waiter. 'I'm sure he was dead.'

'But you're not a doctor, Mr Chau,' said Inspector Zhang, 'In the confusion, it might have looked as if he was dead, but the actual murder was committed later.'

'That's impossible,' said Mercier. 'He was definitely dead when I got here.'

'And you were here soon after the waiter made the call to reception?'

Mercier nodded. 'You saw the CCTV footage. Everybody was there within a few minutes at most.'

'He was definitely dead,' agreed the manager. 'You only had to look at the body. At the blood.'

'But there was a moment when the waiter was alone with the body,' said Inspector Zhang. 'When he made the phone call. At that moment, he was alone in the room with Mr Wilkinson, and we have only Mr Chau's word that Mr Wilkinson was dead.'

'I didn't kill him,' said Mr Chau hurriedly, his eyes darting from side to side.

'I didn't say that you did,' said Inspector Zhang. 'I merely stated that you were alone with Mr Wilkinson and you had the opportunity of killing him if he hadn't been dead already. It is one way of solving a locked room mystery. The room is locked, but the person who discovers the body is the killer. He kills the victim then calls for the police.' He shrugged. 'It happens, but I do not think it happened in this case.'

The waiter looked relieved and loosened his shirt collar.

'Besides, if you did kill Mr Wilkinson, where is the knife?' asked Inspector Zhang.

'Actually, Inspector Zhang, we haven't searched anyone yet,' said Sergeant Lee.

'And there is no need to search Mr Chau, Sergeant,' said the Inspector. 'What we need to do now is to go back downstairs to the security office, for it is there that the solution lies.'

'All of us?' said the manager. 'Surely we don't all need to go?'

'It is the tradition, Madam,' said Inspector Zhang. 'The detective gathers together the cast of characters and explains the solution to them before unmasking the killer.'

The manager laughed, and it was like the harsh bark of an angry dog. 'Inspector Zhang, this is not some country house where the butler did it. Just tell us who the killer is.'

'It is not a country house, that is true, but a five-star hotel is the closest thing that we have in Singapore,' replied Inspector Zhang. 'Now please humour me and accompany me down to the ground floor.'

The Inspector led them out of the room and down the corridor to the elevators. He took the first one down with Mercier, the waiter, Miss Berghuis and one of the two uniformed policemen. Sergeant Lee followed in a second elevator with the two assistant managers and the other uniformed policeman. They gathered together outside the security room and Inspector Zhang led them inside. He waved a languid hand at the chair in front of the monitors. 'Mr Mercier, perhaps you would do the honours.'

The head of security sat down and ran a hand over his scalp. 'We've already looked at the CCTV footage,' he said.

'We looked, but did we really see what happened?' asked the Inspector. He waited until everyone had gathered behind Mercier's chair before asking him to begin the recording from the point at which Mr Wilkinson and the prostitute stepped out of the elevator.

'Here we can see Mr Wilkinson and his guest arriving at 8.30' said Inspector Zhang. 'Very much alive, obviously.'

He watched as Wilkinson and the woman went inside. 'She left an hour later. Please skip to that point, Mr Mercier.'

Mercier tapped a key and the video began to fast-forward. He slowed to normal speed just before 9.30 in time to see Ms Lulu leave the room.

'Now, at this point Mr Wilkinson ordered his club sandwich and coffee from room service, so again we know that he is still very much alive.'

'So who killed him?' asked Miss Berghuis. 'If the woman left the room, and no one goes in before the waiter, who stabbed him?'

'That is an excellent question, Madam,' said Inspector Zhang.

'But can you answer it, Inspector?' asked the manager, tersely.

'I think I can,' said Inspector Zhang. 'They key to solving this mystery lies in understanding that it is not who goes into the room that is important. It is who does not go in.'

'That doesn't make any sense at all,' said the manager crossly.

'I beg to differ,' said Inspector Zhang. 'It makes all the sense in the world. It is as Sherlock Holmes himself says in Arthur Conan

Doyle's masterpiece, *The Adventure Of Silver Blaze*: it is the fact that the dog did not bark that is significant.'

'We do not allow dogs in the hotel,' said Mercier. 'There are no pets of any kind.'

Sergeant Lee looked up from her notebook, smiling, and Inspector Zhang sighed. 'I was using the story as an example to show that it is sometimes the absence of an event that is significant, which was the case in *The Adventure of Silver Blaze*. If I recall correctly, it was Inspector Gregory who asks Sherlock Holmes if there is anything about the case that he wants to draw to the policeman's attention. Holmes says yes, to the curious incident of the dog in the night-time. That confuses the Inspector, who tells Holmes that the dog did nothing in the night-time. To which Holmes replies, "That was the curious incident." Do you understand now, Madam?'

She shook her head impatiently. 'No Inspector, I am afraid I do not.'

'Then, Madam, please allow me to demonstrate,' said Inspector Zhang. He put a hand on Mercier's shoulder. 'Please, Mr Mercier, fast-forward now to the point where the waiter arrives with the room service trolley.'

'This is a waste of time,' said Mercier. 'We did this already.'

'Please humour me,' replied the Inspector.

Mercier did as he asked and they all watched as the video fast-forwarded to the point where Mr Chau arrived with his trolley and began knocking on the door.

'Normal speed now, please, Mr Mercier.' The video slowed as they watched the waiter use his key card to enter the room.

'At this point, Mr Chau is discovering the body and calling down

41

to reception.' Inspector Zhang waited until the waiter appeared at the door and began pacing up and down. 'As you can see, no one enters the room until the hotel staff appear.' On the screen, Miss Berghuis and her staff appeared and they all hurried into the room. 'At this point, you phone the police,' said the Inspector, turning to Miss Berghuis. The manager nodded. Inspector Zhang patted Mercier on the shoulder. 'So now fast-forward until my arrival, Mr Mercier, but not too quickly. And I want everyone to note that no one else enters the room until I arrive with my sergeant.'

The door to the room remained closed for twenty minutes until Inspector Zhang and Sergeant Lee stepped out of the elevator.

'Normal speed now please, Mr Mercier. Thank you.'

Mercier pressed a button and the video slowed. Inspector Zhang walked up to the door and knocked on it. It opened and he went inside, followed by his sergeant. The door closed behind them.

'So, now we are inside, talking to you and assessing the situation. We talk, then I go to the bedroom with you, Miss Berghuis, I look at the body, I talk to you, I walk back to the sitting room, and then I walk out with Mr Mercier.' On the screen, Inspector Zhang and Mercier walked out of the room and headed for the elevator.

'You can stop it there, Mr Mercier,' said Inspector Zhang, patting him on the shoulder.

The picture froze on the monitor, showing Inspector Zhang and Mercier walking towards the elevator.

'So here is the big question, Mr Mercier,' said Inspector Zhang. 'You walk out of the room now, but when exactly did you walk into the room?'

Mercier said nothing.

'You did not arrive with Miss Berghuis.'

'He was already in the room when we got there,' said the manager. She gasped and put her hand up to her mouth. 'My God, he was in there the whole time.'

'Apparently so,' said Inspector Zhang.

Mercier stood up and tried to get out of the door, but the two uniformed policemen blocked his way. Mercier turned to face Inspector Zhang. 'This is ridiculous,' he said.

'Now Mr Mercier, I am going to make two predictions, based on what I think happened,' said Inspector Zhang. He nodded at Mercier's jacket. 'I am certain that you are carrying the murder weapon. You have had no chance to dispose of it, so it must still be on your person. And because I do not believe that you planned to kill Mr Wilkinson, I think that the weapon is actually something quite innocuous. A pen maybe.' He registered the look of surprise on Mercier's face and he smiled. 'Yes, a pen. But I also think that you have a camera, perhaps even a small video camera. Am I right?'

Mercier didn't answer, but he slowly reached into his inside pocket and took out a black Mont Blanc pen. He held it out and Inspector Zhang could see that there was blood on one end. Sergeant Lee stepped forward and held out a clear plastic evidence bag and Mercier dropped the pen into it. Mercier then reached into the left-hand pocket of his trousers and took out a slim white video camera, smaller than a pack of cigarettes.

Inspector Zhang took the camera from him. 'And Ms Lulu, she is in this with you?'

Mercier looked away but didn't answer.

'She is not involved in the murder, of course. She doesn't know that Mr Wilkinson is dead because he was still alive when she left the room.'

Mercier nodded. 'She doesn't know.'

'Because you never planned to kill Mr Wilkinson, did you?' said Inspector Zhang.

Mercier rubbed his hands together and shook his head.

'You were there to blackmail Mr Wilkinson?'

'Blackmail?' said Miss Berghuis.

'It was the only possible explanation,' said Inspector Zhang. 'He was in the room when Mr Wilkinson arrived with Ms Lulu. I am assuming that he wanted to video them in a compromising position with a view to blackmailing him. He was a married man, after all. And divorce in America can be a costly business. The only question is whether Ms Lulu was party to the blackmail or not.'

Mercier nodded. 'It was her idea,' he said.

'You were her client?'

'Sometimes. Yes. Then she said that she had this rich customer who treated her badly and that she wanted to get back at him. She wanted to hurt him and get money from him. She said she'd split the money with me.'

'So she suggested that you hide in the closet and video them together?'

'She had been in his room before, and she knew I could easily hide in the closet. She called me when she was on the way back to the hotel, and I was in position when they arrived. She made sure that he could never see me. It was easy. But then she was supposed to get him into the shower so that I could slip out, but he wouldn't have it. He said that his wife was due to phone him, so he practically threw her out of the room. Then he phoned room service from the sitting room so I couldn't get out, and then his wife called. I was stuck there while he took the call.' He ran a hand over his face. He was dripping with sweat. 'Then it all went wrong.'

'He opened the closet? He found you?'

Mercier nodded. 'He shouldn't have, but he did. All his clothes were in the suitcase and his robe was in the bathroom. I don't know why he opened the closet, but he did and he saw me.'

'So you killed him?'

Mercier shook his head. 'It was an accident.'

'You stabbed him in the throat with your pen,' said Inspector Zhang.

'He attacked me,' said Mercier. 'He opened the closet door and saw me and attacked me. We struggled. I had to stop him.'

'By driving your pen into his throat?'

Mercier looked at the floor.

'I think not,' said Inspector Zhang. 'If you stabbed him at the closet, there would be blood there. The only place where there is blood is the bed. Therefore you stabbed him on the bed.'

'We were struggling. I pushed him back.'

'And then you stabbed him?'

'My pen was in my top pocket. He grabbed it during the struggle and tried to force it into my eye. I pushed it away and it ...' He fell silent, unable or unwilling to finish the sentence.

'You stabbed him in the throat?'

Mercier nodded.

'And then rather than leaving the room, you hid in the closet again?'

'I didn't know what else to do. I knew that he had ordered room service, so I couldn't risk being seen in the corridor.'

'So you waited until the room service waiter discovered the body and while he was phoning the front desk, you slipped out of the closet?'

Mercier nodded. 'I went through to the next room but there was someone in the corridor, so I couldn't leave and I had to pretend that I'd just arrived. It was an accident, Inspector Zhang. I swear.'

'That's for the judge to consider,' said Inspector Zhang. 'There is one more piece of evidence that I require from you, Mr Mercier. Your handkerchief.'

'My handkerchief?'

'I notice that unlike your colleagues, you do not have a handkerchief in your pocket. I therefore assume that you used it to wipe the blood from your hands after you killed Mr Wilkinson.'

Mercier reached into his trouser pocket and pulled out a bloodstained handkerchief. Sergeant Lee held out a second plastic evidence bag, and Mercier dropped the handkerchief into it.

Inspector Zhang nodded at the two uniformed policemen. 'Take him away, please.'

The officers handcuffed Mercier and led him out of the room. Inspector Zhang nodded at the two evidence bags that Sergeant Lee was holding, containing the pen and the handkerchief. 'You can send them to your friends in Forensics,' he said.

'I will,' she said.

'I suppose it does prove one thing,' said Inspector Zhang. He smiled slyly.

'What is that, Inspector?' asked the Sergeant.

'Why, that the pen is indeed mightier than the sword.' He grinned. 'There is no need to write that down, Sergeant Lee.'

STEPHEN LEATHER is the author of more than twenty novels, including *Private Dancer* and *Confessions of a Bangkok Private Eye*, published by Monsoon Books in Singapore, as well as the Dan 'Spider' Shepherd series and Jack Nightingale series, both published by Hodder and Stoughton in the United Kingdom. You can find more details of his work at *www.stephenleather.com*.

Lead Balloon

Lee Ee Leen

'Cover her face!' yelled a male voice from outside the classroom. Life imitates art more than vice versa, according to Oscar Wilde. At that moment, I was teaching *The Duchess of Malfi*, and when I heard part of the most famous quote from the play suddenly uttered in real life, I just had to excuse myself from the lesson. I looked down into the quadrangle from the common corridor area. However, there was no rehearsal for Jacobean tragedy in the quadrangle.

Three male students were carrying Mrs Dora Lau's body towards a wooden bench. They arranged her lying face-up on her improvised gurney. I assumed she had fainted while crossing the quadrangle, but she remained too still, with one of her feet missing a chunky brown leather shoe. Mr Caulden, one of the Economics tutors, dashed to Mrs Lau's side with his beer belly bouncing under his plaid shirt. The material under his armpits darkened with sweat, he gazed up at me watching him, man to man. He put his fists on his hips and the gesture told me that he wished that it were I down there instead of he.

The students of 96A05 stood to each side of me, enjoying the spectacle provided by the disruption of their A-level Literature class. It was 1996, and ten years later I heard that A-level papers were replaced with a different set of exams. Gayatri, 96A05's class monitress and sole scholar from India, pointed downwards. 'Mr Caulden's down there with Mrs Lau.'

'Why don't they get her to a hospital?' Naomi Koh asked.

'She's lost enough weight so they can squeeze her into the ambulance.' Soraya deadpanned.

'Ladies, *tsskk*!' Cordelia Lim chided in mock dismay, 'show some respect for the dead.'

As she surveyed the quadrangle, Cordelia bunched her lips together as if she had bitten down on a hard seed; I had seen that expression before when she had received unexpected midterm test results. I ushered my class back inside the classroom and tried to steer them back to *The Duchess of Malfi*. Their minds had already bolted and remained down in the quadrangle with Mrs Lau's body.

* * *

The world was rumbling during the mid 1990s. Ebola virus outbreaks and the imminent Hong Kong handover all scheduled a year before the 1997 recession had sent Southeast Asia into economic free fall. These events were dress rehearsals for similar future incidents early in the next century, but at the time, I interpreted them as pre-millennium tension. External tensions combined with personal tensions drove me away from London. I left the UK with the same attitude as I left my ex-girlfriend: both of us needed a time-out, an intermission in our relationship for an unspecified duration. Wary of the threat of mad cow disease, shootings in primary schools, and IRA bombs in London, I applied for a teaching contract in Singapore.

I received a reply letter in dot matrix print, requesting my attendance at an interview. I showed my interviewers evidence of my PGCE, teaching experience in comprehensive schools and two summers at adult education colleges. I appreciated routine, but I mistook it for structure. I was a polymath, dipping my toes into too many areas for my own good. My scattered interests showed in my magazine subscriptions: *New Scientist*, the *British Medical Journal* and the *Times Literary Supplement*. After my change of country, there was an additional charge for overseas delivery and the magazines arrived a month late.

My first semester was three months long. I was assigned to 96A05, a class of girls orphaned before the holidays when Mr Greenfield, their former Civics tutor, collapsed of a heart attack outside his rented apartment. When accepting a new position, never step into a dead man's shoes because you are expected to continue his legacy, of which you know nothing. But no one mentioned that I also had to sit at his desk. Nevertheless, the Humanities staff was already thinly spread.

* * *

When I entered the double swinging doors of the staffroom on my first day, the place was more like a police station on a busy night: telephones and pagers going off, and students standing around desks as if they were suspects hauled in for questioning. Stacks of unmarked papers teetered on in-out trays, filing cabinets lined the walls, their drawers jutted open like mortuary freezers and exposed their contents to the Antarctic air-conditioning. Wednesdays were the worst: memos materialised on my desk and assignments from Monday clogged up my pigeonhole. By Friday afternoons, staffroom activity normally wound down. I spent the time in my cubicle, reading my magazines and marvelling at the latest wonders of science, such as Dolly the cloned sheep.

My first impression of Mrs Dora Lau was also my first brush with her. After my first week on the job, she asked to see me in her office. A large woman like her should not get agitated. The thick layers of foundation streaked down her double chin making her face resemble an animated tribal mask. Once I was inside her room, the glass walls looked like a police captain's office. I hoped the walls were soundproof and smiled to show my new colleagues that I was enjoying myself.

'Lydia Ang attempted suicide over the weekend—are you aware of this?'

I had called Lydia Ang's house number in my new tenure as Civics tutor of 96A05 after she was absent for two days with no explanation. I did an exaggerated slow nod to show concern and reported that I had sensed nothing amiss in Lydia's conduct in the week before her absence.

'You should be more observant. As a Civics tutor, one of your main responsibilities is pastoral care,' Mrs Lau emphasised. 'Both mental and physical welfare. More serious personal problems should be referred to counselling.'

I walked out of Mrs Lau's office, trying not to notice the heads retracting into cubicles as conversations suddenly resumed. A petite woman with dark curly hair walked over from the Science section and leaned over my cubicle wall, sympathetic and conspiratorial.

'Hi, I'm Maria De Silva, Chemistry.' She arched an eyebrow. 'Is this your first week here?'

'Does it show?'

Maria nodded in the direction of Mrs Lau's office, 'Dora likes to roast the fresh meat as soon as it arrives. My Science Head of Department only troubles us if we do anything to trouble him.'

I summarised the details of my 'roasting' to Maria.

'Everyone knows about Lydia Ang.'

'The suicide attempt?'

'No, *lahh*!' Maria tapped me on the shoulder with the A4 file she was carrying. 'She's a lesbian! One Saturday after CCA, Mrs Lau saw Lydia kissing another girl at the bus stop.'

'I've just started working here and Mrs Lau is trying to hold me accountable for Lydia's behaviour after school hours? That's unreasonable!'

'Human nature is never reasonable—you never noticed Mrs Lau looking at you during assembly while the college band plays? Mrs Lau wants what she cannot have. That's why she's so hard on you.'

'But I'm not hard on you,' I said.

Maria hid her blushing behind the A4 file, but she remained professional. 'Then do me a favour and make your working life easier. Flatter Mrs Lau the same way you flatter me.'

'I'll do my best,' I called to Maria's departing shoulders and elegant neck. I opened my desk drawer and took out my modest rock collection. Like a meditation, arranging the specimens on my desk calmed me: a cluster of quartz, an ammonite and a chunk of galena encased in transparent plastic.

*   *   *

I wrote the word 'REVENGE' on the whiteboard as Gayatri handed out the photocopies.

'Has anyone here heard of Francis Bacon?'

'Is he related to Kevin Bacon?' asked Soraya.

'Francis Bacon, the writer, died in 1626. He'd be more than six degrees separated from Kevin, the actor.' I tried to avoid discussion of unrelated topics in class, but the atmosphere was more relaxed during my Literature Clinic on Friday afternoons. Lit Clinic was not compulsory, but I had four regular attendees. Yet, I wondered whether these girls had something better to do.

'So, you've all read *Of Revenge*?' I asked.

A chorus of hesitant 'yeses'.

Naomi Koh adjusted her tortoiseshell spectacles and put her hand up, 'I read it, but I'm not sure what it means.'

I asked Naomi to read aloud the first line about revenge being a wild kind of justice, before I distilled Bacon's essay to its essence: revenge, though sweet, may not be the best way, and committing an act of revenge does not ameliorate the outrage.

'In the texts you have been studying, such as *Hamlet* and the *The Duchess of Malfi*, you will find that revenge is a Pyrrhic victory. Even if the characters could achieve vengeance and get away with it, there is a great personal cost.'

They jotted in their foolscap pads and swished fluorescent pink highlights onto their hand-outs.

Cordelia spoke for the first time from the rear row. 'What about real life?'

'It's so nice to hear from you at the back,' I teased. 'Well then class, what about real life? Is there anyone you want to take revenge on?'

'Mrs Lau,' replied Cordelia after a pause.

I detected a dangerous moment that threatened to dominate the class, especially when she said it with a complete lack of jest and hesitation. The others sensed the unease too.

'That makes everyone in this room,' Naomi declared, but she then considered my presence. 'Except for you, sir.' I gave a noncommittal shrug.

'Can't stand the old bi—' Cordelia stopped herself from saying the word. 'When she became HOD of Arts and Adviser in Student Matters since the start of term.'

I knew 'adviser' was an euphemism for enforcer of disciplinary issues. Cordelia's remark set off a ripple of unanimous agreement. I decided to indulge them or this sentiment would simmer and manifest into disruptive snide glances and notes.

Soraya went first. 'Last semester, she banned us from sticking posters on our lockers.'

'I'm sure she wanted to conserve their appearance?' I sat on the desk nearest to the whiteboard and folded my arms.

'No! Sticking posters on the inside!' Soraya continued, 'Haven't you noticed sir? She conducts these random spot checks and makes someone open up their locker. It's worst now. She's got a thing about lateness. If the boys are late for her General Paper class, she makes them do ear-squats outside the classroom for every minute they're late. For the girls, she makes them sit on the classroom floor for the entire lesson.'

'In the case of your locker, she was looking for stray Kevin Bacon posters!' Naomi tossed a crumpled Post-it Note at Soraya's head, who ducked out of the way.

'One lunch hour, she made us attend one of her talks in lecture theatre 2. She said, "Judging from the sort of posters in your lockers, you all are getting too many 'corrupting' American influences!"' quoted Gayatri.

'Then I wonder why this college hired Mr Caulden?' I mused.

'And remember the blood donation drive before the midterm break!' Soraya said.

The four of them issued a united groan at the memory.

'Mrs Lau said during assembly that we didn't give enough blood compared to the other colleges!' Gayatri protested, 'My living expenses are already high enough without having to give my blood.'

'My father's a doctor, and he says that you can't give blood when you've got your period!' Naomi said.

I held my hands up to indicate that I had heard enough. 'Young ladies, please!' I soothed. 'So far you have mentioned collective grievances. But what about individual grudges? Would you act on those?'

They lapsed into a reluctant but thoughtful silence.

Ever the no nonsense student, Gayatri sighed as if holding grudges was beneath her. 'What is revenge when compared with karma? Divine justice will prevail in the end, sir.'

'That's an excellent observation. The concept of divine justice is prevalent in a lot of other works ...' I leapt off the desk to seize this chance to steer the discussion away from the subject of Mrs Lau. Cordelia looked out of the window as it began to drizzle. After class, I returned to the staffroom and consulted 96A05's student contact details—just in case I had to call Cordelia's parents about her behaviour. After all, I had been instructed to be more observant. Cordelia had provided a postal address of a shop in Johor Bahru called Lee Huat Hong TCM.

I associated the abbreviation TCM with the cable channel, Turner Classic Movies, and assumed it was a video rental shop.

*   *   *

On the Monday after the Lit Clinic on revenge, Mrs Lau summoned me into her office after morning assembly. Maria passed my cubicle on her way to the photocopier and flashed me a thumbs up. I opened the office door and greeted Mrs Lau with my best Hugh Grant impersonation.

'Good morning, Dora. Gosh! You look quite stunning today.'

'Sit down, Mr Simon.' My flattery went unappreciated.

The hard plastic chair teetered on two good legs as I took my seat. Mrs Lau rubbed her temples and reached under her desk. She placed three squat bottles labelled with Chinese characters on her desk and took a sip from one bottle. When Mrs Lau put the bottle back on her desk, I saw dark syrup resettling itself through the glass. Yellow plastic bags were stashed on the carpet next to her desk.

Mrs Lau rested her forearms on her desk, with her hands folded. She leaned forward in earnest as if she wanted to sell me life insurance. 'Mr Simon, I happened to pass by your class last Friday afternoon. It sounded like a very stimulating lesson. When I came back to the staffroom, I checked your personal timetable; you have no classes scheduled with 96A05 on Friday afternoons.'

Mrs Lau's vigilance did not surprise me.

'You're correct,' I agreed. 'That class was my Literature Clinic for 96A05. It's an extra class that's also like a pastoral care session. I give them some supplementary material and we have a discussion.'

Mrs Lau coughed into her sleeve before saying, 'I'm glad to see you have followed my suggestions.'

'I'm just doing my duty as a—'

'But listen to me!' Mrs Lau had no intention of letting me get too comfortable. 'Your students don't require supplementary materials. That's only for the Special Paper in second year. And you don't need to give them extra Literature classes. All these Arts students get A's for Literature, for sure!'

'You want me to stop holding this Literature Clinic?' I asked.

Mrs Lau pointed outside her office to the staffroom. 'It's a good idea that can be applied to other subjects. Such as General Paper. Science and Commerce students always struggle with GP. I'd be more than happy to increase your teaching hours.'

'96A05 doesn't need a GP Clinic. They're smart young students.'

'Yes.' Mrs Lau stretched her mouth into a knowing grin. 'They're smart, young and also quite attractive students. I don't want rumours starting about the new Literature teacher from the UK who's too close with some girls from his Civics class. Reputation is everything in education.'

'I'm a professional; you don't have to worry.'

Mrs Lau picked up the receiver of her desk phone, pointed it at my face like a gun and replaced it with a bang. 'But Mr Simon, *you* should be more worried. It just takes one or two phone calls from me to the right people and the result will be an inquiry into your misconduct. My word against yours and you'll be on a plane back to the UK.'

She coughed again, this time hard enough to make her eyes water. Again, she sipped from the bottle of syrup.

'You should see a doctor, Mrs Lau. You don't look well.'

'No!' Mrs Lau cried, horrified at my suggestion, 'I don't trust Western medicine, the drugs all have side effects. That's how my late husband died! The hospitals only wanted our money! I just know it! Traditional Chinese Medicine is still the best for middle-aged aches and stomach pains. And this new job's giving me so much stress!'

'More serious personal problems should be referred to counselling,' I parroted her exact words to me during our first meeting. Unsure of how to respond, Mrs Lau folded her arms, rocked back in her chair and said nothing.

'I'm sorry to hear about your late husband,' I added out of civility, as I rose from my chair, anxious to get out of her office. I stumbled over one of the bags, and noticed the words printed on the yellow plastic: Lim Huat Hong Traditional Chinese Medicine Shop. This abbreviation of TCM did not have anything to do with classic movies.

Mrs Lau noted my interest. 'You know Cordelia Lim from your Civics class? Her father owns a Chinese medicine shop in Johor Bahru. Last term, I asked her to drop Geography for the second year, because History *and* Geography is a suicidal subject combination, it has a very low pass rate. Next thing I know, her father stormed into my office! No respect for teachers these days. To my surprise, Cordelia started bringing me complimentary bottles of cough syrup and sesame powder for the last three months. Cordelia told me it was her father's way of saying sorry.'

'How thoughtful.' I commented. 'Goodbye, Mrs Lau.'

I returned to my desk and looked at the Teacher's Day greeting cards and paper flowers pinned to the inside wall of my cubicle. As gifts of appreciation, three months of free cough syrup and sesame seed powder seemed excessive—more like bribery than apology.

* * *

The Summer Olympics in Atlanta had long finished and Hong Kong edged closer to its handover when Mrs Lau died. Her only daughter had arranged for a cremation, which all Arts staff were invited to attend. A cremation meant that the family did not want an autopsy. The staff talked with a mixture of feigned concern and *schadenfreude* of how she had looked ill and her sudden weight loss that people put down to a diet or dubious products. I did not join in, although I had much to say.

Later on the day she died, I broke into Mrs Lau's office by sliding an old credit card through the gap between door handle and doorjamb. It was easy with those push-button locks. I had to investigate before they cleared her possessions and handed the office and job over to her successor. The inconsistency between Mrs Lau being so loathed by Cordelia Lim yet showered with the same gifts over three months made me suspect more than mere bribery.

The half-finished bottles of cough syrup still stood on her desk from our last meeting. I lifted each bottle and was struck by their curious heaviness. The plastic jars of sesame meal powder had the same kind of weight. The new bottles and jars were stashed under the desk, and upon examination, I noted the unopened cough syrup bottles and jars had no seal or pop-up button on the cap to indicate tampering, just a plastic stopper on the opening of the inner rim. Dubious products, I knew, had questionable packaging.

I carried the opened syrup jars and the sesame powder back to my cubicle and tested their weight again. Big time scientists and investigators have their expensive equipment, but me, the armchair scientist had to improvise with what was available to me. I laid out three sheets of A4 paper on my desktop and opened the jars of cough syrup. After dipping a pen inside each jar, I dropped syrup from each onto the sheets. I smeared the liquid onto the paper and saw powdery dark grains showing up against the whiteness of the paper. I rubbed my finger on the rim of one bottle and touched my fingertip to my tongue. I tasted a metallic sweetness that was perversely addictive, similar to the gustatory compulsion created by MSG.

I closed one bottle, shook it hard and held it up to my desk lamp. In the sepia-toned syrup, I saw the grains settling down. Mrs Lau would not have noticed these grains if they all remained at the bottom of the jar. Being difficult to pour out, she would have discarded the remaining syrup as part of her usual impatience. I scattered some sesame powder onto another sheet of paper. The grains in the powder had two tones of grey; some light mixed with darker ones. They too, tasted sweet. The weight and colour of the metallic powder matched what I knew of lead. When I looked at my chunk of galena, I decided to ask someone who was an expert.

The next day, I caught up with Maria as she left the Science block. 'Free for coffee?'

'It depends on the coffee.'

There was a small shopping centre up the road from the college. I knew of a posh cafe where no student would go as they preferred the Internet cafés for IRC chat and e-mail.

'Do students have access to the science labs?' I asked her at our table.

'No, not outside lesson time. If so, only with special permission from someone like me.' Maria looked weary and I knew she did not want to talk about work.

'Do you keep dangerous substances in labs?'

Maria measured out a spoonful of brown sugar and tipped it into her coffee cup. 'The acid and alkali solutions used for class experiments are rather diluted. Dangerous and toxic substances such as mercury and potassium are handled by the teacher only with protective equipment.'

'What do you know about lead?'

She stirred her coffee, 'It's cheap, quite available and common. It's in the air, hair dye, lipsticks and car batteries. People even ate it! The Romans used lead acetate as a sweetener and artists suffered painter's colic with prolonged exposure to paint. The Victorians used it to sweeten their wine. Even Chinese medicine uses lead powder as treatment for eczema.'

'Is lead soluble?' I was thinking about the cough syrup.

'Lead is not soluble in water, but with exposure to moist air, lead oxide forms on the surface and darkens the lead,' Maria explained, which accounted for the dual tones of the sesame powder.

'Why? Are you worried about poisoning?' She giggled. 'Don't worry, all the pipes in this country are quite new, not like the nasty old lead ones in London.'

I fibbed and told Maria I was concerned about the chunk of galena on my desk.

'Galena is lead sulphide. As long as you keep it in that airtight plastic case and don't breathe, eat, lick or touch it, you're fine.'

'Thank you, Miss De Silva,' I said, genuinely grateful.

'You're welcome, Mr Simon; now it's my turn to talk about *your* subject area. Have you seen *The English Patient*? What did you think of the movie adaptation of the novel?' And she ordered two more espressos.

* * *

I took the 150 bus to Woodlands Checkpoint and onwards across the Causeway. When I arrived at City Square Complex, a tropical heavy downpour started. As the rain thudded outside, I located Lim Huat Hong Traditional Chinese Medicine Shop on the third floor. The signboard bore the logo of a mortar and pestle that matched the logo on the plastic bags. Inside the dusty shop, a skinny Chinese man was perched on a ladder.

'Pirated videos downstairs!' he called to me as he peered over his clipboard, taking stock of shelves upon shelves of large, bell-shaped jars that contained rhizomes, dried berries and preserved roots.

'Is Cordelia here?' I asked him. When he realised I was not there to browse through his merchandise, he descended the ladder.

Cordelia emerged from the back of the shop. 'Mr Simon?'

The man rushed over and shook my hand; his over-eagerness told me he was her father. 'You're Mr Simon? Cordelia always talks about you! She says you're very good and very smart! Want to go for drinks?'

I declined. 'Thank you, Mr Lim, but I must talk to your daughter about college.'

'She got problems again? What for you come all the way to Johor Bahru?'

'No,' I lied. 'I was actually here shopping. By the way, do you sell lead?'

Mr Lim asked Cordelia what lead was in Chinese. Her eyes widened as she went to the counter and opened a thick Chinese-English dictionary that was next to the till.

'*Qian*,' Cordelia read aloud from the dictionary, but kept staring at me.

Her father nodded. 'Ah yes, I have some stock at the back. Good for itchy skin. You want some?'

'No thanks. I was just asking.' I declined and tried not to sound too leery.

Cordelia was already waiting for me outside the shop, resting her arms on the railing as she watched the shoppers below, her lips pressed so tightly together that they turned mauve. I said nothing, a tactic that makes reticent students talk.

'Remember Francis Bacon?' I asked after a minute of silence.

'About revenge coming at a price?'

'You know what Mrs Lau would cost me by forcing me to drop A-level Geography? A chance to get into uni!' Cordelia shook her head in disgust. 'She told my father that History and Geography combinations showed a poor pass rate from previous years. Three subjects left, and me struggling with Economics.'

'I asked three students from 96A07 to drop Literature in second year last week', I replied, 'but they didn't get as mad as you. They didn't try to give me free food with poison.'

Cordelia gripped the railing. 'Mrs Lau said something that pissed me off after my father saw her. She told me she couldn't understand how someone from my background is so good in English.'

'By background, you mean class?'

'No, school background. I was in a Chinese language school in Johor before I went to Singapore. But I work hard, I do assignments and I read up on a lot of subjects in my spare time. Just like you, sir: you are not from a science background, but you still read your scientific magazines. I see them on your desk next to your rocks and crystals.'

Cordelia looked back to her father's shop and continued. 'Mrs Lau called Lydia Ang's parents and told them about their daughter. It was none of the bitch's business; Lydia was just unlucky that day. She did none of that during college time or while wearing the uniform. Only I knew she was gay.'

'You knew Mrs Lau was already dead when Mr Caulden was in the quadrangle?' I asked Cordelia, ' Is that why you joked about "showing respect for the dead"?'

'You saw her lying there too, sir! It just came out when I wasn't thinking. We all heard Mr Caulden shouting "Cover her face", so it reminded me of *The Duchess of Malfi*.'

I laughed in disbelief, 'Ha-hah! I know how you did it: small amounts of lead mixed into the free medicine and sesame seed powder, increment by increment. You're very hard-working indeed. And patient too.'

'Father leaves me in charge of the shop on Sundays, he doesn't notice a few missing stock items. And I know where he keeps everything.' Cordelia tapped her temple. 'We all knew Mrs Lau was sick, I just wanted to make her sicker. So that we'd have some peace.'

'There's a lot of peace when you're alone in a prison cell, Cordelia,' I rejoined.

'But I'm glad to see you here, sir. It proves you're one of the smartest teachers I've known.'

'Not quite.' I turned around to make sure Mr Lim was out of earshot. 'I'm just the crazy new *ang moh* teacher with a wild theory that his superior got murdered in college by one of the students. Without the autopsy, nothing can be proved. But you know that I know about it, Cordelia. And please don't ask me for a character reference when you leave college.'

* * *

Opting not to renew my contract after one year, I left the college before Cordelia. Maria was disappointed to see me go, but I gave her my e-mail and said that she was welcome to visit me in England.

Eighteen months later, Naomi sent me an e-mail with Harvard University in the email address; she wrote that Soraya was studying drama, Lydia was resitting her A-levels and Gayatri was doing Law back in India. In my reply, I asked Naomi about Cordelia, but Naomi did not know what happened to her.

I was relieved not to know any more about Cordelia; to think of her meant an association with lead. I had grown adverse to my galena after my visit to Johor Bahru and tossed the specimen into the monsoon drain outside my apartment before I left Singapore. And even though I am now back home in London, gifts of food left on my desk by students still makes my stomach leap in alarm.

LEE EE LEEN was born in London, UK. Her first story was published in *Urban Odysseys: KL Stories* in 2008. She was shortlisted for the 2009 MPH Alliance Bank National Short Story Award and has also published reviews for *The Directory of World Cinema: American Independent* (2010, Intellect Books, UK).

Decree Absolute

Dawn Farnham

I was rid of her. I was free.

Now is the winter of our discontent made glorious summer by this … pitch of fork.

I know, I know, but the Bard would forgive me. I smiled grimly to myself. It was simply about endings which rhyme, and he would have appreciated the tragicomedy of this finale.

The spade went into the ground. Under the crisp layer of leaves, it was soft. I knew that was superficial. It would get harder. It might take all night, this unorthodox divorce proceeding, but it didn't matter. Before the sun came a-peeping, the decree absolute would be issued. I would be rid of her and the pendulous, chafing yoke of marriage which had been around my neck for two years. Two years of gradual but relentless friction. Two sides of a grinding stone, our marriage the wheat and chaff caught in between, growing ever thinner, ever dustier at each turn of the handle.

The clod of earth made a satisfying thump as it landed on the ground. The place was deep in rough, jungly land. But the earth was friable.

The spade dug in deeper this time and the clod a little bigger.

When had it started to truly go wrong?

At first, I thought it was when sex became too much trouble. Now, excuse me, but isn't it the contractual duty and actually, the absolute fucking point of marriage that there should be sexual activity? At least in the first few years, for chrissake. The regular and vigorous participation of the marriage partner in sexual intercourse was, essentially, the only reason a young man like myself, good-looking, with prospects, would get married in the first place.

God, she'd been clever there. Hours of kissing, fondling, foreplay and a glimpse at what the whole deal would be like, without, now I had time to reflect, really giving me anything.

Well, not totally nothing. She had fabulous tits which she let me touch as much as I liked. And she gave great head. That was the problem, right there. She was good at it. She once told me that she liked to suck cock because it would horrify her father. Whatever. So long as she kept on doing it, the reasons were really not very important. Men can be slaves to women who give great head. And it led me to understand that, therefore, the whole sexual encounter would be mind-blowing. Mind-blowing sex on a permanent basis. You can see the attraction.

She was an animal, that's exactly what I thought. Underneath the most virtuous exterior, she was an animal. But a woman, too, who wanted security. The security of a permanent relationship, the love and understanding to allow her to blossom, to allow her animal instincts to bloom. Only I would know this. She would give herself utterly to me, keeping unto me and forsaking all others, till death did us part.

Well, you see, that's exactly where we were right now. And I, for one, was delighted.

The spade slid down, soft and yielding as a kiss, and another clod landed on the side of the hole.

It really was a lovely night. The full moon which had been glinting through the trees was now in glorious fullness high in the sky. A light breeze played with the leaves.

It was like the night we first met, minus the meat. Or perhaps not. That was quite funny in a gallows humour sort of way. Still the occasion did rather call for it.

We'd met at a barbecue, you see, organised by our managing director and his wife, in the garden of their black and white house. Over the steaks. We'd both gone for the same piece at the same time and she'd smiled shyly. Adorable. Beautiful. 'Please,' she'd said and pointed to the steak. The thought of food had rushed out of my head. Eyes like an Egyptian princess, luscious lips like an Indian goddess, the full, perfect and voluptuous figure of an Italian porn star. And shyly adorable.

I was in Singapore on assignment. My parents are Singaporean, long since emigrated to the US, and I was raised in America. Now I was back, with a Harvard business degree and a great job. A few girlfriends in high school and university had left me less than interested in the opposite sex. It's not an unusual story. Shy Chinese-American boy meets pert American girl. She thinks that, despite the glasses and the intellect, you will be Bruce Lee. In bed. It's not a good start.

The hole was starting to take shape. The first, soft layer had been removed. The rooty tangles lay below. It would be harder from now on.

But there was certainly no problem on my side. My dad is a big guy. He'd been a judo man in his day. I'd inherited his build. Strong and broad-shouldered. And I'm definitely a laid-back sort of guy. Some say too much, but that comes from the American upbringing. So from high school on, the American girls were intrigued. That movie *Dragon* had just come out, with Jason Lee playing the real life Bruce and it was a massive hit. Tall, good-looking Chinese guys were in. I definitely benefited amorously from that.

So there was no problem with performance-based issues. The American girls had ridiculous expectations, but it wasn't even that. They just seemed bland and lazy. It was me who had to do everything. Arouse them, satisfy them. While they lay there doing, well, frankly, fuck all, as the Brits say. That sort of thing is all right for a while. Lovely bodies are lovely bodies, but, guys, you know it can get old very fast.

Well, we could go on about that, but in the end it comes down to this: Leila was dark and exotic and the loveliest creature I'd ever seen. And, after the second date, modestly but enthusiastically proactive.

An owl hooted and the wind picked up. The moon cast long beams down into the clearing. The sky was filled with stars. The night is nice, you know. Nobody gets out enough in the jungle at night. Certainly I had not appreciated it until now.

Where she was clever was the gradual revelation of her glorious body and her sublime skills. From kissing, we had progressed over more than ten dates to touching. Me, allowed to touch her; she, shyly touching me in more and more intimate ways. God, it was arousing.

After two months, I met her parents, who were really delightful and welcoming. Her father is Anglo-Indian and her mother is English, so I hadn't expected such warmth, what with the different cultural backgrounds, but perhaps the middle-class, English-speaking, educated, foreign-raised children of all nationalities have a more common culture than we think.

Anyway, things got a lot more serious. I'd hesitated at that point. I wasn't sure I was at all ready for marriage and she was definitely leading that way. I didn't get it at the time, but she'd read this hesitation and that was when she had suddenly upped the ante by unzipping me.

Initially, she was pretty good fun. A little humourless perhaps. We enjoyed movies and nice restaurants. Not always the same ones, but still. She liked rich toys and I had money, so I was happy to oblige. Have you remembered why? Occasionally, very occasionally, she would show a flash of temper if I didn't do something she wanted, but it was so rare as to be almost adorable.

The spade got stuck on a big root and it took some vigorous hacking to get through it.

The really smart move was her going away. They all went off on a trip back to the UK to visit her grandparents.

OMG! ... as the kids write. I was randy all the time. I read somewhere that men think of sex a hundred times a day or something like that. Well, let me tell you, that was well short of the number bouncing my libido around like pinball in a penny arcade. When she got back. I was her poodle, her willing lapdog. When she mentioned 'something more serious', I caved.

With the engagement ring on her finger, she was my very own nymph—o—maniac. We never went all the way, but pretty damn close and she promised me that saving it for our wedding night would make everything more spectacular. The date was set and I was champing at the bit.

The hole was now exactly the right length and width. Down was now the only way to go. Nice and deep. I chuckled to myself. I'd never have to see her face again. Gone, gone.

The wedding was expensive. Her father pushed the boat out. He didn't seem upset at losing a daughter. He kept on shaking my hand. I'd really felt part of their family. I just didn't see it coming.

To be fair, the wedding night was pretty good. Not spectacular perhaps ... but maybe I'd built it up too much. All that waiting. Perhaps I'd been a little too fast. Not stoked the flames enough. I put it down to bride's nerves. Still, when you slide into a woman for the first time, it's heady, no doubt about it. The submissive liquid and yielding softness. Man, that's the fire of life.

And things did get better. In fact, I'd like to think we were both really enjoying each other for a while there. I was allowed unfettered access to my wife's body and she was pretty hot to trot most of the time. It felt happy. We set up home, bought an apartment in Singapore, got a maid.

Leila gave up her job three months into our marriage. I was pretty surprised. We hadn't discussed it. She just came home one day and announced it. From then on, she spent time with her friends and went out a lot—lunches, spas, that sort of thing.

So I thought the beginning of the end was when sex was too much of a bore, but now, taking the time to reflect here, under the stars, the sex became a bore after we had the money talk.

The earth was flying out. Thump, thump ... it was ready. A bit shallow perhaps, but it was tiring work and it would probably do.

Now here was the problem: her father was rich. She was used to a certain lifestyle. I couldn't supply the lifestyle. I was useless and what's more, I'd asked her to go back to work. We'd talked about none of this before our marriage. After all, I saw now, talking wasn't really what I wanted her mouth to be doing most of the time. Well, that particular pleasure went right out the window.

Reality set in. Marry in haste, repent at leisure. My lord, how true are those words.

And there you have it. We dragged the marriage around like a dead cat. She went back to work, and we stopped having sex. Not immediately, but inevitably, like a train rapidly running out of steam. Her temper got worse. Her contempt for me was obvious. Going home was the last thing I wanted to do. I think she was seeing someone else behind my back. I began to hate her.

Finally, that was it. I'd had enough. Actually, it was only this evening that I'd really, truly had enough. Such a short time ago, and the events of five minutes had led here, into this jungly space with a large hole in the ground big enough to put a body inside. No one was more surprised than me.

Divorce. I'd flung the word at her like a knife. Her face had been a picture of appalled dismay. I loathed her and wanted her to suffer. Divorce. Even in this dissolute age, in her family it meant disgrace. It did in mine too, but I no longer cared. I needed to get out, get out, get rid of her.

I left her standing in the kitchen and went to take a shower. I'd expected the usual show of incandescent temper, but she had said nothing. Maybe we were finally there: she had seen the sense of it

73

and she wanted out too. Get on with our lives. I'd sleep on the sofa tonight and move out tomorrow.

Ah, but that was not the way it was to be. When I came downstairs, she was gone. Out to cry on the shoulder of one of her rich friends, doubtless. The new boyfriend? I just didn't care. I called her name but I seemed to have the house to myself.

The shallow grave was filling up fast. Much easier to fill in than dig out. Each shovel of earth meant only one thing. I would never have to see her again.

Without warning, she'd come out of the darkness, hand raised, knife flashing. I fought off her flailing arms, twisting and turning. Then there was blood everywhere ... and silence. Instant divorce.

It was done. The last of the earth fell into place. Pat, pat. The rustle of leaves. Calm fell on the moonlit clearing.

She walked away. A car started up. The earth felt warm and as I settled comfortably into this final sleep, I thought, she'll never get away with it.

But it didn't matter.

I was rid of her. I was free.

Singapore-based DAWN FARHAM is the author of three historical novels set in Singapore, *The Red Thread*, *The Shallow Seas* and *The Hills of Singapore*, published by Monsoon Books, and an Asian-based children's book, *Fan Goes to Sea*, published by Beanstalk Press, Kuala Lumpur. She is working on a crime fiction series set in Western Australia, as well as several screenplays, for which she has received grants from the Singapore Film Commission. Website: *www.dawnfarnham.com*.

The Corporate Wolf

Pranav S. Joshi

On that Monday morning, CEO David Quek did not summon his managers to his Jurong office for a weekly progress review meeting. Today was not his day, he had realised.

And today was not the day to leisurely sip piping hot latte in his leather armchair, read *The Business Times*, hug his BlackBerry or comb through his appointments with his beautiful secretary, Pearl Ow.

April sun, freshly liberated from a prison of clouds, was peeking through a window blind in his spacious office with its eternal warmth, trying to enliven his mood. But the atmosphere in his office was filled with tension. Escalating. Unusual. Unnerving.

In front of David sat Mr Yeo, the purchasing manager of David's company, Lov-Ely Face Pte Ltd, which manufactured cosmetics and personal care products for the retail market in Singapore.

Yeo was a fifty-eight-year-old, lanky man with thinning grey hair, drawer-like mouth and yellow teeth. Dressed in a badly ironed shirt, he looked as though he had not slept for a few days and was witnessing the fulfilment of a Nostradamus' catastrophic prediction.

'Wh-what do you mean?' David nearly yelled, his face morphing into a picture on a poison warning label.

'As I said, our company is going to kill about a thousand women. Thousand!' Yeo whispered, urgency dripping from his voice. He glanced at the closed door of the office and made a laid-in-a-coffin gesture using his hands. 'In fact, some may have already died!'

'Oh-h!' David straightened his posture with a violent jerk. His chair hummed with a little bounce.

'I came back from China yesterday. My wife is—'

'I know. She's having some health problems,' David interjected and tapped his finger on his desk. 'Look, I'm not interested in your personal matters. Let's focus on the main, killing issue.'

Yeo swallowed a gulp of spit. He hated being insulted by his new boss who was thirty years younger than he was. But this was not the time to register his displeasure. 'Do you remember, in January, you'd told me to change the supplier of nano-minerals that we use in our anti-aging cream?' he asked.

'Which one?'

Yeo dug his hand into his trousers' pocket and brought out a fifty-gram, saucer-shaped bottle. 'This one, super strength revitalizing nano-energy cream. For ladies.'

'Umm, that supplier? Oh ya!' David nodded, remembering the incident in which he had lectured Yeo about the techniques of best sourcing and instructed him to buy raw materials from a supplier who had quoted the lowest price. 'Because the other Chinese company offered us a heavy discount.' He defended his decision.

'Ya, but do you know why?' Yeo jabbed his pen at the quotation of that company, kept in his file. 'They *sabo* us. Their ex-production manager, Mr Tsoi, met me secretly in Guangzhou. He said the clay that his company had used to manufacture nano-minerals came from a site which was polluted with toxic industrial waste.'

'How's that possible? It was an ISO 9001 company.'

'Mr Tsoi said some monkey business was going on.'

David's MBA trained mind tried to digest the information. OK, calm down, calm down, he said to himself, taking deep breaths. He then decided to buy some time to think over the whole issue. 'Give me a full report on this matter, so that I can do an in-depth analysis,' he said, a frown pulling his brows together.

Usually, in his report, he would ask for details encompassing '5 Wives and 1 Husband', or '5 Ws (When, What, Why, Who and Where) and 1 H (How)' as a part of the information gathering exercise, followed by root cause analysis, lessons learned and action plan to prevent such an incident in future.

'No point preparing any report, *meh*.' Yeo, who was not academically inclined, shrugged with his coarse mannerisms, trying hard to comply with David's instruction not to use *lah*, *meh* and other Singlish words while talking to him. He continued, 'According to Mr Tsoi, those cheap nano-minerals contained toxic heavy metals and pesticides in some activator matrix that would allow them to be absorbed deep inside the skin, without producing any burning sensation. From there, the nanoparticles would enter the blood stream.'

'So, are you saying that all those women who have used our cream need to go for blood purification?'

'No, it's not as simple as that. The nanoparticles will accumulate in vital organs like the liver, kidney, heart or even brain, and then poison them over time.'

'Then how come we haven't heard any complaints so far?' Memories of a Hollywood movie scene showing a massive pile of women's corpses flashed in David's mind. He shuddered.

'Because those particles are very small. They won't show up in the routine pathological tests or body scans due to their small size, and so the doctors won't be able to diagnose accurately. Besides, the nano size at which they exist, their toxicity is much higher than if they were absorbed in their normal size. The person will ultimately die.'

'Why should Mr Tsoi tell you this, after four months? That's absurd!' David threw his hands up in the air angrily.

'It's a long story. His ex-company has silenced him. A big cover-up!' Yeo's eyes narrowed to slits.

'How? How did they silence him?'

'By stuffing his mouth with money.'

'Oh!' The corners of David's mouth drew back in a snarl. He quickly recomposed and grabbed his pen. 'How much?'

'He didn't tell me the exact figure, but he said he got a few million yuan to keep his mouth shut.'

'So much money!' The pen dropped out of David's hand.

'One Singapore dollar is about 4.8 yuan.'

'But still, it's a lot of money.'

'It was his price, because of the seriousness of the matter. Several old ladies had died after they'd used the company's nano-mineral clay.' From his file, Yeo brought out a newspaper clipping showing a woman's photo in the obituary column. 'One of their victims!'

David glanced at the woman's tormented face, which looked puffy. A thought came to his mind that in future, he would be looking at photos of Singaporean women in obituary columns, with an underlined remark that David Quek's company had poisoned them. The media, sensing an easy meat, would tear apart his company's reputation, calling the episode 'The Ugly Face of Lov-Ely Face Pte Ltd'. He sighed.

'Two other staff of that company also knew about the problem—their CEO and QA manager.'

'How they discovered the problem?'

'The QA manager was the one who first came to know that the site was polluted with toxic waste. That was why they were getting the high-mineral clay from their supplier at a dirt-cheap price. She ran the necessary tests and confirmed that the nano-minerals produced from that clay by their company were also contaminated. But the contamination wouldn't show up in routine tests. She alerted Mr Tsoi who then alerted the CEO.'

'Then why didn't the CEO inform us?' David loosened his tie. 'Horrible!'

'It was a small company just like ours. The CEO, who owned the company, quickly sold it off after learning about the deaths. Now it's a part of a big organisation. The clay which they sell to us now is of high quality.' Yeo took out a paper from the file and showed it. 'The new management had informed us about the change in ownership.'

'So, now what?' David was frustrated. He pressed his head with his palms as if he had developed a severe headache. 'How many bottles of cream had we manufactured using that contaminated batch?'

'One thousand. I've checked with our sales department. The

retail shops have sold all the bottles by now.'

'That means we're in deep trouble!' David shook his head. 'Have you talked to our sales staff and the production manager about this problem?'

'No, I thought I should first talk to you. Right now, just like the Chinese company, only three persons in our company know about this problem. You, me and Madam Poh, our QC manager.'

'Poh! The one we're going to retrench?'

After taking over the reigns of the traditionally run company, David had begun to introduce sweeping changes in its operations to do a complete makeover of its corporate DNA. Paradigm shift, brand differentiation, New Age thinking, human capital ... the industry buzzwords had entered its old-fashioned world and created a commotion among the employees. To *resize* and *right-size* the company, David had prepared a list of 'old timers' whom he deemed frogs in the well who were incapable of thinking out-of-the-box. His plan was to gradually get rid of those staff and hire younger, better educated staff, the best of the breed. In fact, a few frog-employees had already been replaced. Madam Poh and even Yeo, who had been with the company for the last thirty-one years, were on his list.

'Ya, I had no choice.' Yeo nodded. 'I had to tell Madam Poh to analyse the samples that we've kept for traceability purposes, under the GMP system. She confirmed that the batch contains toxic compounds. She couldn't test all of them, but she's sure that it's full of nasty stuff!'

'Will she leak the information to anyone?'

'Nay, she's very loyal to our company.'

'Are you sure?'

'Ya, very sure.' Yeo nodded vigorously. 'She has promised me that she won't tell anyone about the problem. She has access to our confidential product formulation database, but never ever she has leaked any such information.'

'That gives me some comfort.'

'But the problem is, my wife Siew Eng, and Poh both have been using the same batch of cream. They bought from the market, after you stopped the staff from buying our company's products directly, at a discount. They paid about $22 each. And now, both of them are sick. Their livers are affected.' Yeo pointed at his abdomen and then at the bottle. 'This is Siew Eng's bottle. She has already used half of it.'

'I see!' David understood why Yeo had earlier talked about his wife. 'Have you told her that the cream is toxic?'

'No, otherwise, she'll create a storm and will become even more sick. Besides, I've my own rule. I don't discuss company matters with my family members. It's not ethical.'

'Hmm. But I'm surprised that Mr Tsoi met you secretly to expose his ex-company, even after being paid to shut his mouth. That means he's not ethical.' David made a sharp observation.

'Oh no, actually he was not going to meet me. Just by coincidence, we bumped into each other in the hotel lobby. He told Siew Eng that she was looking younger than she had looked when we met the last time, in Singapore. So, she proudly said that she was using our company's anti-aging cream.'

David stared at the offending bottle, his hand absently rubbing his cheeks as if they had come into contact with the cream.

'Afterwards, when Mr Tsoi learnt that we were going to consult a TCM expert in Guangzhou for her liver treatment, he thought that it was his duty to alert me, before it was too late.' From his breast pocket, Yeo brought out a name card of a TCM professor associated with the Guangzhou University of Traditional Chinese Medicine. 'Siew Eng's local TCM physician had recommended her to consult this professor.'

'Well, I'm sorry to hear about your wife's problem.'

David's half-hearted 'sorry' did not impress Yeo. 'It's OK. Our fate, what else to say?' He sighed. 'Now, the question is, do you want to recall all the bottles from the consumers and inform the Health Sciences Authority?'

David's body shook as though it was electrocuted. 'I ... I need to think about the consequences.'

'Frankly, a recall will be very difficult, because according to the sales staff, many tourists buy our products as well. That means we'll have to advertise the recall not only in the local, but also in the foreign media.'

'What if some women have already died, huh? Their families will sue us, accusing us of being negligent. No, I don't think our sales staff can handle this. Some more, we don't even have a PR manager, unlike those big companies.'

'This is going to be a tough challenge.'

'Have you heard of the cockroach theory?'

'About those cockroach fighting competitions in Beijing?'

'No, no.' David pointed at the floor. 'When a person sees a cockroach in any place, the person will think that there'll be many more cockroaches hiding and breeding in the crevices. In this case, if such news will come out, people will think that there are many more bad news that we're hiding. Our pots are not clean!'

'This is not a cockroach. It's like a dinosaur!' Yeo stretched his arms apart. 'Actually, the whole company will collapse and become extinct. Some of us may even land up in jail. People will call us murderers. And we're not only talking about just the death. What about the pain and suffering of the victims, like what my wife is experiencing? And those expensive medical treatments? Some families will go bankrupt, I tell you.'

David stared at the ceiling. He had worked on a number of problem-solving and decision-making assignments during his MBA, using techniques such as SWOT Analysis and Decision Grid. But this real life problem in the dog-eat-dog world hit him with an impact for which he was not prepared. In fact, the situation had already escalated from being a problem into a crisis. It was now a question of the company's survival.

'Could we cover up?' he asked after a long pause. He justified his question: 'I'm just exploring various options, so don't get me wrong.'

'It's up to you.' Yeo pointed at a photo of David's father, whom they called towkay or, simply, Mr Quek. 'I've served your father since the day he started this company. You were not even born at that time. He loved this company from his heart. It'll be very painful for me to see his lovely face baby dying so fast after his departure.'

David's father had died suddenly during a heart attack last year, in December 2009. The incident had forced David to return to Singapore from New York, where he had just completed his MBA.

'Hmm.' David sighed. Yeo's last sentence knifed him. If he

opted for a recall and caused the company to collapse, the whole industry would think of him as an incompetent son of a competent father. Now, the only option was to cover up the matter like the CEO in China had done. It was either sink or sail.

Yeo continued his assault on David's abilities. 'That's why I'd told you not to just focus on price while buying raw materials.'

'I know.' David bit his lips. 'Now don't do blamestorming. Let's focus on the crisis management.'

'There's a Chinese saying, "The sheep has no choice when in the jaws of the wolf." I think we're already in the jaws.' Yeo coughed.

David thought for a while. Then with his innate shrewdness, he asked, 'Let's say if we want to "silence" Madam Poh, will she agree to it?'

'In what way? The way they did in Guangzhou?'

'Ya, I mean, how much you think we'll have to pay to her?' David was certain that a few thousand dollars to the old woman would suffice. After all, the company paid her a salary that was way below the market rate for her position, but that was also the reason why she had survived all these years in the company, even during recessions when sales had hit rock bottom.

'In China, the CEO didn't pay anything to the QA manager.' Yeo waved his palms.

'Then? Then?'

'He offered her money, but she refused and threatened to expose the matter.' Yeo brought his face closer. 'So he personally silenced her. Forever.'

'How?'

'He ran his car over her in a street, at night. Like a cucumber, her body squashed under the tires.'

'Oh!' David was stunned.

'Do you want to explore such an option?'

'No, no.' David shrugged vehemently. Goosebumps rose on his arms and neck as he imagined himself running his BMW over Madam Poh. This was not an option recommended by his MBA books.

'Actually, Poh wants to cooperate. She can secretly discard the toxic cream from the sample that we've kept for traceability purpose. She said she could fill the bottle with a good quality cream. Nobody will know.'

'If that's the case, then ask her what's her price for helping us?'

Yeo nodded. 'I'll ask her after lunch, when she's in good mood.'

'Hmm.' David cupped his chin in his right palm. 'How about Mr Tsoi? Do you think he'll inform our authorities?'

'No, he said he doesn't want to risk his life. Also, he doesn't want us to get into any trouble. He's a gentleman. Do you want to speak to him?'

'No-o!' David's palms pressed hard on the armrests. 'Look, as far as this issue is concerned, you've never ever spoken to me. I know nothing about it. Understand?'

'I got it.' Yeo again nodded. 'You want to keep your hands clean.'

'Absolutely. Now, to be honest with you, I doubt whether Mr Tsoi's ex-company would have paid him a few million yuan. You said the company was small, right?'

'David, China has changed so much! People have become

very smart there. When CEO found out that the nano-mineral was exported to our company in Singapore, he panicked because the incident could affect China's entire raw material export market, which is worth billions of dollars. Plus, he was worried that the authorities might hang him upside down.' Yeo cleared his throat and continued, 'I don't have MBA and cockroach theories to tell, but I know that bad news travels faster than good news.'

'You're right.' David nodded. 'OK, let me do a kind of cost-benefit analysis. In the meantime, you check with Poh. Don't mention about our plan to retrench her. She'll become upset.'

'Sure. Do you want to talk to her directly?'

'No, it'll complicate the matter. As I said, I don't want to get directly involved in the issue. And ya, another thing. Be very careful. This news should stay with us. Only the three of us.' David pointed at his PC. 'Don't send me anything through e-mail or in writing about the matter.'

Yeo nodded. 'So, no report?'

'No!'

Yeo stood up to leave. 'Actually, I'm very worried.'

'Will such a scenario happen again in the future? I mean, we sweep it under the carpet now, then after one month, we face a similar problem. Then, there'll be no end. We'll always be boiling the ocean and doing fire fighting!'

'Very unlikely.' Yeo shrugged. 'Product quality problems like colour fading and all that we do encounter sometimes, but these are small problems, easy to resolve. Once, we also suspected that a batch of lipstick might have been contaminated with lead metal. But it wasn't true.'

'Has anyone died after using our product?'

'Never!' Yeo pointed at the bottle of cream. 'This is the first time I've heard of such a serious health problem. But I must tell you, the nanoparticles and all those modern day stuff are very unpredictable. Cannot *play-play*. In future, we shouldn't buy just based on price. Cost shouldn't be the only deciding factor.'

David swallowed the scorn. He had gone against the time-tested purchasing techniques of the old man, and so he deserved to face the consequences and manipulate his ego. 'Yep, I was wrong,' he admitted.

'Do you want to keep this bottle?' Yeo pointed at the bottle of cream. 'My wife thinks that we left it in the hotel room in Guangzhou, by mistake.'

'Ya, leave it here.'

Yeo stepped out of the office, his eyes downcast.

Pearl rushed in to inform David about his appointment with a client.

'Postpone all of my today's appointments,' he instructed her with an unfriendly wave.

Pearl retreated to her chair with a large scowl.

For the next few hours, David paced in his office in circles, with his arms crossed on his chest. Occasionally, his palms wiped droplets of sweat, both real and imaginary, from his forehead despite a full blast from the room's air-conditioner. He was a tall man with a prominent forehead and an athletic body. An ugly scar that he had acquired on his chin during his National Service had forced him to settle for a lesser degree of handsomeness than what he would otherwise have achieved.

After settling down in his new role as the CEO, he had set several ambitious goals for the company, such as to expand business across the whole Southeast Asian region, to double its revenue and profit in the next three years, and then to float the company on the Singapore Exchange. Leveraging on the glamorous image of the industry that his company served, he wanted to uplift himself to the elite club of movers and shakers in the country. After all, he was a man of many ambitions.

Two years back, after receiving his bachelor's degree from the Singapore Institute of Management, he had tried to help his father in managing the business. But his management style had not gone well with his old-fashioned father. Unwilling to engage in a confrontation with his father, David had therefore backed off willingly though bitterly, and packed himself off to USA for an MBA.

Now, all the cards were in his hands for the company that had come a long way. Started in 1978 in a humble container by Mr Quek, it had grown slowly, and now it was a nine-million dollar company that employed a staff of about forty. It occupied a manufacturing facility and a two storey office building in Jurong, and a satellite office-cum-warehouse in Simei. The strength of the company lay in manufacturing and marketing products made from natural ingredients. Positioning itself as a supplier of safe products, it had built a loyal client base in Singapore over the years.

And now, that reputation was at stake. In fact, the company's future was at stake, and so was Mr Quek's legacy.

David deliberated in his mind about the options that were available to him. Later, he checked on the Internet to gather more information about similar case histories and effect of toxic nanoparticles on vital organs in the human body. Majority of the women who used anti-aging cream would be older women hence, the adverse effects would be far more significant, he reasoned. Lawsuits were inevitable if the matter was exposed, as evident from the numerous high-profile cases involving diet pills and drinking water, such as the Slim 10 saga in Singapore and the Erin Brockovich case in the USA.

Apart from the legal costs, the compensation to the victims could run into millions of dollars, especially if any celebrity had bought the bottle of contaminated cream. Also, if by sheer coincidence, any of those women had fallen ill from some other cause after using the cream, they would squarely blame the cream for their health problems. No wonder the Chinese company paid millions of yuan to Mr Tsoi to keep his mouth shut.

As David further evaluated the consequences, it became clear to him that if he was not careful, the crisis could throw him—together with his ambitions—into a valley of shame and self-destruction. He was standing on the bleeding edge. His decision to change the supplier for the simple reason of price could catapult him into future MBA books for the wrong reasons: as a case history of what could possibly go wrong when a new, inexperienced CEO was given an opportunity to run the family business. No amount of reputation repair strategies would help him out. He probably needed to lift a shovel and bury the secret of the toxic batch, to save his dignity and his company.

But the question was, could he cover up the matter? Could a smart doctor establish a link between the cream and the deaths and the diseases? What if the authorities found out that he had withheld the information and put all those women at a high risk? Would Madam Poh or Yeo secretly inform the authorities if they were unhappy with the company?

Trapped.

He was indeed trapped. He felt nauseous.

That day, except for a short toilet break, he did not step out of his office. Energy bars and a soybean packet drink constituted his lunch. All files on his desk and all e-mails in his inbox remained untouched.

He was trying to think outside the box but somehow, the box was putting him back inside its chest. The MBA was not helping him in the way he had expected.

Thinking about Yeo's wife, he remembered what his father had told him on the first death anniversary of his mother: 'David, losing your Ma, Ely, was the most painful day of my life. Sometimes, the old man inside me feels very lonely. I really miss her.'

Would Yeo lose his wife? David bit his lips as the thought kept on flooding his mind over and over again.

* * *

The next day, Yeo and David met again to discuss the matter. Worry was written all over their faces.

Yeo placed two samples on the desk. 'You see, this is the nano-mineral sample from the contaminated batch that we've kept in our lab for traceability, and this other sample is from the good quality batch. Nobody can tell the difference.'

David stared at the two samples. Yeo was right. The samples

looked the same.

'Did you talk to Poh?' he asked, his bloodshot eyes hinting that he had either drunk alcohol that morning or had spent the night staring at his laptop.

Yeo nodded. 'We're in deep trouble.'

'Why? She doesn't want to cooperate?'

'No. She's asking for a ridiculous sum, since she knows the extent of problem.'

'How much?'

Yeo blew air from his mouth. 'Umm, more than a million.'

'Basket!' David felt like rushing to the greedy, reclusive woman and slapping her. She had been employed initially as a cleaner in the company. But Mr Quek had encouraged her to study part-time and later promoted her to the post of QC manager. David disliked her, as he thought of her as a stubborn and slow-paced employee, lacking in business sense. During meetings, she would stare blankly ahead and avoid participating in any discussion. Smile? 'Ah, I've yet to see a smile on her face!' he would lament.

'I tried to explain, but she ...' Yeo shook his palms.

'I tell you, that stone-faced woman wants to blackmail the company. So ungrateful!' David hammered a fist on his desk.

'Careful!' Yeo moved away the sample. 'This is far more toxic than the cream.'

'Never mind. How much is it she wants?'

'Two million.'

'Ha!' David nearly choked. A few American expletives emerged from his mouth. Yeo stared at him, astonished by what he had heard.

Realising that his outburst was not so appropriate, David

apologised. 'Sorry, sorry.' He shook his head and continued, 'Now coming back to the issue, let me be very honest with you. I've no intention to pay her such a ridiculous sum. We're not operating a charity!'

'Actually, for herself, she wants only one million. She's afraid that she may have to undergo surgery, which is quite expensive. And she doesn't think that the company will allow her to continue due to her poor health.'

'I've no sympathy for her. If you ask me, I would like to sack her right now.'

'David, you should control your emotions. If you try to fight with her, you'll certainly lose your shirt on this issue, I must warn you. Remember the Chinese saying that I told you: "The sheep has no choice when in the jaws of the wolf." I hope you understand what I'm trying to tell you.'

'Yeah, no point fighting with her. But frankly, she should use her personal insurance like MediShield to pay for her medical bills, rather than trying to milk money from the company.'

'I didn't talk to her about MediShield, since you'd told me not to upset her. Since it's the company's product that has made her ill, I thought she might not like the idea of using her own insurance money.'

'Hmm.' David rubbed his eyes with his fingers. 'Anyway, why does she need that extra one million?'

'Well, she's a crazy woman.'

'Since the day I met her, I knew something was wrong with her. Anyway, she's single and thrifty. So why is she asking for a million more? For her secret lover?'

'No. For her friend.' With a little hesitation, Yeo added, 'I mean my wife, Siew Eng.'

'Your wife!'

'Ya. Because Poh thinks that I won't provide her proper medical treatment. I'll try to save money and so she'll suffer and die in pain.'

'But didn't you explain that you won't do such a thing?' David's voice rose to a high pitch. 'In fact, even in Guangzhou, you tried to get the best TCM treatment for her!'

'Actually, we'd gone there to attend my cousin's wedding, but since her local TCM physician had recommended her to consult that professor in Guangzhou, we tried our luck. We don't know yet whether the treatment is working.'

'Since Poh is so concerned about your wife's health, I think she'll tell her about the contaminated cream. Ah, we're in a mess!'

'No, Poh won't do that without checking with me. She has her own rules, like mine.'

David reached for a Panadol and gulped it down with water. 'Well, I need some time to rethink about the options. But I want to ask you personally: Do you also want any money, like Poh and Mr Tsoi? Please don't lie to me.'

Yeo shot a wounded look, as if David had just spat in his face. 'I'm not a liar,' he said.

'No, I didn't mean that. I just want to know, so that we've a common understanding.'

'Honestly, if I'm given money to keep my mouth shut, I'll happily accept it.' Yeo made a mouth-zipping gesture using his fingers. 'I've worked here for so many years. I know you're trying to introduce changes in the company and want to bring in new, more energetic staff. I'm also tired of trying to keep up. The company can give me a golden handshake and we'll have a win-win situation.'

'How much do you want?'

'I can't think of any figure, but it shouldn't be lower than that given to Madam Poh. Otherwise, I'll lose my face to her.'

'You want more than two million?!' David's eyes enlarged.

'No, I'm not greedy. After all, if you're going to give one million for my wife, I can't ask for so much. I've my own ethics.'

'Just tell me, what's your price?'

'Give me one month's salary for every year I've worked for the company. That's why I said golden handshake. That way, I'll also be able to keep my face among my colleagues, since they'll ask me why I'm leaving the company.' Yeo paused, then added, 'To Madam Poh, the company can give her half month's salary for every year she has worked.'

'Hmm. That sounds more reasonable.' David thrust his hand under his desk. 'I'll do my calculations and let you know. If I decide to pay the million-dollar, under the table money, I'll pay in cold hard cash from my personal account. I don't want to involve our finance manager in that issue. He'll handle your golden handshake details with our HR executive.'

'I'll wait for your decision.' Yeo stood up.

'Leave this contaminated sample here. Tell Poh to replace it with a good quality one.'

'Sure.' Yeo leaned over the desk and whispered, 'I'll make sure that there's no trace of any such sample in the lab or the warehouse.'

'All right then. I'll count on you,' David whispered back. 'Destroy all the evidence, once and for all.'

'Consider it done.' Confidence dripped from Yeo's voice.

As he slowly stepped out of the office, David placed his hands on his head and closed his eyes. He was feeling peaceful and tired in equal measure.

*   *   *

After a couple of days, Yeo received a phone call from David informing him that he had tested the sample in an independent laboratory and confirmed that it was heavily contaminated. Hence, he had made a decision to do COCA—Cover Our Collective Asses— in order to save the entire company. He was going to pay one million dollars to Poh to shut her mouth. To Yeo also, he was willing to pay one million in under the table money for his wife. Plus, both of them would be given golden handshakes by the company, as per what Yeo had suggested. But both would have to sign an undertaking that they would not divulge any confidential information relating to the company to any external party.

The under the table money would come from David's own pocket. He had wanted to buy a condominium in District 10 as an investment. But now, he would use that money to close the matter.

Hopefully, forever.

'Tell Poh that the amount that I'm willing to pay is non-negotiable. And oh ya, tell her that if she asks for more money, I'll not agree to it. The company will collapse and all the employees will become jobless. It'll be the greatest sin of her life.' At the end of the call, David made his point using a hostile tone.

'I'll tell her,' Yeo assured him and put down the receiver.

In his calendar, he then marked a date for their farewell parties. He also rehearsed how to smile without baring his yellow teeth, and what things to say during the event.

'My life's paradigm shift!' he murmured and headed towards the lab. An old Hokkien melody leaked from his lips.

* * *

A month later, Poh and Yeo met in a private room of a restaurant in Chinatown. They sat on a sofa chair, acknowledging mysterious smiles of Shanghainese girls from the wall posters around them. Above them, a red lantern cast a soothing glow on them.

Poh looked at Yeo with her signature blank stare. 'I've sleepless nights. I feel like a criminal,' she said.

'Don't worry, you've already covered your tracks. Nobody will be able to catch you.' Yeo raised his cup of tea. 'Cheers!'

With hesitation, Poh raised her cup. Both clanked their cups.

'One more cheers to all those healthy and younger-looking ladies who have used the anti-aging cream,' Yeo announced, and both sipped their tea in unison.

'I ... I still can't understand how did you manage to bargain so much money for us,' Poh said. 'I was thinking that at most, David will give me about $25,000.'

'Impressed by my game plan?' Yeo smiled and pointed a finger at his chest. 'I told you, if you cooperated with this *ah beng*, he would make you a millionaire.'

'I salute your negotiation skills.' In an odd fashion, Poh raised her hand to her head. With the other hand, she picked up a peanut using her chopsticks and dropped it in her mouth.

'Since the day David insulted me, and told me that I was a frog in the well, I'd decided to take revenge on him. *Beh tahan.*' Yeo punched his face.

'I was so scared when I added those extra toxins in the samples. What if David finds out in the future?'

'Look, you never did anything like that. You understand?' A streak of anger scurried across Yeo's face.

'Ya.' Poh lowered her head. 'But my whole body shakes whenever I think about it.'

'*Aiyah*, as a retiree, you should think about money, not about the work you did in the past.'

'True. With so much of money, even if I spend $2,500 every month from now, it will last for more than thirty years.'

'If you think that it's too much, just give me whatever you can't spend. Do you remember the day when we were young and I had proposed to you?' Yeo winked. 'If we had so much money at that age, hoo-oo!' He made a loud, joyous sound.

Poh blushed like a small girl. 'No point talking about the past. Now, already so old.'

'Old, but with a pot of gold.'

'Ya.' Poh nodded. 'How will you spend the money? Go on a tour of Europe and America, or try your luck at the Resorts World casino?'

'I've some secret plans. Can't tell you,' Yeo said with a mischievous glint in his eyes.

'Don't overspend.'

'Of course, I won't overspend!' Yeo dismissed her with a wave of his hand. 'Anyway, talking about America, Crystal wants to go there to do her MBA. I want to give her a surprise by sponsoring her course. Later, I want to tell David that my daughter can also earn an MBA, just like him. I want to see his face!'

'I heard Siew Eng doesn't need any surgery, just like me.'

'Ya. Thank God.' Yeo brought out a book on Chinese proverbs from his backpack, and gave it to Poh. 'Returning you the *yanyu* book. It came in very handy.'

'How?'

'Read this.' Yeo opened the book and pointed at a proverb.

'The sheep has no choice when in the jaws of the wolf.' Poh read the proverb and shook her head. 'I don't understand.'

Yeo straightened his posture. 'David forced me to turn into a corporate wolf from a frog, and I dragged him into my mouth, under the pretext of being a sheep. Mr Tsoi was my fake tooth, while you were my real teeth. Do you get me?'

Poh looked around with a stealthy look. Then, with a naughty grin, she declared, 'No matter who you are—wolf or sheep or frog—but for me, you're the man with a heart. Next time, if you want to use me as a tooth, make sure that your mouth is clean. I don't want to get involved in any dirty, criminal stuff.'

'Sure, sure, Miss Millionaire.' Yeo laughed heartily.

PRANAV S. JOSHI is a multitalented environmental professional, novelist and poet. His multicultural novel, *Behind a Cultural Cage*, which presented the life story of a Chinese-Indian man, was heartily received by the literary circles. Pranav holds a PhD in Chemistry and an MSc in Environmental Engineering.

The Murder Blog
of Wilde Diabolito

Chris Mooney-Singh

'EACH MAN KILLS THE THING HE LOVES'
13 JUNE 2010

I plan to kill someone. That person is very close to me. If you want
to know who, when and how it will happen, then stay in touch with
my blog and see what you can figure out. It will be a conscious act.
A matter of honour. You may believe you can stop me, but ... In
fact, for the record, let me categorically state:

*I, Wilde Diabolito, being of sound mind and body, am writing
with a sober disposition, without evidence or any diagnosis of
insanity—congenital, inherited or otherwise—lodged against me at
this time, that I am planning a murder.*

I will openly tell you the steps, the time and the means by which
I will commit this act and none of you will be able to do anything
about it. Don't bother reporting my Net address to the police or any
other authority. I have technically ensured that you will not be able
to track me online. This site is now being routed through countless
servers across the globe. I could be anywhere, although I may drop

some hints about my location, just for the hell of it. You see, I will prove to you that a crime can be done in full public view—and what better way in this day and age than to document it online?

I reiterate: none of you anywhere will be able to stop this murder from taking place.

posted by Wilde Diabolito 3.30 p.m.

2 Comments >>

13 June 2010, 7.31 p.m.
Black Sparrow said:
Is this for real? You sound like a maniac.

13 June 2010, 9.27 p.m.
Wilde Diabolito said:
What is real, Black Sparrow? You yourself are hiding a 'real' life behind a fictive name. Thanks for stopping by.

— —

'BY EACH LET THIS BE HEARD'
14 JUNE 2010

Although I have not written anything before, I believe I am as much a writer as any one of you. I have the intention to be a writer, albeit a murderous one, and I declare it now. Who can stop me from publishing myself and documenting this upcoming crime and turning it into literature? (The quality of which, I will leave to others to decide.) I have only to state my intent and create immortality through words.

I am not some brainless thug moved by animalistic urges. Quite the opposite. And there are solid reasons for this coming execution; you will understand later why I have chosen to 'blog it', as they say.

Let me give you a literary precedent for my crime. Oscar Wilde, my namesake and the presence hovering over this screen once wrote: 'Each man kills the thing he loves.' He was reporting a real life crime that he learned of during his stint in Reading Gaol between 1895-7. For those who don't remember, the authorities incarcerated Wilde for 'obscene acts' and while inside, he witnessed the hanging of one Charles Thomas Wooldridge, who had at one time been a Trooper in the Royal Horse Guards. The unfortunate man was convicted of cutting the throat of his wife, Laura Ellen. He was thirty years old when sent to the gallows. Of course, it was a 'crime of passion' and yes, she was having an affair with someone else at the time, which the young and impassioned husband came to know of.

Meanwhile, Oscar Wilde was so moved by the circumstances of this young man's act that he wrote it all down in a pamphlet poem called *The Ballad of Reading Gaol*. (A pamphlet being, in those days, equivalent to the immediacy of an online blog.)

When it came out, it was an overnight sensation.

The poem was published under the pseudonym of C.3.3, Wilde's block number during his two years of hard labour. Anyone could have done their homework and discovered the author, but the poet remained undiscovered, proving a basic point of my thesis— that one can write or commit acts under the noses of the public and not be found out. The name Oscar Wilde did not appear until seven editions later.

I have shared this information simply because Oscar Wilde's line, 'Each man kills the thing he loves' is a grim reality that you, Reader, should remember. It is not outside the reach of any man or woman, when pressed, to contemplate such an act. No, I do not advocate murder just for the sake of it. Yet one day, you may also be subject to similar internal pressures, emotions and circumstances, and this blog may become a useful frame of reference, a crib for your crime, so to speak, and guide you through the darkness at such a moment.

For my part, I admit to making one similar mistake in my life that now needs to be rectified. Perhaps too preoccupied with a life of military service, I realised the years had flown and then, at a late age, I had no child to carry on the family name. Although I have never been much interested or experienced with women, the fact is, I wanted—no, needed—a son to give me a sense that my name would remain in the world. One night, I met a young waitress who seemed the answer to my need. After showering her with gifts and promises of comfort and life-long security, she agreed to marry me, despite the vast difference in our ages. This is what I am documenting here, Dear Reader. Take note: this is the story of the restoration of honour following an old man's folly.

Thus, I now see writing this blog as my public duty. Having served my country all my life, it is now time to serve a wider humanity by sharing the past two years of a hell no decent man should have to endure. No, this is not a serial crime that I am embarking on: I plan to produce a one-off, clean-cut masterpiece as perfect as the deep affection I once shared for the One in question before love soured life. I wish to share it also as some kind of cautionary tale, inspired by Wilde's next line: 'By each let this be heard.' Yes, I, like him, have a moral purpose: he felt human pity for Wooldridge and his poem is a slap on the bearded jowls of the British legal and penal system. I also wish you to understand that the person I am about to commit to the next world was once the dearest thing I possessed in the world.

The last thing I wish to say, by way of explanation and not defence, is that a murder is, by all social norms, an unthinkable act; and yet, such unthinkable actions are committed daily by some of the most thoughtful and handsome-minded people. I do believe motive and act should not be separated in this discussion and that what we hold as dear and sacred may not stand up today under forensic investigation.

posted by Wilde Diabolito at 9.30 a.m.

2 Comments >>

14 June 2010, 11.31 a.m.
Way of the Panda said:
You compare yourself with Oscar Wilde. You've even taken his name as inspiration, an authority figure to justify what you say you are going to do. Wilde was just some sick dude who got a bad taste of prison life because he played naughty with his boyfriends. You have no authority either. Your blog is wack and should be shut down.

14 June 2010, 12.57 a.m.

Wilde Diabolito said:

Dear 'Way of the Panda': I am sorry you obviously haven't read much and have no liking for the works of Oscar Wilde. Others have. In any case, I am not blogging to entertain you or any other Panda in cartoonish ways. I am simply stating facts and there will be a reckoning if you have the guts to stick around.

— —

'SOME DO IT WITH A BITTER LOOK'
15 JUNE 2010

Of course, we kill each other daily with a sour apple glance. It grows like a bad seed, appearing after the rosy period of romance has fallen off the tree. Then the season of cynicism sets in, like an overcast sky when the hard wind rolls into town one day and you find yourself in the grip of someone's displeasure, short temper and accusations, someone's slight, yet gigantic irritation.

You don't quite know how and when it began. Was it an accumulation of small irritants that gradually all piled up? The way I tended to leave my wet towel on the bed after a shower, or my quiet, methodical reading of historical books in my study? Then, there was my snoring. This was the excuse she used to finally move into the baby's room, our darling Baby's room. I could take all that. I was a patient man. I could put up with nights alone in our double bed, while from the next room, I heard laughing and ... I do not want to talk here of the all disgusting things that I heard. But even that I endured, rationalising as an older man must when he is no longer as 'useful' to a young woman at her sexual peak.

But when she began to divulge our private life and her disgust for me, I knew she had no shame. It had gone too far. I began to look sourly back at love and the one I had opened my life, home and bank account to. Yes, she knew I was observing her, yet she literally laughed in my face.

'Well, what can you do about it?' she said. 'I live in my own house now. If you try to divorce me, you'll be the loser: I will wipe you out!'

A man can only stand so much of a woman's cuckolding and contempt before something snaps and he finds himself waking up in the middle of the night seething with a rage and darkness that he did not know existed in him. It hits one like a delayed knockout punch—how she loathes the feel of your old body, its flabby flesh, greying chest hair, the bald spot and now the sourness coming from your armpits, which she said was the smell of your slow decay. She cannot stomach you. That revulsion happened almost the day after we lost Baby, that beautiful boy, waking up one morning and finding a tiny corpse in the crib. It was as if the little one had opted out of this life of impending problems and died anonymously, a cot death.

She blamed me, of course, as a woman must and I blamed her inwardly for her lack of motherly affection—how Baby was so often left alone crying in the crib, while she was either on the computer or talking on her phone. Yes, I was to blame. It will always be a man's fault.

After that, she went into a shell and clamped up. Now she claimed that she couldn't stomach the idea of having sex with an 'old person'. In fact, she said she was too depressed to think about relationships anymore. That was a lie. But what can one say under such circumstances to a girl more than thirty years your junior, yet still your legal wife? She had been my latter-day mistake. I'd fallen head over heels out of my safe boat of bachelorhood into the choppy ocean of marriage. However, a man, even an older one, has rights too, doesn't he?

From that time on, despite her claim about the end of relationships, she began a double life of late night online meetings and rendezvous. She would go shopping and accumulate unnecessary clothes, handbags and shoes. I don't know where she got the money from, as I had capped her allowance. Perhaps it was to spite me, but I could hear her in the next room loudly getting ready to whore around with almost any wolverine she met up with—perhaps in a club, or friend's house, even in some public park up against a tree. I imagined all the possible scenarios.

I am a true product of the State I have lived in and served most of my life, and all my experience has prepared me for the coming role of judge and executioner. No one else knows her as I do and can fairly adjudicate in this case. It is up to me alone to set the balance of nature right. Death is a part of life. Violent death is a law of the jungle, and there are still in this country pockets of green liana and viper nests. I would have felt such ideas repugnant before, but now I realised there was no other way. It was now a matter of honour as well as justice.

From this point, I was no longer looking to the future of the relationship: I was actively planning the end of it. This is the nature of the beast I am reflecting upon for your benefit, Blog Voyeurs. I mean, isn't it a fact that all this personal material is becoming the province of your interest? Are you not now compelled to return for regular updates on the life and times of Wilde Diabolito, the man who will, in the near future, commit a murder?

posted by Wilde Diabolito at 11.17 a.m.

2 Comments >>

15 June 2010, 1.31 p.m.
Little Twilight said:
Dear Mr Diabolito, are you trying to scare us? I mean I've watched movies where girls get their necks chewed open by vampires and seen the daily news with suicide bombs going off all over the Middle-East. So what's the big deal, huh?

15 June 2010, 11.54 p.m.
Wilde Diabolito said:
Indeed. What is the big deal? You think that all this is some game, something to entertain. You think of this as on the same soulless level as some thrill-seeking advertisement for Red Bull. You only seek the result of titillation, not the motive behind why I would kill someone. I believe you are too young to understand what might happen to you one day in the arms of your own future Love Mugger. May you grow up fast, Little Twilight.

- -

'SOME DO IT WITH A FLATTERING WORD'
16 JUNE 2010

I am glad some interest is stirring. It flatters me a little I admit to think that after just three postings, I am building a small readership and that some of you are moved, or at least interested enough, to be repelled by what I am saying here each day. Yes, Commentators, you are becoming my accomplices, although you can't see that far into the future. Yet by coming to this blog site, your mental energy is already beating in time with the pulse of a crime in the making.

So dear Blog Followers, your comments, ideas, however reactive, childishly sentimental or puerile are appreciated by this writer. You are now part of the fabric of what I am proposing here. I speak out for cold-blooded honesty, clean-cut results born from clear motives. This is my personal matter, yet political to the extent that bigger crimes than mine are committed by murderous regimes in the name of Harmony and World Peace. Let us stand against hypocrisy: To kill for love is a purer kind of killing than for power or economic annexation, wouldn't you say? Love is my motive. In my own way, I am still in love and will kill the thing I love out of a belief in the same lasting sentiment.

posted by Wilde Diabolito at 4.10 p.m.

6 Comments >>

16 June 2010, 8.12 p.m.
Black Sparrow said:

I'm outta here, you dumb fuck.

16 June 2010, 8.27 p.m.
Way of the Panda said:
If you think we are going to play your game and create bad karma for ourselves, you have another think coming, Diabolito. I am not coming back!

16 June 2010, 9.45 p.m.
Little Twilight said:
I don't know, you guys. Some of what he writes makes sense. Maybe we can reason with him. Maybe it's not too late.
16 June 2010, 10.58 p.m.

Wilde Diabolito said:
Well thanks for your votes of disapproval, Sparrow and Panda. You reveal your own lack of fortitude. No loss there. And Little Twilight, aspiring vamp, I thank you for your small support.

16 June 2010, 11.03 p.m.
Precinct Angel said:
I have been lurking here without commenting and reading your blog, Wilde, and I must say your thinking, although flawed, is not without its strong points. The overriding and obvious error is clearly that you think you are a moral being and that your wife an irrevocably immoral one. You have already proclaimed sentence on her, just as a government would proclaim capital punishment for an act of first-degree murder. What you are proposing is self-justified,

premeditated execution. Why have you not allowed her to reform? Yours is not just hypocrisy—it is an illness. You are a sick, sick man.

17 June 2010, 1.23 a.m.
Wilde Diabolito said:
Precinct Angel, I do not need any other person to tell me what is moral and immoral. I know the difference, as does my young wife. She clearly believes, however, that she can break the ancient rules of fidelity, trust and loyalty. She does not realise how much I believe in action and honour. She should never have abused my generosity, siphoned off a lot of my wealth to her siblings and grasping widow of a mother. But that is another story, and I have closed that account. Let me throw down the cyber gauntlet to you or anyone: I will commit my crime within five days and will prove without a doubt online that my One is not honest with me and can never be so, because she is lascivious and rapacious by nature.

- -

'THE COWARD DOES IT WITH A KISS'
17 JUNE 2010

Blog Readers and Lurkers, here is your chance to play Judas and kiss my cyber cheek. If you can, reveal me to the authorities. That is my challenge to any one of you. Precinct Angel seems up for the task. All right, we will see who else is willing to face me in this cyberworld. As this medium is no less real to the millions who spend as much time online today as they do in their physical towns and cities, I give you an invitation to play.

First—a rapid round up of the past year or so of our life together. I was forced to become familiar with the Internet as a tool of investigation. My wife, as I mentioned, spent nearly all her free time online. It was always her hobby, I guess, but she had become more secretive about it. She had taken over Baby's room and had turned it into her private boudoir-study, enrolling (she said) for some online degree in Social Communications from a community college in the USA. (Yes, we are not living in that country.) She also said she had to do online tuition at odd hours. I had seen the printed assignments, but the online tuition part was not listed on their website curriculum, except for special subjects outside the scope of her degree, which was mostly coursework by e-mail. Yes, I quietly checked into it all.

A few nights back, while she went out to dinner, I logged on to her computer. Looking for clues for any obvious liaison she might be having, I went directly to her e-mail inbox. There was some correspondence from Camberway College, but nothing that aroused any suspicion and I admit to feeling some surprise. Then, I checked her MSN chat portal and chat logs and found them all largely to be local girlfriend talk. I was puzzled. I scanned her documents and picture files. Nothing. Then I searched the desktop, opening the icons one by one until I clicked on one like two conjoined heads looking in opposite directions. It was the Janus symbol, though I doubt that many would know the Roman mythological significance: how the symbol was inscribed in doorways, on gates looking both to past or future, the all-seeing eye on safe passage through portals to other universes. It immediately opened to the application browser of Double Life (DL), the online 3-D community.

As fate or luck would have it, I had a little knowledge of DL. It's an online networking playground where identities or 'avatars' form friendships, even work, marry, live in virtual houses and go about virtual lives with all the fun and social adventure limited only by the imagination. I had read some article about this in our local papers and even seen a TV programme on this site.

In the bottom window of the browser were spaces for a first name ID login: 'Indigo' was written there and in the second slot was a strange word: 'Wishpool', then a place for a password. I tried it. The password registered. Although I could not read the asterisks representing the seven letters of the secret word, I saw Indigo materialise from a cloud of vibrating particles, taking shape as a naked grey female form to someone dressed in the most extraordinary, slinky red dress. Her breasts were full, her lips and hips tantalisingly ample and her features not of my race—she was clearly Caucasian. The voluptuous cut of her dress rode straight up to hip, exposing in perfect 3-D a sensuous line of tanned leg reeking of invitation. This avatar was of middle height, not short and slim like my real life wife. This is how she clearly desired herself, standing in the middle of a luxurious apartment. On each 3-D wall, there were erotic paintings. If you clicked on them, two intertwined figures began to gyrate in sexual coition. There were virtual statues of semi-transparent nudes, both male and female, facing each other.

I moved my cursor, accidentally walking through one. The male figure with a large erect phallus grabbed at my virtual 3-D female body as a voice spoke, saying. 'Come on, baby, be my fuck buddy.' But there was nobody here. It was all just sexual fantasy furniture, like the lounge suite shaped in the form of a giant sideways penis.

Meanwhile, I perused her DL inventory files and discovered her ID details, who were her DL 'Friends' and the places she spent time in. The name of this place was 'My Nest'. By the look of her Signposts' History log, I could see this was a very familiar place. Perhaps even her online 'home'. After quickly reading up on the DL User Guide, I realised that to be associated with someone here, you had to become their 'Friend'. Somehow, I had to 'meet' her online and get her to add me to her Friends list. Only then could I begin to have regular association with her.

Meanwhile, I e-mailed all her Friends, Signposts and Groups to my own e-mail; then, suddenly a chat window opened from an online Friend:

Lance Pumason: You're back. I thought you said you were having a 'sex-free' day today, resting up for the big weekend. Hey, I've just lined up ten customers and they want a group rate!

He was clearly her pimp. I was dumbstruck. My fingers on the keyboard began to shake, my eyes popped open and my head was making ready to explode. She who refused me, saying she was beyond sex and relationships, here she was clearly involved in a dirty world of cyber prostitution! Was she, in fact, earning real money for this? I had noted that in DL, people ran businesses, sold cyber merchandise, offered services, etc. Was this how she was becoming financially separate from me, buying all those expensive shoes and handbags now stored in Baby's room? I wanted to tear apart the room.

Then I remembered her threat of dragging me to court. It would obviously be on the grounds of violent abuse. How could any judge not believe a pitiful-looking young woman over an old baldy like me? They might drag up my service record and cite that case twenty years back, when I once lost control and struck a young officer.

Smashing up the computer and room would certainly make it easier for her to file a case against me. It was difficult to hold in this frustration and anger. All I could think of was cutting her up into small pieces and throwing her remains down the rubbish shoot of my apartment block, but my crisis training finally kicked in. I took a breath and calmed down. This would not do. This would ruin my good standing. I had not served in the military to be demoted like this by a good-for-nothing cyber whore.

Lance Pumason: What's wrong, honey? Is your old creepy husband around? Can't talk? Anyway, see you this weekend. Bye.

I kept a grip as these last words punched up onto the chat window. It was a stroke of luck. The strategist in me remembered how in the history of battles, there's always an element of uncertainty—the way the wind blew up a storm in the face of the Spanish Armada, or the fateful course of that stray arrow that lodged in the eye of King Harold at the Battle of Hastings, opening an era of Norman conquest. I immediately knew that Lance Pumason was going to be my way to get to Indigo. I was not yet ready for a direct confrontation online or off.

It was time for me to go offline, so I hit the Quit button. I had gained valuable information and felt quietly jubilant. Wilde Diabolito had become his own private investigator.

posted by Wilde Diabolito at 10 a.m.

'THE BRAVE MAN WITH A SWORD'
18 JUNE 2010

Now my purpose is plain and honest: with these same cutting words, I will do battle on Double Life, a world made of language and ideas encoded into 3-D images. Thus, I proclaim again today, that this blog is mightier than the threat of a police break in through my door, or pistol pointed at my head and set of stainless cufflinks manacling me from behind. You have no chance of finding out about the real me, even in this real life country where the law enforcement officers are all dressed in dark blue-black. (Another clue, Blog Sleuth.)

Yet, do not discount the fact that I am a collector of actual razor sharp weapons, from the claymore to the battle-axe, or the scimitar to the famous samurai blade. These and other works of sword artisanship I keep locked up in three constructed, polished cedar cabinets in my own study. Sometimes I simply take out a sword at random just to feel its primal power fill my veins. Yes, a sword has a voice and soul, and it can be heard and must be obeyed at the right moment. A sword is the symbol of a man's honour.

Thus, when I went to my glassed-in office in what shall remain an unnamed grey building with high fences and security cameras around it, I was armed with a new power. I set my profile and password and entered Double Life. As time is of the essence now, I will summarise some of my experiences on becoming a DL resident. There is some learning curve in the beginning. One must master a new set of minimalist mouse skills, just as one must know how to hold the shorter samurai, the length of a forearm used in a small combat zone like a traditional Japanese house with paper walls.

It took me some weeks to become fully conversant with the style and manners of the place. First, I had to choose a body, a skin to match the identity of Wilde Diabolito. I developed My Form with the application function buttons choosing the 'male sexy body type' and dressed myself in white collared shirt with a long gothic black coat and grey trousers, leaving my hair rakishly long in memory of Oscar. In addition, I tried on a feminine avatar form. After all, my name was sufficiently androgynous to pass as a woman if and when required. I dressed my feminine self in a blue short skirt, white top, short hair and then gave myself green eyes. With a little fumbling, I was able to move forward, back, turn left and right, but knew little of what to do here and where to go.

The interesting thing about playing with masks, Blog Sleuths, is that one assumes something of the identity you are pretending to be. Not sure of what to do and where to go, I would see other figures materialising from white glowing clouds of swirling energy particles. From ethereal brown forms, their actual DL identities would come into being—male and female, human and sometimes strange and playfully fantastical or demonic. I was soon surrounded by an interesting group, all with strange hybrid names like Ripple Platonic, Hermione Seagull, Anton Uranis, Gorgi Mansong, Liptonia Gryphondale, or more recognisably derivative names like Smooth Operator, Moonlight Sonata, Happy Toknowya, Hope Eternalia and so forth.

There were others who I began to chat with like Butter Aphrodite, who I soon learned spoke broken English and was from Saudi Arabia. I was able to ask her in my female avatar form whether she wore a full, head to toe burqa or the head scarf in her real life. She said, yes, hijab. This could mean not just a scarf, but also being fully covered up. She had three 'sisters'— wives who were all married to the same very rich oil man who was strictly orthodox in public and made them wear the full black dress with eye-slit whenever they went to the shopping mall, one of the few places they could move about freely. 'What did she do most of her time in DL?' I asked.

'Shopping,' she wrote in her chat window and added 'LOL.' She also wrote that she loved it here because she could do much more and meet people—'Guys especially-smile-'. The best thing, she added, was that she felt free because everyone's cyber body was, in fact, a kind of hijab, cloaking inner identity, so she felt truly equal for the first time. It was interesting to learn this from her and I later reflected upon how much sexual identity switching was going on here as people played out secret fantasies. It was with this ID firmly logged in that I embarked on my first DL adventure.

posted by Wilde Diabolito at 12.12 p.m.

– –

'SOME LOVE TOO LITTLE, SOME TOO LONG'
19 JUNE 2010

It was time to move in on Indigo Wishpool. I was soon able to fly to many of the intricate regions of the Double Life map. I kept the particular locations I wanted to return to in my Signposts folder and began to familiarise myself with the vast shopping malls, accumulating woman's dresses and male apparel, meeting different people along the way. It was an especially strange experience role-playing as a female, as I had to take on feminine mannerisms and ward off male advances. I had also joined the Groups that Indigo and Lance Pumason were members of and went to some of their favourite hang out places to prepare myself for eventual contact. Yes, I was ready to put my battle plan into action.

posted by Wilde Diabolito at 10.36 p.m.

4 Comments >>

19 June 2010, 11.23 p.m.
Way of the Panda said:
You know nothing about yogis in caves, levitation or walking through world walls. You are a fake, Wilde.

20 June 2010, 12.07 a.m.
Wilde Diabolito said:
You are absolutely right, Panda. And by the way, welcome back.

20 June 2010, 12.17 a.m.
Precinct Angel said:
I see you.

20 June 2010, 1.03 a.m.
Wilde Diabolito said:

Good for you Precinct. As for the rest of you Blog commentators: Thank you for visiting my modest web page. I am gratified. However, I apologise but from now on, I will not be able to publish or respond to your comments. There are just too many coming daily. I did not know The Murder Blog would become so popular; my humble chronicle is becoming a small sensation on the Internet. Stay tuned. The day of reckoning is at hand!

- -

'SOME SELL, AND OTHERS BUY'
20 JUNE 2010

I knew it would be easier to make contact with Indigo through Pumason, so I tracked him down to one of his favourite haunts, 'The Garden of Beastiality'. The garden was out the back of a sex shop selling animated sex toys. Like many of the shopping and other environments, appropriate music or sound-scapes played on in the background. Here was a taped recording of a bondage game with a man whipping a screaming woman. He was saying, 'Oh, you like that, don't you, baby. Yeah, squirm, you dirty little whore', followed by more screaming.

I descended a long set of stairs into the garden where there were 'rides' and sex-animation animals like sheep and zebra women waiting to be penetrated and to penetrate. It was a popular place and the public chat was busy, mostly male locker room talk. And there, standing and watching voyeuristically, was Lance Pumason. I sensed that he was here shopping for customers to engage in private sex parties so I came up to him and opened a private chat.

119

Wilde: Hi there, Lance.

Lance: Hey!

Wilde: Interesting goings on.

Lance: Yep.

Wilde: To be honest, I'm not too much into the sheep and zebras.

Lance: No? What do you like?

Wilde: Nothing with animals.

Lance: Boys or girls?

Wilde: What do you take me for?

Lance: Hey man, it's all here in Double Life. Anything you want.

Wilde: Women. Strictly women. I don't swing.

Lance: Sure, I'm like you. I'm a ladies man.

Wilde: So far, I haven't really found any.

Lance: What?

Wilde: Women who ... are ready to ...

Lance: Hey, they're everywhere. Maybe you're not looking in the right places.

Wilde: What do you mean?

Lance: Well, you need to use your charm and personality.

Wilde: Afraid I'm rather new at all this.

Lance: Oh I see ... Look, maybe I can help.

Wilde: Help?

Lance: Help you get started ...

Wilde: What do you mean?

Lance: Well, I have this ... working girlfriend if you know what I mean. She's very friendly. Can teach you some girl tricks and also do you at the same time.

Wilde: You mean a prostitute?

Lance: Instructress. A special girl. Helps guys find their dicks in DL, so to speak.

Wilde: I see.

Lance: Yes, and she's sexy. You get fully simulated audio chat sex with or without voice modulators. 120 different sex animation positions, and my girl will talk you right through it all. By the end, you'll be so relaxed, you'll be able to chat up even the keyhole of a locked door. Women will fall for you like flies.

Wilde: Just say I was interested—how much would all this cost me?

Lance: Well, it's a specialised service and there is a queue. She's very popular. Perhaps tomorrow, I can squeeze you in. A small party. It would only cost 3,500 DL dollars.

Wilde: That's a lot.

Lance: Well, she is the best around here. Look, I'm prepared to give you a special—a one-on-one with her for another twenty-five minutes if you like. No extra charge.

I was silent.

Lance: Hey, no obligation, Wilde. You come, you check her out first. Watch and listen to the others. If you want to join the party, then we'll talk biz. OK?

With that, I saw an offer of Friendship appear on my screen. I had a choice to click Yes or No. This was the moment. At last, I would be able to confront Indigo.

I clicked his offer.

Lance: OK! Now we're moving. Look I'll meet you this time

tomorrow. Come online and get in touch, then I'll take you to my girl, alright?

Wilde: OK. Tomorrow then. Goodbye.

posted by Wilde Diabolito at 10.30 a.m.

- -

'SOME DO THE DEED WITH MANY TEARS'
21 JUNE 2010

I prepared the following e-mail from an anonymous account and saved it. I would send it at the right and appointed time. Or maybe I wouldn't.

Dear Indigo,

This is my first and last letter to you. I am both saddened and mortified at the kind of life you have begun to lead in your online world. I had no idea that such dirty smut filled your heart and that you could whore yourself so willingly for a few DL dollars. Had you cooperated better, treated me with due respect and honoured my good name, we might have had a beautiful life together. However, there is nothing more to say. Goodbye.

posted by Wilde Diabolito at 3.29 p.m.

- -

'AND SOME WITHOUT A SIGH'
22 JUNE 2010

As Ecclesiastes says: There is a 'time to love and a time to hate, a time for war and a time for peace.' Today was a time to hate dispassionately the act of bought love. It was a time to go to war and then experience the carillon sound of peace ever after in this cyber life and in my own house. After closing the door of my study, I ceremoniously took a sword and placed it on the table, then picked it up, touched my forehead to its jeweled hilt, bowed my head to the west and put it down again. Then I went to my computer, powered up and logged on to Double Life. I put on the headphones and sent a private message to Pumason.

He came back almost within the count of three, as if he was a retriever bringing back a bird in his mouth to drop at my feet.

Lance: Hey! Glad you could make it. Sending you a transfer.

With that, I saw the transfer window pop-up and accepted the offer to visit 'My Nest'. Suddenly I was travelling and arriving in my white materialising particles, then forming a greyish body putting on clothes in Indigo's special apartment. I recognised the big bed, the penis sofa, the erotica on the wall and the transparent sculptures. Then, there she was in skimpy virtual underwear that one could easily see through, sitting on the sofa with a man on either side. Both were naked. I switched on the audio chat and heard soft music in the background and heard her voice. There was no doubt: it was my wife. She was giggling and joking with one of the men. Suddenly, I saw Lance was also in the room, standing behind me.

Lance Pumason: Hey! Wilde. You won't be disappointed. She

is a real professional.

Indigo stood up at that moment, and I saw her underwear disappear and the emergence of a voluptuous, full-bodied nude woman with dark curls falling on her neck and legs designed to be spread-eagled. She was rosy and roomy. Now, the men on the sofa also stood. Their shirt and pants evaporated into cyber air and then a penis appeared on each and became immediately erect. Was this the best they could do with 3-D animation, I thought? One decided to play the erection game, flicking his animation switch off and on. His member drooped and stiffened, drooped and stiffened until I heard Indigo's audio chat voice.

Indigo Wishpool: OK, Mr Summertime, are you going to fuck me?

Two small balls, a pink and a blue, were suddenly floating just above the penis sofa.

Indigo Wishpool: You get on the blue one.

He obeyed and soon his avatar was sitting on it while Indigo's nude avatar was mounting the pink. In another few moments, they merged in cyber intercourse on the penis sofa.

Indigo Wishpool: Hey, don't you want to join in, Wilde?

Lance Pumason: What do you say? This is your chance. See that other blue ball near her face? That's the blow job animation.

Through my stereo headphones, I now heard the moans of simulated sex frenzy coming from both Summertime and Indigo. Hannibal Wormal, the other man, had decided not to wait and must have pressed the 'sit here' command on his own module, as now he was receiving fellatio from Indigo while she was getting ass-fucked by Summertime on the penis sofa. This all looked and sounded quite ridiculous to me. I looked on, wondering how on earth people could get any thrill from this pretend sex, unless they were masturbating themselves in front of their computer screens.

I could understand friendship and talk chat, but to try and re-enact 3-D cybersex like this seemed not just sordid, but disturbing in its implications. How far had we come with all this, living vicariously in our own home spaces, but enacting fantasy lives when one could go outside? What's more, they all seemed to be enjoying it immensely. Yet none of it touched me at all. In fact, it repelled me.

Here was my wife selling her body online to all comers. I knew it was like a spreading cancer in the world, and here were the sick results of what was happening to my own wife right in front of me. It was unnatural and she would not be able to stop it. She would become more and more sex-addicted. Some say this is all just role-playing and fantasy, but did that make her betrayal any less real? Betrayal is betrayal, whether online or off. There was nothing left to do but to end this twisted business now, and perhaps even save my wife's perverted soul.

Lance Pumason: Well? Are you in or not? I think you've seen enough to make a decision.

Wilde Diabolito: Yes, I have. More than enough. Each man kills the thing he loves.

Lance Pumason: What? What did you say?

Wilde Diabolito: You will see soon enough. And you too, Indigo.

I said this with a cold and chilling ring to my voice, allowing the anger and disgust to rise up. I did not care whether or not Indigo recognised my voice over the sex sounds of the fornicating threesome.

With that, I unplugged my headphones but let my avatar stand there to watch on. I turned around to my sword table and picked up the blade. It was the short samurai sword. I had selected it for this purpose, suitable for use in a small space. I unsheathed it and tested the air with two swallow-swift cuts in opposite directions.

Sword in one hand, I opened the door and ventured into the hall outside Baby's room. I could hear her side of the sex orgy going on. I turned the door knob, entered and there she was: sitting in her flimsy nightie, one hand on the cursor, another in her groin, touching and stimulating herself. She was too absorbed to see or hear me as I stalked in and took the high raised killing position behind her. Suddenly, I could see my own reflection in the computer screen lifting the short samurai blade, ready for decapitation. If she couldn't see me before, she certainly could see me now. Trying to turn, she screamed so loudly and differently from her sexual moans, yet the avatars on the screen did not shift or budge from their acting as I swung the blade with all the force of my position, my training, and all the sense of righteousness I could muster, then separated her petite head from those slim shoulders with one clean, irrevocable swipe.

It was done. Justice had been served, honour restored.

Her head hung a moment in the air and then dropped suddenly, relieved of its kicking body like a bloody soccer ball onto the ceramic tiles. The headphones were still on, cut from their cord—a grotesque and fitting emblem to the end of a cyberlife, severed not just from her body, but the emotional life line of a computer. I switched off the screen, not wanting to see any more of this simulation, and then sat down on the floor with the sword across my knees and wept.

posted by Wilde Diabolito at 10.25 p.m.

– –

'YET EACH MAN DOES NOT DIE'
23 JUNE 2010

It is True, Dear Blog Companion, what Oscar Wilde once said: 'Yet each man does not die.' Each of us lives on in another form—cyber or other. What is it that we are made of? Whizzing particles, antimatter, vibrations of syllables? At least my blog counter proves that I am truly worthy of being called a writer, as the total tally of visitors has reached the 100,000 mark in ten days and I know it will increase exponentially. Perhaps I should consider syndicating The Murder Blog as living proof that a crime can be committed in full public view and no one can stop such a thing from happening. Will there be a sequel? Who can say? Having committed one brilliant murder in such a unique and original way, I am charmed by the idea, Dear Reader.

As for the case of the woman in the story, you will never know what her fate was. Did I cut her body up into little bits, put them in a truck and throw them off the prow of a hired fishing vessel into the South China Sea?

Last clues, dear Sleuths. For those who fruitlessly went on Double Life in search of Wilde Diabolito or to warn Indigo Wishpool directly before her impending execution, the incidents depicted did not happen within the stated time frame. You have been duped in time as well as place.

No such characters exist now in that 3-D playtime realm. Did they exist at all? Do any of us exist for that matter? I write, therefore, I and you, Blog Reader, *are*. But now everyone is logged out on this matter.

In any case, I was not so stupid to have let anyone interfere in such an important incident. Maybe what you witnessed happened in the past. Recently, perhaps? Or three years ago? You will never know whether the particulars of this chronicle are true as stated, or just shaped from vague imaginings into playful fiction.

One thing is certain, the country in which this tale is set is that tiny city-state in Southeast Asia with its red and white flag wilting in the humid breeze. This is the unimaginative land known as Singapore. Am I living there? Perhaps. But it is unlikely. Maybe I have migrated to greener pastures or prairies like so many of this nation's citizens have.

Why am I divulging this? Because, Blog Sleuths, even an online murderer needs a back story, just as a budding writer needs a by-line. But that is all you have to go on. All the rest must remain a vague and airy set of cyber question marks stamped on your brain.

posted by Wilde Diabolito at 3.30 p.m.

CHRIS MOONEY-SINGH is a full-time writer, teacher and publisher and co-edited *The Penguin Book of Christmas Poems* (Australia). Two of his stories were featured in *Best of Singapore Erotica* and and another in *Best of Southeast Asian Erotica*. He is presently doing his PhD in creative writing at Monash University, Australia.

A Sticky Situation

Alaric Leong

Theodosius Kwan was very glad it hadn't rained as promised that morning. He had asked the taxi to drop him off four streets short of his final destination, and he hated walking in the rain. Especially when he was so unfamiliar with the area and had to search out the address scribbled on the small scrap of paper he was holding.

The address he was seeking was in the sleazy area of MacPherson. The buildings all looked as if they had not been cleaned or even dusted in years. Finally, he was close to his target. Number 27, 23, 19. He frowned when it became obvious that not every building here had a house number posted. No major calamity though; he was close, he knew that, and was only a little late.

He looked down at the address again, just to be sure. Right at that moment, something tugged at the sole of his foot. He smiled. This must be the place. He turned and looking up, saw a big, green number 15 facing him. Yes, this was the place.

He opened the tall front door painted in four totally incompatible colours and walked in. Several steps in, he saw an open door from where, a moment later, a man in a security guard uniform jumped up from a desk.

'Yes, sir, can I help you?' asked the uniformed man. Kwan

replied with the code he'd been given. He hoped this fellow would recognise it.

'I'm here to see an old friend from an old, old story.'

The 'security guard' flashed a smile that wrapped all the way across his thin face and nodded enthusiastically. 'Oh yes, sir. Yes, indeed. The train you want is waiting for you upstairs.'

'Room Number 18?' Kwan replied.

'That's right, sir. Second door to the right after the stairs.'

Kwan thanked him and headed up the steps with a slow but determined stride. As he approached the landing, he saw two other men standing guard at Room Number 18. These men were not wearing security guard uniforms. In fact, they were dressed in well-tailored dark suits, but it was clear that they were also serving as guards. Neither budged an inch as Kwan approached.

'I'm Mr Kwan. Theodosius Kwan. I believe someone inside is expecting me.' The guard on the left nodded to the other, who then nodded at Kwan and they both stepped aside. One of them even opened the door and held it for the new arrival.

As he walked in, Kwan saw an unexpectedly large number of men sitting at a round table. In the middle sat a man who was obviously the leader of this group. This was the man who spoke.

'Mr Kwan! How nice to meet you in person finally. Please take a seat.'

Kwan nodded, smiled and started looking for an empty chair. At the outer edge of the circle, he saw a long-time associate, Krishnan Nurdi. They exchanged smiles.

'Theo. How are you today?

'I'm fine; how are you, Krishnan?' Nurdi nodded and then

indicated an open seat near him. As this seat also directly faced the man Kwan had come to do business with, he accepted Nurdi's suggestion.

Kwan turned and looked directly at the man directly in front of him. 'Mr Lok. I also find it a pleasure to meet you finally. I have heard you are a man to be respected and even admired.'

'And I have heard the same of you, Mr Theodosius Kwan. That's why I thought you were a man I should be doing business with.' Lok then noticed that Kwan was furtively casting looks at the other men around the table. 'Oh, I hope you don't mind that I asked a number of my close friends and some of my interns to join us. I always get a little edgy at business meetings, so I like having people who like me to be there when I conduct business. Especially with the kind of business I do.'

Kwan nodded to show he understood Mr Lok's situation. He then glanced at the men lending moral support to Lok. Two of them were actually not sitting, but standing against the wall. Like the two doormen, they wore well-fitted suits. With arms crossed tightly across their torsos just south of the diaphragm, they displayed slight bulges on their upper chest, right side.

Kwan's gaze lingered a bit longer on these bulges: these men either both had some strange abnormal growth, or they were both keeping some kind of weapon there. The way they held their arms so tightly and the defiant looks on their faces told Kwan that they were intentionally making no secret of the fact that they were packing weapons.

At first, Kwan found this thought disconcerting, intimidating even. But very quickly, he smiled and relaxed. Of course, that's why they were there ... for intimidation's sake. But to intimidate others: maybe other gang members, or the police, or the border guards. Intimidation would be counter-productive with Kwan himself. After all, Lok needed him more than he needed Lok: Lok had to find someone reliable and reasonably safe to distribute his goods. Kwan could just walk away from this meeting and not be any poorer; he would certainly be in less danger from the police if he did leave with no more than he came in. The more he considered this, the better he felt. This was a buyer's market, even if Lok didn't care to admit it yet.

Kwan decided that the two men standing against the wall looked like they might be from Myanmar, though he wasn't quite sure what Myanmarese were supposed to look like. He also thought that two of the five men sitting with Lok—three to one side, two to the other—might be from Myanmar. He wasn't even sure where Lok himself was really from. Though he claimed to be from northern Malaysia, a full Peranakan, Kwan had severe doubts about that.

Lok was conversing with two of the men flanking him at the table in a language Kwan was unfamiliar with while Kwan and Nurdi exchanged a series of meaningful looks. Finally, Lok turned back to his two guests.

'So, gentlemen, shall we be getting down to business? It pains me that we can't be making small talks and get to know each other better, but I have other appointments today.' He nodded. 'Other business partners coming to see me.' He smiled, with that smile which tries to convey layers of meaning it just can't bear.

'Yes,' said Kwan. 'We can now discuss all the details and try to close the deal.' Krishnan nodded and turned to Lok with a smile to match Kwan's. He wanted to show that they formed a united front.

'I had actually started discussing matters with your friend, Mr Krishnan, before you arrived. He told me that you will be responsible for most of the finance on this deal.'

Kwan threw a quick sideways look at Nurdi. 'That's right. I think I can handle most of that part of the transaction.'

'Yes, my ... sources tell me that you are a man of some means. They also have informed me that you have this vast network of outlets where you can distribute our product.'

Kwan shrugged and gave a smile that feigned modesty. 'I don't know that I have a *vast* network. But I do have a large number of customers in small shops all across Singapore. And my friend Krishnan has a good-sized network himself.'

'Mainly Indian and Malay shops, but I have quite a few Chinese customers as well.' Nurdi was thoroughly proud of the multiethnicity of his customer list.

'And many of those customers would be interested in offering *their* special customers something like what you offer.'

'And now you can provide it to them,' Lok said with a proud nod.

'Which is why we're here, of course, Mr Lok.'

'And you won't have any difficulty seeing that this particular product gets to your customers?'

'It shouldn't be any great problem really. After all, your product is small and easily transported. We can squeeze several packets into one of our regular, legal deliveries.'

'Of course. The ability to conceal our product is one of

133

its main advantages really.' He leaned back in his chair, as far back as it would go without falling. One of the men standing at the back stepped over and made sure the chair didn't go too far. 'So Mr Finance Minister, do you think we can do a deal then?'

Kwan smiled, turned to Nurdi, then turned back and smiled again. 'It's very possible. We would first have to agree a price though.'

'Of course; price is the spinal column of business, isn't it?' Lok then turned to the person to his right and said something in that language which Kwan couldn't understand. Man to the Right nodded, then plucked a folded sheet of paper from a dark blue folder and slid it across the table to Kwan. Kwan picked it up, unfolded it and held it out so that both he and Krishnan Nurdi could read at the same time.

'As you can see, gentlemen, there are a number of prices there. The price per unit goes down depending on the number of units you purchase at any one time.' Lok then smiled broadly and raised one finger high like a young child who had just learned a new phrase. 'Economies of scale, you know.'

Krishnan Nurdi sputtered a laugh. 'Very resourceful. It's like you were selling digestive biscuits, or crisps, or cigarettes.'

Lok beamed a boyish smile and nodded. 'Yes. It is the same principle anyway, isn't it?'

'Not here in Singapore,' Kwan countered. 'The authorities here do not look on your particular goods as acceptable.'

'Of course. Which is why we must charge much more for our goods than the basic production costs. Risk is a costly extra.'

Kwan nodded, then went back to perusing the price list.

'Actually, it's more likely that we will purchase a smaller amount. At least for the first few deals. We want to be sure that our customers are willing to take this risk themselves, and also that we can sell everything we get from you.'

'Oh, I'm sure you'll be having no problem there. It is a very popular product. And, of course, forbidden fruits always taste more sweeter, isn't it?'

The only immediate reply from the Nurdi-Kwan duo was matching smiles. After a few moments, Kwan nodded to Nurdi and turned back to his supplier. 'I think for the first consignment, we would be looking at 200 kilos. If the uptake is there, we can increase the amount on further purchases.'

'As you wish,' Lok replied.

'Now, about the price. I think we would be most comfortable with $50 a kilo less than what you have listed here.'

Lok looked like he had just swallowed a large bullfrog. He coughed and took a deep gulp from his teacup. 'Fifty dollars less. That's quite a reduction.'

'But I think that brings us to a fair price. Something we can all be happy with.' Kwan then added a smile to sweeten the challenge.

'You seem to have a different way of viewing happiness, Mr Kwan. Fifty dollars a kilo less than our already generous offer is more in the range of a grimace than a smile.'

'But the price you have here would cause us much unhappiness, Mr Lok.' Kwan paused here and delivered a regretful sigh before continuing. 'Only because it would cause our customers pain when we ask them to take on this product. Risk *and* the price we would have to ask might be more pain than our customers could bear.'

The two sides then stared at each other across the table in silence. When Kwan felt they had held that silence for just the right amount of time, he spoke again. 'And on the subject of risk: I imagine that you have already brought adequate supplies of your product into Singapore.'

'Of course. You can take delivery tomorrow morning if you like.'

Kwan raised a hand to slow Lok down. 'You must then factor in the risk of taking all those boxes back across the causeway. The Singapore authorities will again give you a good going-over as you return to Malaysia. Surely the lifting of that risk should be worth at least $50 a kilo to you.'

On that note, the two sides slipped back into the exchange of silent stares. However, Krishnan Nurdi softly tapped his fist twice under the table to express his admiration for Kwan's negotiating skills.

On his part, Kwan knew that silence was now his ally. He would wait for Lok to break it. Which he did barely twenty seconds later, accompanied by a forced smile.

'OK. Yes, we can accept that price. But only for the first consignment! After that, we will need to have new negotiations and see what agreement we reach then.'

'Of course,' replied Kwan. 'The whole picture will be much more clear then.'

'So, my friends, we have a deal then? You will take 200 kilos at that giveaway price?'

'Well, there is one other matter that we have to look at,'

Kwan answered.

Lok's smile vanished as quickly as a magician's lit candle. 'Oh? And what is that?'

'The product itself.'

'The product? I don't …'

'We want to be sure of its purity. In this particular line that you deal in, Mr Lok, there are many counterfeits. They come from places like China … Myanmar.' At this, the two minders suddenly showed minimal shifts towards discomfort in their poker faces. 'And these counterfeits are not of the same quality. They have problems—in taste, in texture, in strength. Sometimes there are even harmful additives used.'

'Gentlemen, I can assure you that our product is 100% genuine. It all comes from the original source, not from some dirty shed in Burma or China. What we are offering is the real thing. Of that, you can be sure.'

'So you say. But *how* can we be sure?'

At that moment, Lok shifted back very comfortably in his chair, a genuine, relaxed smile on his face. It was as if Kwan had just dealt him the last card of a royal flush. 'Would you like to sample the product yourself?'

'Sample?' replied Kwan. He exchanged looks with Nurdi.

'Yes. As my guests. It will be my treat.' He then leaned forward, his folded fists stretched as far across the table as they could reach.

Kwan recovered and nodded confidently. 'Yes. A very good idea. That should remove all of our doubts.'

'Absolutely.' Lok then signalled to the man on his far left, who hauled up a largish box heavily sealed with grey masking tape. The man then suddenly produced a cutter that looked like an appendage of one of the Transformer figures and started slicing along the top of the box. Lok turned back to his two guests.

'You will see that we have brought along as samples a rich variety of what we are offering our friends and customers. We have more than one product in our product line, you know.'

The man with the cutter was just then completing his energetic slicing. As if on cue, the two suited fellows at the back had swung into action. One moved two steps closer to Lok himself, while the other glided around the table to an open area; both had their eyes fixed intently on the closed door. They had also placed tensed hands on their chests, close to the bulges under their jackets. It was clear that no unannounced visitors would receive a friendly welcome from these fellows.

Standing, Lok himself dipped both hands into the now open box. He was beaming all over. 'Yes, you will certainly be able to judge our product from this sampling.' He gazed into the box. 'Let's see ... Yes, we have Juicy Fruit, Spearmint, Doublemint.' He then pulled out a double-fistful of chewing gum packets. 'And we even have here some of the more exotic flavours: Flare, Elixir, Lush, Zing, Cobalt. And ... Hubba Bubba. So which would you gentlemen like to try?'

Kwan, staring at the wares in Lok's hands, considered for a moment before answering. 'Could I try both the Juicy Fruit and the Spearmint? I can make a good comparison and judgement with that, I think.'

'Fine,' replied Kwan. 'I like your thoroughness, Mr Theodosious.

And you, Mr Krishnan?'

'Just the Juicy Fruit, thank you.'

Lok nodded, opened two packs of gum, then deftly slid out three sticks. He handed them to his assistant on the far end, who duly passed along one to Nurdi, two to Kwan. 'Gentlemen, enjoy your chews.'

The two guests nodded. Nurdi kept his eyes fixed on Kwan, following his lead precisely. He watched as Kwan slowly peeled off the silver foil wrapper, rubbed his fingertips carefully along the sugary dusting on the gum, took a few educated sniffs, then placed one stick on top of the other in a kind of chewing gum sandwich. He broke the sandwich in two and held up one half. 'I want to save this part for later.'

'I understand entirely, Mr Kwan,' replied Lok.

Kwan slid the double sticks of gum in and started masticating. Nurdi had meanwhile inserted the whole stick into his mouth and begun his own test. A minute later, Lok flipped his smile into high beam.

'Mr Kwan—you chew that gum like an old master of the form.'

Kwan nodded. 'When I was at uni, I studied for eighteen months abroad, in Australia. Me and my some of my friends spent a lot of our time and money chewing. Sometimes we would chew three or four times a day. It was ecstasy.'

'And your customers will soon know that same ecstasy.' He paused and lowered his tone. 'That is, if we can come to some agreement here.'

Kwan glanced quickly at Nurdi, then back at his host. 'Oh, I think we can reach an agreement now.' He turned to Nurdi to signal that he approved. 'But you can assure us that the entire shipment is like this: the best quality?'

'Absolutely!' shouted Lok. Kwan nodded, half-closed his eyes and began chewing more slowly, deliberately, savouring every squeeze of his teeth into the pliant flesh of the Juicy Fruit and Spearmint. It brought him back to his glorious student days in Oz.

From there, the three men managed to wrap up the whole deal within ten minutes. As they triumphantly shook hands, Kwan commended Lok for the efficiency of his operation. Lok smiled and took a slight bow. Nurdi asked if he could try a stick of Hubba Bubba before leaving, and Lok insisted that he take a whole pack along with him, as a gift, to celebrate their new business relationship.

Krishnan Nurdi was still chewing his Juicy Fruit as the two visitors made their way back down the staircase. Theodosius Kwan had removed his well-masticated wad of gum and put it in a safe place. He hand-signalled Krishnan to hide his before they stepped outside; Nurdi then swallowed the whole in one bold gulp. 'I think,' Kwan whispered to his associate, 'we have just formed a business partnership that can really stick.' Nurdi, choking slightly on the gum, could only nod.

The two stepped out into a brilliant shower of sunlight; not a hint of rain anywhere in the magnanimous Singapore sky. Theodosius Kwan turned to his now partner in crime, flashed a thumbs up sign and for five chomps mimed the energetic chewing of a contraband substance.

Krishan winked in return. If he wasn't still struggling with the gum lodged in his throat, he would have added a hearty shout of 'Hubba bubba!' to that.

ALARIC LEONG is a proud Singaporean and aspiring author. Having worked as a PR writer, he decided to gravitate into a brand of fiction that hews a little more closely to reality. Another of his first attempts at fiction has been included in the Monsoon Books anthology, *Best of Southeast Asian Erotica*.

The Madman of Geylang

Zafar Anjum

Zul scratches his balls for the umpteenth time, but the satisfaction, the sedation-inducing contentment, of a well-scratched scrotum eludes him once again. He has been feeling this itch for God knows how many hours now, but the handcuffs have been making the exercise difficult. His hands are big and scruffy and the many years of cleaning dishes and mopping floor—his line of work ever since he was a teenager—has made them calloused.

He wants to feel his bum too—it must be sore, of a pinkish hue by now, like that of an orangutan, he thinks. But it's impossible for his hands to reach his rear. He has been sitting on the floor of a ten-by-twenty room for hours, maybe even days, weeks, his hands cuffed, feet chained. He has no sense of time, he does not know if it is day or night, morning or afternoon, but he has felt spells of extreme cold and heat in the time that he has been trapped in this rabbit hole. It has been like a year of many summers and winters for him, the season changing every few hours, the change every time breaking something inside him. He has no watch, nothing except the rags of a prisoner on him. Like the four walls of the windowless room where he has been cloistered, his mind is blank and all he has with him is an image—the image of Melly.

'Ah,' he grunts, a sense of frustration making him twinge with rage. Then, taking his head between his hands, he lowers his body onto the floor and begins to sob. 'Melly, Melly,' he cries out loud, pulling his bristly hair with his cuffed hands. 'What have I done, what have I done, Melly!' His body moves to and fro, throbbing as he lets out his muffled shrieks. A rivulet of drool flows from a corner of his mouth.

A few minutes pass like this, then Zul calms down, half awake, half asleep, like a sedated animal in a cage.

In his state of delirium, memories of Melly come floating to him as if in a dream. Her plump, round face, her long dark hair, her big black eyes, her supple body with big, round, pendulous breasts envelopes his consciousness and as he tries to hold her in his imagination, she slips away like a ghost, like sand slipping through the fingers of a mirage-struck traveller lost in a desert.

The first time he had set his eyes on Melly was when he was walking back from work and she was standing in a playground in Whampoa. The playground was close to Spice Junction, an Indian stall in a hawker centre where he worked as a cleaner. She was chaperoning a five-year-old boy who was playing with other children. While the boy played, she talked to another maid who was standing guard over a baby in a stroller. Melly talked a bit loudly, at a faster clip and laughed heartily—the mark of a generous woman. It was her laughter that had attracted him. When she laughed, she threw her head backwards and her breasts arched out, like two huge cannon balls.

And the balls had struck him right in the heart—the seductive pallets arousing in him the cacophony of love, stirring him in a

143

totally new way. Since that day, he had made it a point to pass through the playground and linger around it to take a good look at her on one pretext or another. Sometimes he would bring along a plastic bag and collect the fallen leaves scattered in the playground. On other days, when he felt tired, he would just sit on one of the benches among the old folks and pretend to play a game on his handphone, stealing glances at Melly as often as he could dare. It was a hopeless situation—why would anybody, even a maid, notice a short, snub-nosed, grizzled hair, thirty-year-old, good-for-nothing like him—but the sight of Melly was the only thing that gave him pleasure after a hard day's work.

One day an impossible thing happened, just like his mother used to say. 'Son, Allah has strange ways of doing things,' she would say. 'If you set your heart after something and pray to Him, asking for it, He would give it to you before you know it.' And when it happened, it was incredible. He then had no doubt that his desire for Melly, verbalised in earnest entreaties to Allah in the Friday prayers week after week, had reached the skies.

That afternoon, Shekhar, his employer, had scolded him for being lazy in his duties and in a huff, he had left the stall, not caring for what the Indian chef thought of him. Soft and saturnine, he was a man with a weakness—his rage—and when it ballooned in him, he leaped out of his senses as readily as a cleanliness-loving man would discard his dirty pyjamas. In those moments, even he wouldn't know what he would do. It was like a streak of madness in him. His mother had warned him against it, a madness that had chequered his career, walking him from one job to another over the years.

When he reached the playground, luckily there was no one around—only Melly and her ward in the leafy playground. There were no other maids and no toothless old men hanging around like hungry wolves gawking at young maids.

He was feeling depressed after having fought with his employer. He sat down on one of the wrought iron benches in the play station. Wearing a T-shirt and shorts, Melly was sitting on another bench, under the shade of a tree. Left to himself, the boy was jumping around the play station. As a mischievous idea came to the boy, his eyes glinted and he began to climb over the monkey bars.

'Careful, Zack,' Melly said as she sauntered towards the boy. 'That is dangerous ... stop doing that—'

Even before Melly could complete her sentence, the boy lost his balance and toppled over the bars. 'Thwack!' The boy's body tumbled down to the ground, face down.

'Zack!' Melly cried, rushing to the boy. The boy didn't move at all.

'Zack, Zack!' Melly shook the boy. She took his head in her lap and shook him by his chin, and gently tugged at his hair. No movement.

'Zack! Wake up, open your eyes, Zack,' Melly cried desperately. 'Oh, God,' she sobbed. 'What do I do now?'

Horrified, Zul was watching all this from where he was sitting. Without a thought, he ran over to the boy. Hovering over him, he took a good look.

This was exactly what had happened to his younger brother, Zul remembered. Scenes from his childhood days replayed before his eyes. The only difference was that his brother had fallen from a tree in a *kampung*, his village which was no more, vanished under the skyscrapers of the Lion City. His brother had later died. He remembered the unforgettable words spoken by the most educated man in his *kampung*: 'He would have lived if he had been brought to the doctor a bit earlier.'

'Move!' Zul shouted, pushing Melly away, 'I know what to do.' He felt the boy's pulse, took him in his arms and began to run.

'The doctor, the doctor,' he said and sprinted towards the nearest clinic in the Whampoa market. The maid ran after him, panting. He did not stop running until he had reached the clinic. He put the boy in the doctor's chamber and stepped aside.

When the boy regained consciousness after medical help and the boy's mother came over to the clinic, Zul slipped away unobtrusively.

For the next few days, he did not go either to Shekhar's food stall or the playground—he just slept at his mother's place at Geylang Serai and gallivanted around the food stalls looking for cleaning jobs. His employer had not called him either. 'Shekhar does not want me to work with him anymore, so why bother going to him,' he thought.

But he was wrong. One day when Zul was cleaning his canvas shoes at home, Shekhar called.

'Aye, Zul,' he said, 'Where are you? Why aren't you coming to work?'

'Boss, I thought you didn't want me work with you after what—'

'Aye, what gave you the idea? Come to work from tomorrow, *lah*. OK?'

146

'OK, boss,' he said.

'You are still upset about the things I said to your face the other day, eh?'

Zul didn't say anything. There was a beat of silence over the phone.

'Never mind, *lah*,' Shekhar said. 'People say things when angry. Understand or not?'

'Hmmm ...'

'By the way', Shekhar said, 'a maid had come looking for you.'

'Which maid?'

'Don't know, *lah*,' he said. 'A plump-sized one. Said lives in Block 77. She was saying you saved her job.'

'Is that so?' he said, his heart suddenly swelling with happiness.

Next day, after work, when he went over to the playground, he had a pair of *masala dosas* wrapped in brown paper.

'Who is it for?' Shekhar had asked him when he was leaving the counter.

'For a friend.'

'The plump one?' he joked. Zul had got out of the shop without answering Shekhar, just throwing him a mysterious smile.

Melly came running to him when she saw him approaching the playground. 'Where have you been ... Zul?' she said.

So, she knew his name. Must be Shekhar; otherwise, how would she know his name?

'Ummm ...' he searched for appropriate words. 'I was away for a few days.'

'I've been looking for you for days,' she said, her eyes dancing with joy after having found him. 'Thanks for your help the other day. You saved the boy and my job.'

Blushing, he sat on a bench next to her, passing the food packet. 'What is this?'

'A little gift for you.'

She accepted the gift with a smile. 'Thank you,' she said. He could see her stubby finger poke around the warm packet, but she did not open it in front of him.

He had left soon after handing her the gift. While he was seated next to her, he had felt his body shaking with desire, and not knowing what to do with the heat numbing his mind, he had said, 'I've some errands to run. So, I will take your leave now.'

He could read the disappointment in Melly's eyes. Still, he walked away. He had his own castles to build in the air.

The next day, they met at the playground again. She thanked him for the *dosas*. 'Zul, I love that Indian food. Bring it for me everyday, will you?'

'Why? Are we friends?' he said.

'Of course, we are,' she said, putting her hand in his. Melly's fellow maids giggled at a distance seeing the two shaking hands.

From that day onwards, bringing a gift in folded-up paper became a routine for Zul—sometimes he would bring *dosas*, sometimes *vadas* and *idlis*. The good thing was that Shekhar did not mind Zul's wrapping the food items for his girl.

'How is the romance going, lover boy?' Shekhar would tease him.

He didn't mind his employer's joke and would leave the stall with a bowed head.

Day after day, he kept bringing gifts for Melly. On the days she would not come to the playground, he would go to a leafy glade by the Whampoa canal and gobble down the soft and warm *dosas* or *idlis*, daydreaming about her, remembering her smile, her talks, her gestures.

One day, she brought him a return gift: a T-shirt. It was yellow, with a picture of Superman on it.

Accepting the gift, tears welled up in Zul's eyes, which he tried to hide from her. But she caught him averting his eyes. 'Oh Zul, you are so sentimental,' she said. The remark comforted him, allowing him to let the tears flow down and form a small delta under his eyes.

He could not stop crying because he did not remember anyone giving him a gift, not since the days when he was a child. His father brought gifts for him: clothes, small toys, sweets from the hawker stalls. But his father was long dead.

'Thank you for the gift,' he said, choking with emotion.

One month after that, they had met on a Sunday and she had spent the whole day with him, walking around Geylang and then Toa Payoh. He told her everything about himself: his dead father, his dead little brother, his ailing mother who was a cook, and his security guard big brother Ali. She also told him about her dead father in Indonesia, her seamstress mother and her school-going little sister, Tissie. In the evening, before going back, she had kissed him on his cheek. 'I want to marry you, Zul,' she declared.

First, he could not believe her. But then, when he realised what he had heard, he felt as if he were a cup of bland, warm water into which Melly had thrown a spoonful of sugar.

He didn't know how to reply to her or what to say.

'You are kidding, wa?' he said, kissing her. 'I would do anything to get married to you.'

'Then marry me,' she said, throwing her plump figure against him. It was either the weight of her body, her tight hug, or the ache of happiness in his heart that made him swoon. His head on her shoulder, he saw a small girl running after a balloon in the park. The red balloon was going up in the air, away from the girl's grasp. He felt as if he were that balloon, full of the air of happiness.

The following day, he confided in Yousuf—his Friday prayer *kaki*. Yousuf worked in an office opposite the hawker centre where Zul worked and often came to eat his lunch at Shekhar's. 'I'm a social worker'; that's what he had said in his introduction to Zul. He was a tall, lanky man with a kind smile. There was something honest and humane about him that gave Zul the confidence to confide in him.

'It's good that you are in love, Zul,' Yousuf said, smoke curling forth from his mouth and nostrils. 'But yours is a tricky situation.'

'Why do you say that?'

'The girl, Melly, is a foreign worker, a domestic maid, isn't she?'

'That's true. So?'

'Don't you know that you can't marry a foreign maid just like that?'

'Really, brother?'

'Yes, foreign maids here are not allowed to marry Singaporeans or even permanent residents. They can't even get pregnant while they are working here.'

'Tch,' Zul sighed, wringing his hands. 'What to do, brother? Just tell me what to do and I will do anything to make the marriage possible.'

'You will have to get government permission for this.'

'*Gahmen* permission?' Zul said with disappointment. He stayed away from *gahmen* as far as possible. But now he had to deal with the *gahmen*.

'Yes, *gahmen* permission,' Yousuf said, patting his back. 'You need to get that. Is she educated?'

'Who?'

'The girl you want to marry.'

'Yes, more than me. She is half a graduate, she went to college in her country.'

'That is good,' Yousuf said, drawing on his cigarette.

Zul looked on at him like an innocent pup, waiting for his lord's command.

'Not to worry, brother. I will write you a petition, a letter, and you go and meet the local MP.'

'Who?'

'MP. The Member of Parliament of your constituency, the guy you had voted for.'

'I don't even remember who I had voted for. I think that fellow lost the election.'

'Never mind.'

'Where?'

'What where?'

'Where to meet this MP? Go to Parliament or what?'

'No, no, brother,' Yousuf said, touching his hair. 'In one of his Meet-The-People sessions.'

'Where?'

'Meet-The-People's session!' Yousuf repeated himself, taking a hard puff. 'That's where people go with their problems to their local political leader. You've never been to one?'

'I don't remember going to one.'

'Anyway, you don't worry,' Yousuf said, crushing the cigarette butt in a makeshift ashtray made of a used can of Milkmaid. 'In a day or two, I will bring you a written petition and you go and meet your local MP. OK, brother?'

Zul had nodded his head, but he was already feeling uncertain about this whole meeting with the MP business. He wanted to marry a girl and that's a simple thing that every man does. Then why should the *gahmen* come in between the marriage of two people, he thought.

A few days later, with great trepidation, he went to meet the MP and gave his assistant the petition, a page of typed gibberish that he could not read, but he trusted Yousuf to have captured the pain of his heart in it. The MP had taken the sheet from him with a smile and put it away in a file.

'The government will let you know about it,' the MP's assistant said when Zul asked him what would happen next.

'You mean a letter would come to me?'

'A letter or a call,' said the man, dismissing him.

Weeks passed, but he did not hear from the *gahmen*. He was seeing Melly everyday and they both talked about the letter from the government that never arrived. They dreamed about their future together, about their home, their kids—it all filled his heart with a desire to live his life that so far, had seemed so meaningless to him.

Weeks turned into months. He tried to see the MP many times during the Meet-the-People sessions, but every time, access was denied him. 'You've given your application, and you will hear from the government.' That's all he was told by the MP's assistant. His cup of patience was almost empty.

Following Yousuf's advice, he decided to meet the MP one last time. He had decided that he would fall at the politician's feet and ask for his help in his matter.

On the evening he was going to meet the MP, Melly called him.

'What are you doing, Zul?' she asked him.

'Getting ready,' he said, tying the laces of his shoes.

'Where are you going?'

'To meet the MP.'

'Be careful, Zul,' she said, her voice touching his ears like a soft feather. 'Be polite, don't lose your temper in front of the MP or any other officer, OK? I know you are angry. There has been no response, but you don't show your anger. You show you are a responsible person, that you want to start a family ...'

'OK,' he blurted.

'Must call me later to tell what happened, OK?' she said.

'Sure, *lah*, darling,' Zul said, getting out of his house.

Melly whispered a kiss into Zul's ears before ending the call. Then, with quick steps, he walked towards the elevator.

Then a thought clouded his face and he went back to the house. Like a man possessed, he went through the contents of his drawer in his room. His facial muscles relaxed when he found the object that he was looking for and carefully tucked it into his socks. With a song on his lips, he strutted out of the HDB block.

The MP, wearing an untucked white shirt and a pair of white trousers, was making a small speech when Zul entered the room.

The room was full of people, the MP standing up in a corner of the room. Zul stood at the back of the crowd, near the door. He felt uncomfortable in the room. The crowds, especially of educated people, made him nervous.

'With the new policy of active aging, we want to change the dynamics and the lifestyle of our silver population ...' the politician declared. He was speaking in English mixed with Mandarin, and whatever he was saying made little sense to Zul.

When the MP's speech ended, people clapped. Zul joined them in the clapping. The MP, a balding man in his late forties, pursed his lips in a smile, shook his head and looked at the crowd triumphantly. Then he took a seat on a chair and visitors, in groups of two or three, mostly aged Indians, Malays and Chinese, started approaching him with letters and papers in their hands.

When he tried to leap at the MP, jumping the queue, a man dressed in white stopped him. 'Wait for your turn, will you,' he growled.

'It might be too late, sir, if I do.'

'What do you mean?'

'The last time I came to meet the man, I was asked to wait, and by the time my turn came, it was time for him to go somewhere else.'

'It must be some emergency if he had to go like that last time, you understand? He will meet everybody who comes to meet him.'

'I must meet him, sir,' he tried to sound as sweet as possible. 'It is an emergency for me. I've been trying to meet him for weeks ... '

'Then wait for your turn,' the man shouted. 'Wait. Order. Discipline. That's how business is conducted here.'

The high-pitched oration of the man's voice caught the MP's attention. He looked at the two fellows engaged in a verbal duel.

'Hold it,' the MP said, 'and come here.'

'Wa!' Zul was mad with joy, his prayers were going to be answered. He gave a condescending look to the man he was quarrelling with and walked over to the MP.

'Haven't I seen you before?' the MP asked him in a flat voice. 'What can I do for you?'

'Sir, I had given my application some months ago,' be blurted.

'Application for what?' the MP said, looking at him quizzically. Then he looked at his assistant.

His assistant whispered something into the MP's ear. A smile spread on the politician's face.

'So, you are the man,' the MP said, looking him up and down as if he were sizing up a man whose gumption outstripped his calibre. 'The man in love with an Indonesian maid?'

'Yes, sir.'

'Very well. What do you do?'

'I work in a restaura—'

'Yes, I know what you do for a living. You are a cleaner,' he said, emphasising the word 'cleaner'. 'My question was only rhetorical.'

'Sorry, sir?'

'Never mind,' the MP said, looking intently at him. 'Look, you are a cleaner, and you want to marry a foreign maid ...'

'Yes, sir, I want to start a family,' Zul repeated the line that was taught to him by Melly. 'Together, we will start a family.'

He remembered her words. 'You must say to the MP "I want to start a family." The government wants more babies born in

155

Singapore, understand?' Yousuf had approved the line.

'But how?' the MP asked him. 'How do you want to start a family? Do you know what it takes to start a family.'

'Hard work, sir. Both of us are working ...'

'Hah,' the MP threw his hands in the air in exasperation. 'What future do you have? A cleaner and a maid. What future, eh? I cannot ask the government to change rules for you.'

'But I must marry Melly, sir,' Zul cried, tears welling up his eyes, his voice cracking.

'But why a foreign maid?' the MP shouted, his face red with anger. 'Can't you find a woman in Singapore? We've plenty of women here who can't find ...'

'Because I love her, sir' he cried, falling at the feet of the MP. 'And she loves me.'

The scene between Zul and the MP interested everyone in the room. A real life drama, a rarity in Singapore, better than the farce on the local TV channels. Someone took out his smartphone and began to shoot the sequence—good material for YouTube.

While Zul sobbed at the MP's feet, he felt a hundred pairs of eyes boring into his back. But all he could see then was an image of Melly—she was being pulled away from him by a group of monsters dressed in white. She was crying helplessly and the only person who could help her was Zul. And for Zul, the only person who could help him was this man on whose feet he was hunched over.

'Look at you,' the MP said. 'Today, you want me to help you marry a foreign maid. Tomorrow, you will come asking for some HDB flat, then you will come asking for financial help, then you will have children. What will you do ... homeless, jobless? Pitch a tent at East Coast Park? How will you afford a good education for your children? What will they become when they grow up? This vicious circle of poverty will go on.'

There was silence in the room and everyone hung on every word that was coming out of the MP's mouth.

Then he heard the MP laugh like a hyena. 'This man here says he loves a maid,' the MP cackled. 'Love! Ha ha ha! Don't you know that romance is the privilege of the rich, not the profession of the poor? Can somebody tell him that?' A pause for effect, and then he continued, 'Don't you have a sense of responsibility? How come a maid and a cleaner want to start a family?'

While he sat curled at the MP's feet, the MP's laughter triggered something inside him. Click; something snapped in his brain's machinery, like the popping of a grenade's clip. 'Don't the poor have a chance at love?' he wanted to shout. 'Don't they have the right to raise a family? Why must the world and its happiness belong to the rich only?'

His body began to shiver with rage. His mind started whirring, things began to appear blurry before his eyes. He saw monsters pulling Melly away from him and a man in white seemed to laugh at his helpless situation.

His hands reached for the folded object in his socks. And as the MP bent down to pull him up, his hand worked like a bolt of lightning. Before anyone could realise what was going on, he shouted, 'Monsters!' and in a sally of anger, plunged a knife into the MP's soft belly.

The knife belonged to his little brother, and had survived from his *kampung* days. His brother always carried this knife whenever

157

they went around hunting birds, stealing fruits in the *kampung*.

The MP's eyes bulged in surprise as if a pair of invisible hands was at his throat. A jet of blood forcefully spurted out from the MP's abdomen, covering Zul's face in a warm, red splash. Howling, Zul gasped for breath, kicking his hands and feet around. The MP flopped on the chair. The room filled up with shrieks, cries.

'The mad man ... stabbed the MP.'

'Crazy man!'

'Beat the bastard!' someone shouted.

A kick landed on Zul's tummy, followed by a punch on his face. He fell on the floor and passed out. Next time he came to his senses, briefly, he heard the wail of an ambulance. Then he found himself in a hospital and, later on, in a prison cell. Three winks, three different places.

* * *

Zul wakes up as the guard beats on the iron bars of his prison door. A key turns in, the prison door is thrown open and the guard walks in. 'Someone is here to see you,' he says, poking him mildly with a baton.

He lifts his head, his hair dishevelled, the fuzz on his face forming a short beard. The guard appears like a ghost to him, blurry, a haloed figure, standing over him. He feels his shirt sleeves, starched by snot and drool, biting into his skin.

'Who?' He hears himself speak in a hoary voice.

The guard helps him stand up, without saying a word. Zul follows him like a zombie and guesses about the person who has come to see him.

Over the weeks or months—he has no idea of time—many people have visited him. Police officers, lawyers, prison guards. They have asked him questions to which he has no replies—educated man's questions. How would he respond? He is not educated, he doesn't know. He doesn't know anything that the police want to know from him. Conspiracy, opposition, communist, terrorist ... What sort of words are these, he wonders.

Among his personal visitors, only his mother and brother Ali have come to see him. His mother did not say anything to him, only looked at him with tearful eyes, and ran her fingers on his hand. His brother had a snarl on his face. 'You ... ah ... a disgrace to our family,' he had growled. 'You dead for us, you know. We don wan to see your face again, understand? So you better rot here and die!'

He didn't feel any anger towards his brother. What anger could he feel for a man whose mind and soul were twisted? His reaction was expected: Ali never liked him anyway. Zul had refused to help him in selling contraband cigarettes from Malaysia—the source of his part-time income after his full-time job in a security company. Zul preferred cleaning tables to selling contraband cigarettes—and his impertinence infuriated Ali.

'Now who is here to meet me?' he wonders as he passes through the corridor to the visiting room. The corridor is flanked by many dark cells, a world of shadows. Is he in Changi Prison already? He has no idea.

Yousuf stands up from a chair when he sees Zul walking into the room. Zul gives him a faint smile. 'I didn't expect you would come here to see me,' he says.

'I had to come, brother,' he says, helping Zul sit on a chair. 'Melly has given me a letter for you.'

'Melly!' Zul's eyes brighten up. 'How is she? Why didn't she come to see me?'

'She went back to her country.'

'Went back?' he says, his fuzzy face a rampaged valley. 'Just like that?'

The brightness of his eyes dies down, like a bulb suddenly losing its burning filament.

'The government sent her back, Zul. She didn't want to go.'

'Didn't want to go. *Gahmen* sent her back,' he repeated after him, like a dazed parrot.

'She came to me before she left for Indonesia,' Yousuf said, putting his hand in his shirt pocket. A letter emerged in his hands. 'And gave me this letter for you.'

'Can you read it for me?' Zul pleaded.

'Of course,' Yousuf said.

'Dear Zul,' Yousuf starts reading the letter, written in longhand. From across the table, Zul can see the scribble. The letters are plumpish, like Melly herself.

'I am so sad to know what has happened to you. You are in prison and I am being sent back home. My employment permit has been cancelled by your government. I wanted to come and see you one last time, but even that is not being allowed. So I came to brother Yousuf for his help.'

Yousuf stopped, cleared his throat and asked, 'You want me to read the entire letter?' His voice has turned shaky.

'Go on, I asked you to read already,' Zul answers gruffly.

'I wanted to come and confess my sins to you because I've done nothing short of sinning against an innocent man. That is you, Zul, my dimwit honest lover. You loved me so deeply, so honestly and there I was, deceiving you, sinning in my greed. A maid by day and a whore by night, sucking the smelly dicks of Chinese men—all for money. I had hoped that you would marry me and through you, I would get Singapore citizenship, and free myself from this life of want and disgrace ...'

'Stop, stop, stop!' Zul shouts like a madman, shielding his ears with his hands, as if preventing them from molten lead that someone was pouring down his ear canal. 'This is a lie, a big lie, my Melly cannot be like that,' he sobs, beating his feet on the ground, his cuffs clinking.

In a swoop, he seizes the letter from Yousuf's hands, crumples it and throws it down on the floor, then tramples on it with his lightly shod feet.

'I thought you a good man, Yousuf.' He spits on the floor. 'But no, you too side with them, you too *gahmen*—all wanting to drive me mad. I am not mad, let me tell you. You mad, you are all mad, you and this guard, and my brother Ali, and the *gahmen* who won't allow me to marry Melly, all are mad. And Melly, she a good woman, and nobody call her a hooker, you hear!'

Yousuf looks at him with his mouth agape, his gorge going up and down. The guard hovers around Zul, ready to catch the gorilla gone berserk.

Zul staggers to the guard. 'Here,' he shouts, foam appearing at the corners of his mouth, 'take me from here. Cane me, hang me, kill me, I don't want to live anymore, don't want to live in your mad, filthy *gahmen*-run world, don't want ...'

The guard grabs a raging Zul and Yousuf sees him walk away from the room. He feels his throat go dry as Zul disappears. His hands reach for the pack of cigarettes in his trouser pocket, but then they remain frozen there for a while, remembering that smoking is not allowed inside that government building. 'Tch,' he clucks, and steps out.

ZAFAR ANJUM is a journalist and author and is the editor of *Kitaab. org* and *Writersconnect.org*. One of his short stories, *Waiting for the Angels,* was a finalist for India's prestigious The Little Magazine New Writing Prize for emerging Indian writers. His stories have been anthologised in Monsoon Books' *Love and Lust in Singapore* (2010) and *Best of Southeast Asian Erotica* (2010). He is one of the recipients of the 2010 Arts Creation Fund grant from Singapore's National Arts Council. 'The Madman of Geylang' was inspired by a Haresh Sharma–Alvin Tan play, *Model Citizens*.

The Lost History
of Shadows

Aaron Ang

The Singapore we know today belongs to a different universe from the Singapore of the prewar era. Especially those last years before war broke out.

In those days, this was a raucous port city, one that richly deserved its soubriquet: Sin Galore. There was an ample supply of all the leading vices, and much of the island was portioned off into jealously guarded fiefdoms of secret societies, gangs and petty criminals, each maintaining its dominion through vicious measures. Robbery, assaults and other forms of casual violence were, if not daily occurrences, nothing out of the ordinary.

Still, even within this rich melange of crime, the slaughter in early December 1938 stood out for both its brutality and efficiency. For a time, this crime captured the public imagination, spinning various myths that defined how people in those days viewed Singapore.

As the colonial police originally reconstructed the events of that night, it ran pretty much like this: Shortly after 1 a.m. on the morning of December 13, a group of five men were gathered around a table in the backroom of a dubious establishment on Keong Saik Road in Chinatown when three other men stormed into the room. Two of the men at the table drew their knives, then quickly realised they were out-matched: the three interlopers drew pistols and pointed them at the group.

The two knife-wielders were promptly persuaded to drop their weapons to the floor and give full attention to the three gunmen. Then, or shortly thereafter, the three gunmen relieved their five victims of all their cash, watches and whatever other jewellery they had—and perhaps some other valuables that police could only guess at.

Had it all ended there, this crime would hardly have stood out amongst the hundreds of other armed robberies Singapore police had to deal with during this period. But for some motive the police were never quite clear about, this robbery went beyond the robbery stage, and that is what pushed it into the realm of legend.

First, the robbers ordered the three men on the left side of the table to put their hands over their eyes, ears or mouths in the classic see no evil, hear no evil, speak no evil triptych. The three robbers then proceeded to shoot their five victims; shoot them in a most systematic way. Each man at the table was shot once in the upper right side of the chest, once through the neck and once in the head, just above eyebrow level.

Police speculate that the first five shots, into the chests, were to stun the men and render them unable to offer any further resistance. But the police Forensics Department pointed out that the third shot was thoroughly redundant: the blast through the throat or the one to the forehead alone would have killed the victims nicely.

This degree of brutality led police investigators to conclude that the shootings followed the robbery: the sizeable wounds from the Webley revolver bullets produced so much blood, especially from the heads, that it would have been too messy, if not visually difficult, to remove money and valuables from the victims.

The three gunmen then quickly left the scene: rushing out into Keong Saik Road, they darted to their left, turned a corner and disappeared. Their escape left a clutch of witnesses. Although it was fairly late, this was Keong Saik Road, and the police later turned up eight people who witnessed the rapid departure of three nervous-looking men and were willing to speak about it. Reports claimed that at least twice as many people were out on the street that night, near the club, and somehow suffered bouts of temporary blindness. All too typical of prewar Singapore.

The crime quickly seized the imagination of the Singapore public. A big part of the reason, most observers agree, was the splash it received in the local press.

In fact, the story was given a big push into legend by the front-page article in *The Straits Times*. This article was written by the famous, or—as some would have it—notorious Paul Haggerty. Haggerty had been a star journalist for the *Manchester Guardian* who'd gotten himself fired the previous year for insubordination. (A charge which included the fact that he was carrying on a sordid affair with his boss's wife.)

Haggerty found himself shipped off to the Far East with the hazy promise of a return to high-end British journalism if he behaved himself out there. But for his first six months here, Haggerty found himself smothered in boring assignments. His tendency to drink too much was stoked almost daily by the tedium. The Keong Saik Road case gave him the opening he needed; this was just the kind of journalistic red meat he loved sinking his teeth into.

His article the following day opened this way: 'The "shortest day of the year" proved to be very short indeed for five men at a private Chinatown opium party, including one of Singapore's richest men.'

That sentence contained two of the elements that catapulted this case into celebrity status. There was indeed some opium paraphernalia on the table when the police arrived, along with small spreads of opium. Even more eyebrow-raising was the make up of the quintet at that party. As Haggerty wrote, one of the five murdered men was indeed one of Singapore's richest local businessmen, Tan Tong Hua. The main owner and head of Samtan Industries, Tan was not known for his visits to sleazy Chinatown clubs and there was a quick flurry of speculation as to why he was there that evening.

Three of the murdered men were more typical denizens of these parts. All were known locally as petty criminals, marginal foot-soldiers of marginal Chinese gangs. These three—Koh Lee Pock, forty-three years old; Seng How Chook, nineteen; and Low Wee Hong, fourteen years old—had few resources, but many contacts within the netherworld of Sin Galore. But just what their association with one of the colony's wealthiest and most respected men was, that baffled many.

But the most intriguing part of the puzzle involved the fifth victim, a German diplomat by the name of Karl-Friedrich Hant von Herzberg. At the time of the murders, Hant von Herzberg was chargé d'affaires of the Bangkok embassy of the German Reich, a post he'd held for just over a year.

Hant von Herzberg had travelled to Singapore on some 'minor business' according to the Bangkok embassy in its brief statement to the press. The exact nature of that 'minor business' was to become a major source of speculation in the coming months.

Two days after the murders, a tight-lipped delegation arrived from Bangkok to retrieve the body. Except for filling out the necessary papers, they offered no assistance to the British authorities and returned quickly with their diplomat's remains.

A Nazi diplomat, a fantastically wealthy businessman, three small-time hoods, opium: it was the perfect recipe for making the case the most celebrated crime in Singapore in that decade. In fact, many Singapore residents, Asians and expats, took a kind of perverted pride in the killings. They felt it showed that Singapore too, could produce criminals whose brutality and cold-bloodedness matched the infamous in other crime capitals.

The crime was even given its own nickname: the St Lucy's Day Massacre. The echoes of the notorious St Valentine's Day massacre in Chicago was purely intentional: the robbery-murders suggested this city too, had a capacity for brutal crime of an epic nature.

Actually, there was a sixth victim that night. While the men were meeting in the back room, a thirteen-year-old girl who worked at the club was in a side room just off the front entrance, apparently trying to catch some sleep. She worked in the club as waitress, cleaning lady, general purpose dogsbody.

Woken by the shots, she came stumbling out of her room to see what was going on. She was immediately rewarded for her concern with three quick shots to the abdomen. Not having been a part of the killers' plans, she was left with that.

She was the only victim still alive when police turned up some twenty minutes later. They found her lying, as Paul Haggerty described it, 'covered with a tidy blanket of her own blood around her midriff.' The police tried extracting useful information from her. Though her English bordered on non-existent, the Chinese officer on the scene did manage to get a few fractured sentences from her.

The girl, known locally as 'Agnes Slop-Mop' was staring upwards as she kept repeating, 'The men ... the men ...'

'Yes,' implored the police officer. 'The men. What about the men?'

'They wanted ... They wanted to ...' And that was where she lapsed into unconsciousness from the loss of blood. She never regained consciousness; she died on the confused ride to the hospital.

The death of a thirteen-year-old girl only made the case more piquant, stoking further outrage at the 'savages' who were responsible.

The local police very much needed to solve this case quickly, but they seemed helpless at first. Having little to go on other than sketchy descriptions of the three nervous men who fled the club that night, they started clutching at anything they could find. All their fragile leads withered and turned into dust as soon as they started looking at them closely. They seemed totally lost.

But then, they caught a lucky break. Two weeks after the killings, there was a bungled break-in at a ball-bearings warehouse. The lone burglar was surprised by police and seemingly cornered. However, he slipped into a back room, kicked out a small barred window and managed to crawl through. Finding a young policeman waiting for him there, he shot and wounded the officer in the shoulder, then turned to find three other members of the police team had arrived from around the corner. He fell to one knee and aimed his revolver.

In the ensuing shoot-out with the police, the burglar was killed. (Shot eight times according to one report.) At the morgue, his identity was quickly determined: this was none other than Zhou Wei Tong, one of the colony's more notorious criminals. His arrest sheet alone would have filled a small booklet. Somewhere along the road, he had acquired the soubriquet 'Poison Claw Zhou'; few who knew him disputed his right to such a tag.

The big breakthrough came when the authorities determined that the large, blood-red ruby ring Zhou was wearing had not long before been a prized possession of Tan Tong Hua. Also, in one pocket, they supposedly found a fancy brooch belonging to one of the three minor criminals killed that evening.

The authorities also noted that the quasi-ritualistic style of the shooting bore the traces of Zhou. He was known for putting his signature on a crime with such nasty touches.

That settled the matter for the police: His record, his reputation and his possession of the two expensive pieces convinced them that Zhou was one of the St Lucy's Day killers.

Eight days later, police got their second break. A small-time hood was found down on the banks of the Kallang River near Thomson Road, a single bullet hole through the head. He had no impressive possessions tying him to the Massacre, but a number of police informants from the underworld assured the police that the dead man had served as a kind of intern to Poison Claw Zhou.

With the death of this man, Chang Ten Li, police promptly declared the case closed. They issued a report saying that their investigations had determined the two killers were Zhou and Chang, and that the crime was a simple robbery-murder. Having robbed their victims, the hoodlums wanted to leave no witnesses who could ever identify them or testify against them.

And what about those witnesses in the street who had seen three men leaving the club? A not unprecedented mistake, the police commissioner explained. Eyewitnesses are notoriously unreliable—especially Asian eyewitnesses out in the wee hours of the morning, probably after excessive drinking or drug use. They see things that are not there. All too typical is that one 'witness' will imagine he saw something, convey this impression to a second, and before long, you'll have the whole lot swearing that the man in the moon had swept down on a diamond-studded broom and stuffed a big wad of green cheese up the nose of one of their plaster gods.

But there was one further complication to the police version. There were eighteen shots fired that morning, and the two Webley revolvers could only carry twelve bullets. Quite easily explained, said the police spokesman: one of the two gunmen simply reloaded after emptying his barrels and started shooting anew.

Far from closing the case, this explanation quickly fuelled a firestorm of speculations about what really happened that night and why.

Conspiracy theories abounded. A police cover-up was a foregone conclusion. One batch of theories argued that some of the local police were actually themselves involved in the crime. Working with the two career criminals, they pulled off a nearly perfect crime—except for the witnesses who happened to see an undercover cop fleeing with his two cohorts.

The police then decided to turn the two full-time criminals into sacrificial lambs and when they were comfortably eliminated, they declared the case solved. The missing money and valuables were then duly distributed amongst all the police involved in the conspiracy.

But another popular theory had the police involved only on the margins of the crime. In this version, some high people in the British colonial administration were behind the killings, and planning and responsibility possibly stretched all the way back to the Colonial Office in London.

This theory turned upon the most baffling of the five main victims, Hant von Herzberg. What was a German diplomat from a refined East Prussian background doing in a sleazy Chinatown club with three petty criminals and a Singapore mogul?

As this narrative went on, it had the German travelling to Singapore with a tidy sum of money to buy cooperation. He was there to form a Fifth Column of paid traitors who would carry out acts of sabotage or organise an armed uprising against the British in the event of a war between Europe's two superpowers. Any serious attacks or disruptions against the Empire in this important colony with its vital port would have to be a major distraction for the British and help the German military campaign in Europe.

Hant von Herzberg arranged a meeting with the respected, well-connected Tan and the businessman brought in the three hoodlums who would actually organise and help carry out any attacks. The Nazi attaché came ready to provide a hefty down payment to Tan and his associates, but that money disappeared into the hands of the three government agents who abruptly ended the deal.

There was one big stumbling block for this theory: there was clear evidence that Tan had himself withdrawn a substantial amount of cash earlier that day and this money had also disappeared. Why did he need all that cash? Was he making his own, parallel deal with the Nazis? There was no explanation for what happened to this money either. Those who favoured the British government conspiracy theory argued that this was just a windfall profit for those involved.

Soon after the murders, the British authorities ordered the police to stymie all real investigations, find a couple of scapegoats, plant evidence on one of them and stamp 'Solved' on the crime. Or so the theory ran. But those who didn't like this version had an inconvenient question for its proponents: Why didn't the police find three scapegoats and close the case even more neatly?

As Paul Haggerty wrote in one of his columns after the official police report was issued, 'How fortunate we all are that our defenders of public safety can close a messy case like the St Lucy's Day so neatly. Of course, they had some kind assistance from the second and *ostensibly* final killer, Mr Chang.

'This Mr Chang was obviously so upset about the death of his mentor at the hands of the police that he made his way to a secluded area by the river, put a bullet through his own head, and then managed to cleverly dispose of the suicide weapon. Other than the fact that the gun he used to kill himself has not yet been found, the case has a perfectly neat and symmetrical solution. Bravo to our boys in the police department.'

The case remained a hot topic of whispers and rumours over the next half year or so. Then war broke out in Europe, and people's attention, even in Singapore, turned to other matters. Not long after that, the Japanese armies started sweeping down the Southeast Asian corridor towards Singapore. In February '42, the colony itself fell to the Japanese and the St Lucy's Day Massacre faded far into the background. By the end of the war, the killing of six innocent people seemed mild, even niggling, in comparison to what most people had seen during the war years. Before long, it was about as burning an issue as the mythical Bukit Merah killing. And much less well-known.

* * *

It might be safe to say that almost nobody thought about or talked about the St Lucy's Massacre again for the next half century or so. That was when Rajesh Datt, a graduate student at the National University of Singapore, happened to come upon the story.

Datt was grinding out his Ph.D. in History, with the subject of his dissertation Singapore's social and cultural life in the run-up to the Second World War. The working title was 'The Last Silly Seasons in Tropical Babylon'. His thesis adviser was, not surprisingly, unhappy with the title.

In the course of his research, Datt started ploughing his way through contemporary news accounts of the massacre that night in Chinatown. As happened to so many of those who had actually lived through the period, Datt quickly became engrossed. Within a few weeks, the Massacre had grown from a footnote in his thesis to two paragraphs and then to several pages. And that was just from gleaning the newspapers, including the obituaries. But this was late 2006, and there were still large portions missing from the story.

Despite the intervening decades, so many unanswered questions remained about the case, especially the first five victims and the twisted forces that had brought them together on that night. Reading every newspaper account he could dig up, Rajesh Datt started giving the case more attention than was advisable for his academic work.

Two years into his dissertation, Datt was knotted in stress, a common ailment for doctoral candidates. He was having trouble sleeping. He had adopted a steady routine of drinking too much alcohol to slide him into some form of sleep and then too much caffeine to get him awake and alert the next day. Weekends were a kind of reprieve where he tried to make up his sleep debt. But that had become a rather huge debt.

And what sleep he managed would often be racked by harsh dreams. Many of them found him on Keong Saik Road back in 1938. (Though, as will happen in dreams, the spectral landscapes were filled with a lot of ringing handphones, flat-screen TV monitors and other toys of our time.) In these dreams, he started seeing some of the victims, Rajesh's friends would show up as witnesses or police officers, and he'd receive desperate phone calls from one of the victims during the shootings. In one dire dream, he walked into the club the morning after the Massacre and made his way through the rooms, all thickly coated with semi-dried blood. His shoes got stuck in the layers of blood and he had trouble moving.

Even his graduate school friends, no slouches at overwork

themselves, had started to get concerned. Datt had become edgy, easily distracted. Finally, his thesis advisor had called him into the office and ordered him to take a two-week break. He was to do no work on the dissertation, no work at all, until the end of that month.

This was actually exactly what Rajesh wanted to hear. He needed someone, someone with authority, telling him to slow down, to put on the brakes for awhile. Still, his strange dreams continued even though he had suspended the actual studies.

At this point, one of Datt's grad school friends returned from a short stay in London. He'd brought back a number of classic DVDs with him, and he invited a coven of his closest mates, Rajesh included, to a Saturday night Classic Film Marathon.

Bernard, the DVD man, carefully selected the order of the films and then proceeded to get up and give a short intro before each one. Early in the marathon, he planted himself in front of the screen and held up a DVD with a noirish cover.

As he started speaking, Bernard had to swat pieces of popcorn tossed by two of the friends who kept barking, 'Show the film! Show the film!' Undeterred, he chuckled and proclaimed that a poll of scholars and critics had chosen this next film as Number One, the best British film of the twentieth-century. 'As opposed to the best British film of the eighteenth-century?' Mark Chan quipped.

'I guess so,' Bernard replied as he slid the film into the slot and they all sat back to enjoy Carol Reed's *The Third Man*.

About halfway through, just after the major plot twist when Harry Lime reappears, Rajesh leaned forward, his eyes doggedly fixed on the screen. He then grabbed the remote control from the coffee table and squeezed the Pause button. The others all turned to him, irritated. He looked possessed.

'Yes!' he said. 'Yes. The third man! There really was a third man!'

'Yeah, thanks for the profound insight there, Raj. It was that Harry Lime guy. Now can we get back to the movie?'

But Rajesh didn't quite hear what he was saying; he was off into his own private orbit. 'Of course.' He turned to his friends. 'Eight witnesses. They couldn't *all* be that wrong. Not all of them.'

'What eight witnesses? It was just that one guy, the concierge. OK? But he was the one who was right.' David Quan then snatched the remote from Rajesh's hand and pushed the Play button.

Rajesh slid back into his nook on the couch and stared at the screen. But he found it difficult to concentrate on the film. His mind kept on darting off elsewhere. When he did start paying attention, he was caught up in the idea of the quest for the truth. Like Holly Martins, he wanted to get to the bottom of the thing. And there, that evening, the subject of Rajesh Datt's dissertation had just shifted dramatically.

* * *

'Any more questions?'

At this, the assembled guests exchanged taut, nervous smiles, looking around at the others in attendance, hoping no one would raise a hand. The heads turned back to the stage and waited expectantly for several moments. Finally, the main speaker nodded. If there were no more questions, he said, they could break for lunch.

The official announcements safely over, most of the invited guests had made their way over to the lunch buffet with mildly restrained haste.

It was February 2009, a week after Chinese New Year, when the Royal Sonesta Hotel in downtown Singapore hosted this small press conference-cum-free buffet. The occasion was to announce the real event: a week-long series of festivities to celebrate the 70th anniversary of the founding of Blue Horizons Pte Ltd. Blue Horizons was one of the Republic's premier success stories, a company with its steady fork in quite a few juicy pies.

The company had been founded by two youngish brothers who had arrived as toddlers in Singapore, then slowly clawed their way up. After a shaky start, Blue Horizons was one of the local firms that actually prospered during the Japanese occupation, then took off dramatically in the postwar years. By the time of independence, it had risen to 'pride of the nation' status: here was an example of what Singapore's people, especially recent immigrants, were capable of. It was the story of modern Singapore writ small.

There for the announcement of the anniversary were Blue Horizon's CEO Bertram Koh and his son, Anson Koh, company vice-president and heir apparent. At sixty-four, the elder Koh had actually been taking a less and less active role in running company affairs since a serious attack of spinal muscular atrophy had confined him to a wheelchair three years earlier. He and Anson had been working closely ever since, as Bertram carefully groomed the younger man to take over the reins completely. A flurry of rumours claimed Bertram Koh was preparing to announce his premature retirement at the 70th anniversary festivities.

Bertram Koh was now working one side of the room while his son worked the other. After moving from a brief exchange with a small investor, Anson turned to see who his father was schmoozing just then, but the older man had disappeared. Not to worry, Anson thought; he'd probably slipped out to go to the toilet.

Anson himself soon found himself talking to two of the company's long-time customers and a new but important supplier. He was trying his best to avoid the journalists in the room, a not too difficult task as most of them were so involved with the free buffet that he felt safe from the scattered spray of their dumb questions.

Just as he was dismissing the impact of some labour action in Jakarta on Blue Horizons's retail arm, Anson's phone rang. He apologised with a nod and a half-smile as he pulled the phone from his jacket pocket. It was his father.

'I'm sorry; I have to take this. My father,' he said with another, longer smile. His two companions smiled back and nodded as he stepped off slightly to the side.

'Anson, I need to see you.'

'Why, what's wrong, Dad?'

'Nothing ... wrong. It's just there's someone here I want you to meet. We're up in Room 316.'

'Room 316? You took a room?'

'He did. Look, please just get up here as quickly as you can. Everything will be very clear when you meet this gentleman.'

'Uh, OK ... I'll be right there. 316, right?'

'That's right. Turn left just out of the lift, it's halfway down the hall.'

'OK, I'll be right there.' He excused himself once more and with a promise that he'd be back shortly, Anson Koh headed to the ballroom exit.

Out of the lift, he forgot his father's advice and started scanning the room numbers on both sides. Still, it took him less than a minute to orient himself and find Room 316. When he reached it, he found a 'Do Not Disturb' sign slung over the knob and wasn't sure that he had the right room. Nonetheless, he gave a light, cautious knock.

'Come in, Anson,' shouted a voice he didn't recognise. 'It's open.'

An uncomfortable feeling gripped Anson, but he opened the door nonetheless. As he did so, he saw his father in the wheelchair, facing the door, about ten metres in. Standing behind him, slightly to his left, was a man he'd never seen before—holding a handgun to the back of his father's head. It was clear the man had placed himself a bit to the left so that Anson wouldn't miss that gun and its ominous position.

'Come in, please. Quickly. And close the door behind you.' Anson, stunned by what he saw, did as he was told.

'Now lock it, please.' Anson hesitated for just a moment, but then he read the nervous impatience in the man's face as he twisted his lips. Exchanging a quick, fearful glance with his father, Anson clicked the lock, then stared at the stranger for further instructions.

'Good. Thank you. I see you can be as cooperative as your father. That's good for all of us.' Anson nodded, then started speaking as quickly as he could.

'Look, whatever it is you want, we'll give it to you. Or we'll get it for you. But please leave my father alone. As you can see, he's an invalid and he needs—'

The man with the gun ignored his near panic. 'Why don't you sit down, Anson. I want you to be very relaxed while I'm telling you the purpose of this little meeting.'

'Relaxed?' Anson replied, in a tightly wrapped tone. The man with the gun smiled.

'As relaxed as you can get. But don't fall asleep on us or anything.'

Anson again nodded and settled into a large, functional chair near the door. It felt like something you'd throw a small bag or clothing onto rather than something you'd want to sit in for very long.

'But please ... like I said, whatever it is you want ...'

The man had now stepped a fist's length away from Bertram, though the gun was still pointed persuasively at his head. Anson kept looking intently at the man, examining that face, wondering whether he had ever seen him before.

His look must have revealed more than he cared to: the man with the gun offered him a condescending smile and said, 'You're wondering if we have ever met before.' Anson nodded stiffly. 'Well, not met the way you probably mean "met". But our paths have crossed.'

Bertram Koh now swallowed deeply and spoke for the first time. 'Our ... host tells me that our families have a shared history. He says he's been at a couple of our functions so that he could get to know more about where that history has brought us.'

The gunman now smiled and nodded several times, like a bobblehead doll. 'That's right. Yeah, so true. And the key facts about that history is right over there.' He pointed with the gun to a writing table across the room. Anson turned and noticed for the first time a thick manuscript sitting on that table, spread open as if someone had just been leafing through it.

'I'm going to ask you to read from that book in a few minutes, Anson. But since we're all such busy men these days, I decided to save some time. Let me give a quick background to the parts I want you to read.' He then looked insistently at his two 'guests', as if asking permission to tell his tale. Bertram nodded in agreement.

The man with the gun then recounted the major details of the St Lucy's Day Massacre, being careful not to jump over any of the messier parts. When he asked if the two Kohs had ever heard any of this before, they both said no, earnestly. After he'd finished, he repeated the names and salient details about three of the victims, including the thirteen-year-old Agnes Slop-Mop.

'Now, Anson, I think you should get up and walk slowly over to the table. Keep it a straight line, though: don't try to get clever. This gun is quite loaded, I assure you.'

'That's a serious crime here in Singapore, in case you didn't know. The law does not look lightly on people who point loaded guns at other people.'

'You know, I think I've heard that somewhere before. But that's OK. By the time our heart-to-heart is over, I think we'll all be willing to keep that little mistake between ourselves.' He smiled again and, with an anxious wave of his hand, indicated that Anson should not waste any more time getting over to that manuscript. Anson nodded, rose from the chair and moved quickly. As he reached the table, the stranger spoke again.

'Oh, I'm sorry, I've forgotten to introduce myself; my name is Kelvin Tan. I think we should all get to know each other better.' Anson and Bertram exchanged looks and Anson squeezed out something between a frown and a smile. 'The pleasure is all mine,' Kelvin said with a dry snicker.

Anson stared at the book curiously, touching the double open pages as if they were some delicate object. He started to turn the page, at which Kelvin Tan cleared his throat in warning.

'You don't need to browse anywhere, Anson. I went to all that trouble to set the pages for you, so don't make it all confused. The story you want starts right there. Second paragraph on page 107.'

'Yeah, yeah, I see it. So you want me to just … read?'

'Out loud. Share it with all of us. It involves all three of us.'

Anson cleared his throat. He found the spot again and began reading. 'So, for all the foregoing reasons, I think we have fully established that there was indeed a third gunman that evening. And my further research from that point established almost as firmly that the third man in the robbery-murder that night was …' Anson stopped and just stared at the page, his eyes seized by the next words.

'Having trouble with the name, Anson? Want me to give you some help?'

'No. I think I can manage this name myself.' He then turned and stared at his father. He continued. ' … the third man in the robbery-murder that night was Koh Kai-Sung.' Bertram Koh sat up, shocked.

'Your grandfather??'

Anson read on a bit. 'Within six months, Koh had founded

a small company with his brother, Koh Tai-Win. That company was later renamed Blue Horizons and went on to become one of Singapore's most successful companies, with a wide range of activities and interests.'

Here Anson stopped and looked up. Kelvin Tan was looking back at him, a self-satisfied smile on his face. He then turned to Bertram Koh to irritate him with that same smile.

'So what the hell is this thing, this shit book?' Though it seemed hardly possible, Kelvin's smile broadened at that question.

'Believe it or not, it started out a Ph.D. thesis. But now it's a key to the Blue Horizons bank vault, I think.'

Bertram Koh turned to him at this point. 'Who's responsible for this thing? Who put this rubbish together?'

'My partner. My silent partner.'

The elder Koh's eyebrows lifted skeptically. 'A silent partner. As in …'

'He wants to keep out of this part of the deal. He's … respectable. But he's also brilliant, believe me.' He looked from one of the Kohs to the other, gesticulating as if he were trying to sell his partner to them. 'You call it shit? I've been told this guy is a very respected researcher and scholar, whatever. He's really good. And obsessed! You spend a hour or two with him, you can't keep up with him. He's amazing: can't sit still, always looking for something, thinking three jumps ahead of you.'

Anson choked on a bitter laugh. 'Well, you can tell your partner he's completely wrong this time. This is nothing but wild accusations. Crazy stuff. With no evidence at all.'

'Oh no? Keep reading, Anson. Just keep reading.'

Anson read on. 'This may sound a rather dubious claim, maybe even an outrageous claim, especially coming sixty-nine years after the police declared the case closed.' Anson gave his own nod to that. 'But I strongly believe it to be a claim supported by all the evidence I have collected in over two years of research.'

'I have now established that Koh Kai-Sung was an associate of the notorious criminal Zhou Wei Tong. He was learning the trade from Zhou. I have spoken with a number of people who knew Koh and examined letters from others. I will just give some samples here.'

At this point, Kelvin Tan raised his gun. 'You can skip over to page 109. There at the bottom, I've got it marked in red. You'll have time to read all those testimonies later, don't worry.' Anson stared at him coldly, though with a twitch of fear still in his face. 'Turn the page. Please. We're all busy and I want to get through this part of the programme quickly.'

Anson turned the page, found the marked passage and began reading again. 'As the nearly blind man told me, Zhou Wei Tong was more than a teacher to Koh; he was more like a father. He spoke of young Koh the way a father speaks of a son, with warmth and pride.'

Anson turned the page and started reading from the top. 'I now have strong evidence that Koh Kai-Sung himself was arrested twice while carrying out petty crimes for Zhou. But at both arrests, he produced false I.D. that we can assume had been provided by Zhou, as this was another of the older man's sidelines. The colonial police did not expend much energy checking out the details of Asians booked for minor crimes here, so Koh's false papers were accepted. The two mug shots which I include in the appendix both bear strong resemblance to Koh, although two different names were used by the same man in those photos.'

Kelvin then told Anson to skip over to page 113 as the next two pages were rather heavy with details. Anson found the passage Kelvin was referring to and started reading again.

'Through this friend, Koh secured a job working for Tan Tong Hua. He'd been working for Tan for just over four months at the time of the killings. It is more than reasonable to assume that Koh, smelling all that money swirling around Mr Tan, contacted his mentor and father-figure, Zhou, and suggested they could find some way of using this connection to make some quick money.

'He then learned, presumably from the chauffeur, that Tan had an unusual, late-night meeting in Chinatown on that evening. Also that he had withdrawn a large amount of money earlier in the day. Zhou would have quickly contacted his other young trainee, the strong-arm Chang, and arranged for the robbery. Whether they had planned right from the start to kill the robbery victims cannot be proven at this late date. But the seasoned criminal Zhou would have realised that there was a real danger of Tan somehow recognising Koh and the whole caper getting unravelled.

'On the other hand, it is likely that the murder of the thirteen-year-old cleaning girl was fully spontaneous as one of the three criminals, probably Koh himself, panicked when she ran out during their escape and shot her without thinking. This, as we shall see, was probably the only part of the massacre that actually stirred deep feelings of guilt in the young criminal.

'The money and other valuables would have been secreted away somewhere, with Zhou and his two 'interns' taking just a small portion to play with at first. Koh was more than willing to take Zhou's lead on this and other matters related to the crime.

'We can well imagine Koh's sense of loss, of despair even, when he heard about Zhou's demise. Without his mentor, how was he to go on?

'We can further assume that Koh, being quite bright if uneducated except in the basics of crime, saw himself faced with a major choice. He could continue pursuing his life of crime with the excellent prospect of more arrests, and at the end of that road, a good possibility of ending up like his mentor—a bloody bulk in a filthy alleyway. Or he could choose to go straight; more or less straight anyway. With a much larger than expected gain from the Keong Saik robbery, he now had the wherewithal to seek to make it in the world of legitimate business. Which is the path he ultimately chose.

'But Koh still faced one large obstacle blocking that legitimate path he now wanted to take: his other cohort in the robbery-murder. Chang Ten Li not only had a rough idea of how much they got away with that night, but he could always blackmail Koh in the future with what he knew. In fact, the more successful Koh became in the legitimate world, the more likely it was that his former accomplice would attempt to blackmail him. And plunge deeper into his wealth with each act of blackmail.

'With several cold-blooded murders already on his hands, Koh would have had no trouble pulling off just one more, especially as he felt this last one would lift him out of the morass of crime he was then stuck in.

'It is a safe surmise, then, that Koh Kai-Sung arranged to meet his only remaining accomplice there by the Kallang River to remove this last threat to his escape. We're on the far edge of speculation now, but it's not unreasonable that Zhou had told this young trainee where the money and other booty was hidden, but not Chang. So Koh most likely lured Chang to his fate by promising to divvy up the remaining wealth with him.

'We can picture the two of them meeting down by the river, remorse at the death of their mutual mentor darkening the moods, but those moods then lifted by thoughts of dividing Zhou's hefty share of the takings.

'We can also imagine Koh pointing upriver and asking Chang to look, so as to better see what he was pointing at. As the brutal but not too bright criminal turned to view the object, Koh swiftly pulled out his revolver, put it right up to Chang's head, the muzzle a little west of the ear (1.8 inches according to the police autopsy report), and fired a bullet cleanly through his former colleague's brain. As the Christian doctor who signed the autopsy said, before the body hit the ground, Mr Chang was already facing his Maker.

'We can even imagine Koh Kai-Sung lingering over the corpse of his former partner, staring at the body with blood spurting out of that neat hole, a certain note of nostalgia playing counterpoint to the more dominant notes of relief and joy. With that sprawled body in front of him, he could imagine himself looking at the end of his own former life, that life of crime that had become so central to his existence. And now it was over. He turned and walked away quickly, feeling he had turned his back on that former life and was now striding into the life of the respectable Chinese Singaporean business class.

'He didn't look back. It now seems fairly clear that soon thereafter, Koh made his way to the hiding place Zhou had shown him and removed all the money as well as the remaining jewelry and other valuables. He traded in the latter with those people who serviced this type of criminal and suddenly found himself a somewhat wealthy young man. And he evidently believed that he had captured all of his shadows and squeezed them into a safe-box.

'Less than half a year later, he founded a trading company with his brother, a company they originally called K,K&Z, later changing the name to … Blue Horizons Pte. Ltd.'

Anson Koh stopped there. 'Alright; you've got one of those thick red lines scrawled under that.'

'Oh yeah,' said Kelvin Tan. 'That means you've covered all the really essential parts of the story up till there. Those other bits, you can read later. They're good too.'

He turned to Bertram Koh, whose stare had been fixed on his son and the all too visible pain in his face as he read. 'That's your copy there. I've actually got you each your own copy. Other one's in the bag over there.' He swung the gun upwards and to the right to indicate a bulky plastic Border's bag slumped next to a chair. He looked back at Anson. 'Some great eye-opening stuff there, isn't it?'

'Eye-opening? I prefer calling it bullshit. Total, libelous bullshit. No, that demeans bullshit; it's worse than that. It's toxic'

'I can understand why you'd like to believe that, Anson *Koh*. It would save you a lot of shame … and even more money.'

'You obviously got inspired by that part about blackmail in this fantasy. But this stuff', he flipped a few pages, 'is worthless. What does this shit mean: "we can assume", "it's reasonable to believe", "we can just imagine"?

Kelvin shrugged. 'He has a lot of hard facts … from there, he just connects the dots.'

'He has wild rumours and then he goes haywire. Sorry, but it is reasonable to believe that this thesis is more like faeces, and we can just imagine that the guy who wrote this was desperate to support a very weak theory and maybe to make some easy money through intimidation and throwing garbage on a very decent man.

'And we can further assume the reason you came here is to try and blackmail us. Well, we can just imagine that you're facing a long spell in jail and many strokes of the cane for kidnapping, blackmail and carrying a deadly weapon.

'Tell you what: You put that gun somewhere safe and let my father and me leave right now, then you follow and never contact us ever again, and we can pretend all this never happened. And that's about the best offer you can expect out of this charade.'

Kelvin Tan nodded, then broke into a rasping laugh. 'You want to hear my counter-offer? It's pretty good, actually. First, you make a one-time, strictly cash payment of 1.5 million. Most of that goes to my partner, but I get a little finder's fee. Very reasonable. Right?'

Anson turned to Bertram. 'Dad, can you believe this guy? He's not only deaf, he's obviously insane.'

Kelvin ignored him. 'And then I get *my* fair share.'

Anson threw up his hands and looked to the ceiling. 'Oh, I can't wait for this!'

'You make me a partner. Oh, don't worry, I'll be a nice, silent partner. But I get a 20% share of Blue Horizons, with all profits and bonuses, and everything that's fair.'

'Fair? You have the guts to talk to us about fair. Look, you asshole, my grandfather and uncle worked really hard to build this company out of nothing. And then my father worked almost as hard to keep it right up there at the top. And that's the work I'm continuing right now.

'Then you come along with some rubbish story and try to grab a piece of what my family has been building and holding for seventy years, and you think that's fair?'

Kelvin Tan gave another laugh at this, which made Anson want to punch him. This asshole was very lucky he had a gun in his fist, Anson thought.

'So your grandfather and uncle built up the company all fair and honest, is it? You think making deals with the Japanese during the Occupation is fair? And what was so fair about reporting other small Chinese businessmen to the Japanese for some stupid remark or minor offence? And when those guys suddenly disappear, Blue Horizons gets a little bigger, a little more successful. Their reward for helping the Japanese kill innocent men.'

Anson looked like he'd just been punched in the face. 'What, you're saying my family ratted out other Singaporeans so they could grab their businesses?' Tan flashed a self-satisfied smile and nodded.

'You're as ignorant as you are arrogant. And for your information, Mr Tan, my grandfather was a hero in the war. So was my uncle. They even got these ... what, these citations from the British.' He turned to Bertram and pointed. 'My father has them framed and hanging up in his office.'

'No, no, wait; my partner has that one covered too.' He reached into his left pocket and pulled out a piece of paper. 'Page

...' He opened the paper and turned it around to read. 'Sorry; I can't keep everything up here in my head. Page 154. The paragraphs are marked.'

Anson turned to page 154. He found the marked passages.

'The man who arranged for the Koh brothers to get that citation was a man called ...' Tan tried to remember.

'He was some very high official. Very *high*.' Anson turned to his father for confirmation. Bertram nodded, then turned to Kelvin Tan.

'His name was Terrence Lampert. First secretary to the Governor here. To both Shenton Thomas and Sir Franklin ... Gibson.'

'Yah, that's right.' Kelvin snapped his fingers in concurrence. 'Lampert. That's the one they talk about. Why don't you read it out for us, Anson.'

Anson turned to page 154 and started reading from the top. He first read the annotation that these passages were from the still unpublished memoirs of the late journalist Paul Haggerty.

'I guess I should consider myself damned lucky that I was kicked out of Singapore just as the war was getting started in Europe. I managed to make my way back to England in early 1940, a couple of years before the Japs took control in Singapore. If I'd stayed around, I would have certainly landed up in one of their POW camps. And from what I've heard, the drinking opportunities in those camps were rather meagre.

'Be that as it may, it stung to get tossed out of my second consecutive country, and this time with no just cause really. I was always convinced the real reason was that I was getting a little too close to the jugular of the power establishment with my investigations into that St Lucy's Day mess.

'Before I left, I'd scavenged together a pile of evidence pointing to someone high in the colonial administration who was working with the Nazis. I had narrowed it down to just a handful of names by the time I got the boot, and continued pursuing the matter as much as I could back in England.

'I finally managed to get it down to two prime suspects, and then my journalistic instincts and a chat with one of his nephews convinced me it was this fellow, Terrence Lampert. Lampert was apparently a virulent anti-Semite and someone who felt the Soviets were the real threat to Western civilisation, while the Nazis were simply the last reliable bulwark against Bolshevik barbarism.

'In 1967, I finally managed to meet Lampert. Using a false name, I arranged an interview on the pretext of writing a book about the defeat of the Japanese in the region and how the British had re-established order in Malaya after the war.

'I drove to Lampert's home in Luton and pulled up early on a crisp but lovely autumn afternoon. Mr Lampert proved to be a gracious host, as I have always found Nazi sympathisers to be. We were both into our second glass of port when I started easing some questions his way.

'Lampert answered all the innocuous, pablum queries in a relaxed manner. It was obvious he'd spoken about these matters many times before. Then I tossed the firebomb into our conversation.

'"You know, it's really a shame you never got to raise a wassail with your old pal Hant von Herzberg when he came to see you there in 1938."

'Lampert looked stunned. I could see from the quiver in his

lips and the cold stare that I'd found my man. I smiled at him, but he just coldly replied, "I don't know what you're talking about." The way he said it, I knew that he knew *exactly* what I was talking about.

'I pressed on a little bit about him and his relationship with Hant von Herzberg. His only response was to call his wife. "Ruth, our guest has to leave. He's not feeling all that clever suddenly." He then turned to me. "I'll call my man; he'll see you to the door."

'I replied with a caustic smile. I had a lot, but it wasn't quite the proverbial smoking gun. So I decided to pull one of the tricks all great investigative journalists use: I would play a hunch and pretend it was established fact.

"Sorry, Mr Lampert, but I've seen those documents. The ones Hant von Herzberg was carrying that night he was killed. The wily Chinese gentleman who sold them to you was just clever enough to make copies before he handed the originals over. They're with my publisher right now. It's got your name on them, your signature and your nasty role in betraying the government you were meant to be serving."

'Now the look on Lampert's face was one of fear—deep, choking fear. I could almost hear his mouth going dry. He had gone pale and started looking to the side as if to find a way out. But a few moments later, he turned back and glared at me with intense anger. "They didn't have these photocopies back then. They didn't exist. Certainly not there in Singapore. You made that up, you devious bastard."

'I then shot him one of the brightest smiles of my career. "Indeed, I did. But you've just confirmed the central truth of the whole matter for me." With that, I turned and started strutting out without waiting for his "man" to guide me. I was afraid he might come running up behind me and try to strangle me. Or stick a dagger in my back. But he did nothing. I swear I could, however, feel the palpable sting of his glare in my back as I left.

'So I had my traitor and everything else had come together. All that was missing was the identity of some Chinaman who had evidently sold incriminating documents to Lampert for either money or special privileges.

'It's probably too late for me to ever track down that Chinaman, but I hope somebody will someday pick up the torch from me. The one thing I'm bloody sure of is that our man got those documents off the dead body of the German diplomat that night in Chinatown. In other words, it was that third killer, whose existence the Singapore Detective Branch spent so much time and energy denying. Whoever this was, he was the last piece of the puzzle.'

Kelvin Tan was absolutely beaming at this point. 'So now we see how those hero's citations were arranged: one very dirty hand washes the other.'

'And this ... Mr Haggerty?' Bertram Koh asked.

'Dead. He died a few years later. I think it was 1971, but that's not the important thing. My partner got a lot of his information from those memoirs. And from me.'

'From you? So how did you work your way into this anyway?'

'He came after me, my partner. Wanted to know what I knew about my great-uncle.'

'Your great-uncle?'

'Tan Tong Hua.' He paused for effect. 'Once one of the richest men in Singapore?'

Anson offered a cynical nod. 'Of course.'

'After he got killed, the business went all to hell. His sons, his nephews ... my father one of them ... couldn't keep things going. Didn't have his touch, I guess. Most of what was left of the company got sold off. Mainly to ...'

Bertram Koh nodded. 'Blue Horizons.'

Kelvin smiled broadly. 'Oh yes; I knew I've heard that name somewhere before.' He then stepped to the middle of the room, halfway between the two Kohs. 'So now you see, gentlemen, why I feel I am well and truly entitled to a share of Blue Horizons. The money my great-uncle had on him the night he died, all his possessions that night, that all disappeared. But then it comes back as seed money for your family company. And money that came out of that was used to buy the rest of my family's company.'

Bertram Koh looked at him hard. 'So you helped your partner find much of what he could regarding our company?'

Tan shrugged. 'As much as I could. But you can believe I got super interested in this case. Especially when I knew how much I could profit from it myself.'

'Yes, indeed. Any more startling revelations about our family?'

'No, nothing that you can't—oh wait, yes; thanks for reminding me.' Tan now smiled like a ten-year-old about to tell a dirty joke. 'Your family has this ... uhh, foundation or something.'

Bertram nodded, already suspicious of where this question was headed. 'The Wan Tze Min Foundation. It makes grants to groups furthering the education of young girls from poor backgrounds.'

'Right; yes; very, very humanitarian of your company. And that

195

was started by …?'

Anson scowled. 'My grandfather. As if you didn't know.'

'Just wanted to be sure … partner. But one thing still not clear … who was this Wan Tze Min?'

'A young girl in southern China. Where my family came from originally. She helped some cousins and an aunt escape just as the Communists were moving into that area. They got away to Malaysia and eventually made it to Canada.'

'And that young girl? What did …?'

'The Communists found out she was helping people from the area escape. And not just my family members. So they tortured her to get information and apparently she died while in their custody. Murdered probably.'

Kelvin shook his head, feigning sorrow. 'Sad story really. So sad.' He looked up towards the ceiling, as if seeking advice.

'And these relatives in Canada, do you see them often? Keep in touch with phone calls, letters?'

Bertram Koh shifted uneasily in his wheelchair. 'No. They … they never kept up contact after making it to North America. I've never really seen them or spoken to them … myself.'

'Oh. What a lack of gratitude. After saving them from the Communists.'

'It happens. Families are not always as tight or as loyal as they should.'

'How true. How very true.' Tan then reached into his shirt pocket and pulled out a few well-folded pieces of paper. 'Oh, before I forget. I have a present for you. Both of you.' He tossed the pages across the floor, towards Anson.

'What's this?' asked the younger Koh as he picked the papers up off the floor.

'It's a copy of a police report. From 1938. You can verify it yourself if you want. Go to the police headquarters, file a request, you have to wait about a month, but ...' He smiled. 'Why go to all that trouble? I swear to you that these are genuine. And if you can't trust your new partner, who can you trust?'

'I'm sure they're authentic,' said the elder Koh.

'It's only part of the entire report. But it has the name of one of the victims and how she died. The girl they called 'Agnes Slop-Mop'. They've got her there under her real name.'

Anson slapped the papers in the palm of his left hand. 'Thank you, Mr Tan. We'll look at these later.'

'You'll find it very interesting reading.'

Anson and Bertram exchanged long looks. Then Bertram pulled himself up slightly in his chair.

'Mr Tan, can I speak to my son briefly? Just the two of us?'

'Why? You think I can just—'

'Sir ... When you first accosted me downstairs, put that gun to my back, you said you just wanted to discuss something with us. Said you weren't planning to rob us, you just needed that gun to assure that we would listen. Well, now we've listened. To everything we need to know, I think. So I would like to discuss the matter with my son. You are not a member of our company yet, Mr Tan. Not yet.'

'Or were you maybe planning all along to stage a small replay of that St Lucy's Massacre?' Anson piped in. 'Unfortunately, we don't have a lot of cash on us at the moment. And I didn't wear my good watch today.'

Kelvin Tan gave a sour laugh, then nodded. 'OK, I'll let you both discuss it. You need, what, fifteen minutes? Is that enough?'

'Yes, I think that will be fine. You can come back in fifteen minutes and we'll see what deal we can work out. Don't worry, we won't try to leave.' He then turned and stared hard at his son. 'Or call the authorities.' He turned back to Tan. 'We'll be right here when you come back.'

'OK, I guess I just have to trust my future business partners, isn't it? Oh, by the way: we have like ten copies of this manuscript. Most of them are with this solicitor we hired. If anything happens to me, like getting arrested or falling down the steps here and breaking my neck, our solicitor turns those copies over to *The Straits Times*, *Business Times*, *Today* newspaper, Mediacorp TV ... well, you know, all of them. Some overseas newspapers too.'

Bertram shook his head. 'You don't have to worry about anything unpleasant happening to you, Mr Tan.'

'Oh, I'm sure I don't. But I just thought I'd mention it.' He made a salute, tapping the gun lightly on his forehead, then backed up slowly, opened the door and stepped out.

Bertram Koh turned, his head held down. Even so, Anson detected a sickly look on his father's face as he crossed over to him. 'Dad, are you alright?' Bertram nodded slightly, but didn't look up. 'You don't believe all this idiotic drivel, do you? None of this would stand up for a minute in a court of law.'

'Probably not, but ...'

'Dad. What is it? You can't believe this crap?'

'When your grandfather was in the hospital that last time ...'

'Yeah?'

'I was in to see him this one time. I caught a glint of something like tears in his eyes. I thought it was just, you know, natural fear, so I reached over, took his hand. He was staring straight out into space ... like he was focused on something. Then he half-turned and told me that when he was gone, I had to be sure to keep giving those regular donations to charity. If I didn't, he said, the company would probably collapse, or something else terrible would happen. He then said the reason for this ... is that there was some terrible crime committed at the very beginning. I asked him what he meant, he just shook his head and said, "Very bad. Something very bad ..."

'After your grandfather's funeral, I asked your uncle what grandpa might have meant. He said it was probably something that went on during the Occupation. He said that almost everyone did something to survive during those days that they are deeply ashamed of now. I thought that was it, just dealing in the black market, something like that. Something everyone did.

'Then when your uncle himself became seriously ill, I was sitting with him. I felt bad about asking him again, but I couldn't let it rest. I asked what happened during the Occupation. He said that your grandfather and him, they passed information to the Japanese, to the Kempeitai. Information about other Chinese, small business people mainly. And then, when these people disappeared, the Japanese rewarded grandpa and Uncle Lim by letting them take over most of those businesses. That's why Blue Horizons was able to grow like that during the war years.'

'Oh God. I can't believe this.'

Bertram reached over and took his son's hand. Anson clutched

Bertram's hand more firmly. 'I didn't want to tell you until I thought it was the right time. Now our friend Mr Tan has forced me to make a very bad time the right time.'

'But all this drivel about the St Lucy's Massacre, that's all ... bullshit, right?'

Bertram shook his head sadly. 'Two days later, I went to see your uncle again. He told me there was one other thing I had to know. About the founding of Blue Horizons. That your grandfather had come into a lot of money suddenly and that was the money they used to get started. I asked him where the money came from, and he said it was not good how your grandfather got that money. I pleaded with him to tell me more, but he was very bad that day, and he promised he'd tell me some other time. But he was gone soon after that, so I never found out.' The elder Koh sat staring off into space for a few moments, then looked up at his son. 'Until today.'

'Dad, I still don't—'

Bertram didn't hear this; his gaze was fixed on the sheets in his son's hand. 'Those papers he just gave us. He said it was the police report?'

Anson reacted as if he'd forgotten about them. He cautiously unfolded two sheets stapled together and started looking through them. 'It's ... like he said, some official document ... from the police.'

'What does it say?'

'Dad, we don't need to know. Really. This has all been enough for one day. Let's just—'

'Anson, what does it say?'

He turned back to the sheets. 'It describes the shootings, where the victims were found ...' He suddenly stopped cold and clenched his lips tightly.

'What is it?'

'They have her name here. Her real name.' Anson looked at his father. A painful silence filled the air. Now, Anson had the glint of tears in his eyes. Finally, Bertam turned and looked towards the door, the one through which Kelvin Tan had departed. He turned back, looked intensely at his son, then spoke.

'It's Wan Tze Min, isn't it? That's her real name?'

'You didn't know, did you, Dad? You really didn't know?'

'I swear on everything precious to me, I didn't. But I knew, just then, why Mr Tan gave that thing to us.'

'Look, Dad, this still doesn't prove anything. So many Chinese names are similar, or the same. It could just be coincidence.'

'Coincidence has a narrow frame. All this doesn't fit in there.' He took a deep sigh. 'There are no relatives in Canada. The lives that girl saved were ours.'

'So ... so what do we do?'

Betram buried the lower part of his face in cupped hands and considered for about thirty seconds. When he spoke, there was a sharp note of resolve in his voice. 'We have to protect the memories of your grandfather and great-uncle. Also, the reputation of the company. This all has to stay hidden. All these shadows, they have to stay buried. When Mr Tan returns, we'll discuss the matter with him.'

'Are you kidding me?'

'We have to. We'll ask him to meet with our lawyers and work out a deal. I don't like some of the numbers he was throwing out there, but I think we have room to negotiate.

But we have to reach some deal with him. Quickly. There are too many shadows coming back now. We have to put them back in their box. Otherwise, we could all be swallowed by these shadows.'

'You realise, Dad, that we're bringing an unqualified asshole in as partner.'

'I won't argue with you there, but that asshole seems to know more about the beginnings of this company than both of us did. That's worth a lot.' He swallowed hard. 'It's worth a lot to me. We just have to make sure that this Mr Tan stays a silent partner.'

Anson was taken aback. 'Do you mean ...'

Bertram shook his head. 'We stuff his mouth with money. That's all it will take with him. Just money. I know his type. Give them a chance, they'll choke themselves to death on the money. They can't appreciate anything else.'

'So?'

Bertram Koh nodded. 'So we let him choke.'

* * *

The 70th anniversary celebration of the Blue Horizons company ended up much toned down from the original plans. There was only a single evening with a slide show of the company history and a small event with drinks and food two days later—at the company headquarters, not the hotel as originally planned.

Press releases and other official announcements put it down to the poor health of company president Bertram Koh, who had stepped down in late March. He then became the head of the Wan

Tze Min Foundation. One of his last acts as Blue Horizon's chief was to make a substantial increase in the company's contribution to the foundation.

Anson Koh took over as Blue Horizons president and announced some substantial changes. By the time of the anniversary celebration, there was a more sombre mood running through the company. Some observers attributed the problems to internal turmoil and poor judgement by the new CEO. Bertram Koh remained neutral, saying he was now retired and out of the trenches: his son had to lead the company into the future.

*   *   *

At the National University of Singapore, a junior faculty member by the name of Rajesh Datt abruptly announced that he would be taking an extended leave due to personal matters. He wanted to do more research on a special project.

At the end of term, he left Singapore to do some travelling. He left no forwarding address with university officials, but a month later, he turned up at Eccles Cemetery in Salford, England. It was almost closing time when he arrived. With some difficulty, and a bit of a bribe, he found the grave of one Paul Haggerty.

The young historian stood over the grave, staring in silence for several minutes, then pulled out a bottle of Irish whiskey and poured the contents onto the sod facing the tombstone. He saved one swallow for himself, which he downed after raising the bottle in a toast. He also pulled out two sheets of paper, which he stuck into the ground, just below the tombstone.

Then, as evening shadows were gathering heavily all around him, Rajesh turned and walked away, a sad smile on his face. He, too, had a long way back.

AARON ANG is a Singapore-based writer with a passion for both Literature and History. He has published a number of short pieces, many on historical topics, including sports history. His short story *A Perfect Exit* (first published in Monsoon Books' *Best of Singapore Erotica*) was adapted for TV and aired on Mediacorp's Arts Central channel in Singapore.

Nostalgia

Ng Yi-Sheng

If this is recording, I need to tell everyone this. There was no other way. You may call me a monster, but the city is hungry and must be fed.

You have seen the consequences. Here in my hospital ward lie the results of our neglect: a plague that has brought Singapore to its knees in the last ten months.

Remember the children? I remember the children. There were so many of them. Filing into my clinic like ants. Girls in pinafores, boys in tank tops. Walking like sleepwalkers, faces printed with the same blank, impenetrable stare.

There was an Indian man who told me his daughter heard voices. What kind of voices? I said.

No idea, he told me. Like someone teaching school. Only everything in Chinese.

Then there was that little boy who told me how he dreamed of crocodiles and tourists and huge glass tanks. I'm full of fish, he said.

I'm full of books, a schoolgirl told me.

I'm full of old people, said another.

There was a six-year-old who said, I'm full of Japanese soldiers. Then she went, Pew pew pew pew pew pew.

Those were the talkative ones. We were grateful for the talkative ones, as the nation had begun its downward slide into panic. The Ministry was closing the schools to contain the epidemic ... as if it struck with any kind of pattern.

I was confounded. And then I met Mr Mohaiemen. He was from Bangladesh.

He was the one who had told us about the outbreak in the migrant worker community. As a rule, the employers had kept it quiet. If a man became unresponsive, they'd just send him home or throw him into the street.

And now he, Mr Mohaiemen, was in the clinic on his off-day, believing, surely, that Singapore must have a cure. He had been working on a site in Kallang, and now he saw planes.

I can hear them whoosh also, he said. Noise very loud. Come, you listen my body. Not only I hear. You hear?

Sure enough, when I pressed my stethoscope to him, I heard that distant buzz in his chest. You can hear, he said, triumphantly. You hear.

So we began testing our other patients. Amplifying the sound of their heartbeats, we saw signals emerge. Mostly household babble. Barking dogs. Religious chanting.

Our breakthrough came with that blond, expatriate child, taken sick after a trip to Fort Canning. He was catatonic by then; he couldn't feed himself or use the toilet, but the recordings were clear. Cantonese opera. Indian ragas. Rock. Classical fugues and concertos.

That was when the Head Nurse spoke up.

The National Theatre, she said. I was there.

With the help of some parents and relatives, we managed to pinpoint some locations. The National Library, of course. The Van Kleef Aquarium. The zinc-roofed huts at Bukit Ho Swee.

It's the government's fault. There was a woman who said that. She was cleaning the pus from her granddaughter's bedsores.

All the government's fault. They knock down buildings. You imagine: you're a building. You won't be angry? You won't want to come back and cause trouble?

Cases have rapidly proliferated since then. The diseased now cover every age and class. There are even celebrity patients. That national sailor, troubled by visions of life on a *kelong*. That Minister, haunted by Tang Dynasty City.

And there are duplicates. Three patients have been identified as the old Changi Prison, five as the old National Junior College campus, two as the original Odeon Theatre—but there are so many old cinemas, no one knows for sure.

And now there's this talk that the very land is rising against us. Rumours of factory workers in Tuas, holiday-makers on Beach Road, all choking on reclaimed soil as if drowning in the sea. And that NS boy yesterday: one of my researchers claims he's possessed by the original palace of the sultans (or Palace of the Sultans) on Fort Canning.

Our nurses work double shifts, triple shifts even, changing IV drips and adult diapers, and still the patients keep coming.

The patients keep coming. Something has to be done. And as chief medical officer of this facility, I have the responsibility to do it.

I had a dream tonight. I was in my clinic, between late night rounds in the hospital. Dozing off, I saw myself on Mount Faber.

White shapes were moving in the distance. I imagined they were cable cars, but I looked again and, no. They were the buildings that had possessed us. The thousands on thousands of buildings we tried to forget, twinkling in this shining city in the open sky.

They were beautiful. The ancient voices: I'd heard them in recording, but for the first time, I understood their language. We are hungry, they said. We are so, so hungry.

Then I woke up. I sprang to my feet. I disabled the alarm systems. I ransacked the pharmacy for volatile chemicals. And as a man of science, I can defend these actions with logic. For if we can appease the spirits of humans with the gifts of burning houses, why not the reverse?

The patients lie sleeping in the ward before me: children, women, men. They are but a humble offering to the indestructible city.

It is not without fear that I strike the match, letting the flames fall onto the bed sheets. For in that world to come, my victims will be my neighbours and may curse me for my act.

Yet it is also with joy that I anticipate my arrival in that shining city, that deathless ghost of Singapore.

I shall sit on my stoop there and observe the towers rising below, like the hills of so many ants.

NG YI-SHENG is a full-time poet, playwright, journalist and minor activist. He is the author of *Last Boy*, a poetry collection which won at the Singapore Literature Prize 2008, as well as the novel *Eating Air* and the bestselling *SQ21: Singapore Queers in the 21st Century*. He blogs at *www.lastboy.blogspot.com*. 'Nostalgia' was inspired by Michael Lee Hong Hwee's artwork, *The National Columbarium of Singapore*.

The House on Tomb Lane

Dawn Farnham

Chapter 1

They were walking and talking, but they were already dead.

He didn't look like a murderer. Of course, it was a cliché that vicious men don't look like monsters. But he *was* monstrous, despite his pathetic looks, his bony, sallow frame, his thinning, greasy hair. Maria watched him step through the gates of Changi Prison to be greeted by his pudgy wife and skinny sister.

Three years. His sentence for beating, burning and murdering his maid, Maria's cousin, Flora. This was the sentence deemed suitable for the torture and death he had visited on a frail, lovely girl in the flush of her youth. For the other two who lived in the house, who said nothing, who watched silently, indifferently, as he crushed her bones and scorched her flesh and let her die starving, in agony—no conviction, no charges ... nothing.

She gazed at the newspaper picture she had brought with her. Cyril Lim, his wife, Pearl, and his sister, Stella. Her eyes rose slowly, her face impassive.

Maria had done her research. She could stay in Singapore for up to thirty days. She had shown the authorities her nursing certificate and the letter of employment from the London hospital, her hotel information and her onward plane ticket. She was stopping off for a holiday on her way to join the thousands of other Filipina nurses recruited by the UK National Health Service. Her last name was not the same as Flora's, whose long-dead mother was her aunt. There was absolutely nothing to link her to either Flora or the Lims.

She watched as the taxi pulled away. She had no need to follow. She knew the address of the Lims' house.

Flora had come to Singapore in the usual way: through an agency, and been placed with the Lim family. It was supposed to be safe, both sides carefully vetted. What a joke. Maria and Martin, Flora's brother, now knew that Cyril Lim had a history of violence with maids but few employers, apparently, were ever blacklisted. Martin had followed the investigation during and after the trial, trying to piece together how Flora had ended up with this monster. Everyone was at fault. The agency who didn't care, the Philippine government who didn't care, the Singapore authorities who didn't care enough.

At the tender age of eighteen, Flora had been utterly alone and defenceless. Absolutely no one was watching—including Maria knew, Flora's own father. He was as cruel and callously indifferent to his daughter's predicament as Cyril Lim. When the hideous facts of the case had been made known to the ordinary people of Singapore, an outpouring of horror, a compassionate disgust, had impelled many to send money to Flora's family. A lot of money. More money than his daughter could have earned in two lifetimes. Maria had watched the old man's eyes glitter at this unexpected bounty.

Maria had dispatched her uncle to the search for eternal riches with a neat air bubble in the vein. It was too easy. He was diabetic. He needed insulin and, being cheap, he expected her to give the injections for free. Maria was a remarkable nurse. She was a cum laude graduate from the College of Nursing and had received the highest award for academic achievement. She prided herself on giving painless injections. He had certainly not suffered enough. Nobody had cried for him.

Maybe no one would cry for the Lims either but she would not be so compassionate with them. They had two children under Flora's care—a baby and a toddler. Cyril Lim had beaten Flora senseless for drinking some of his toddler's milk. The autopsy had revealed a hairline fracture along her jaw. She had been given one packet of noodles to eat each day. In six months tiny little Flora had lost almost half her body weight.

Maria's hands tightened around the newspaper picture. She walked slowly back to the bus stop and waited. Lim had admitted to forgetting how many times he beat Flora. The coroner's pictures showed two hundred separate injuries to her body; bruises, fractures, burned and scalded skin. When he had kicked her in the stomach for the final offence of eating some cold rice, he had burst her duodenum and left her. She had died alone in an agony of peritonitis. Lim had gone to the police station and given himself up.

And now he thought he was free.

Chapter 2

She gazed into the mirror. Things change you. It was an immutable truth. Horrible experiences harden you, turn you into a different person. She looked into her eyes and saw herself, the same features, the dark brown eyes, the same full lips, the rich black hair. She seemed the same but underneath the skin she was fundamentally different, as if her cells and sinews had been subtly rearranged.

She took up her brush and began to stroke it through her hair. She had no regrets for the Maria who had gone. That one had served her well. But experience and time add layers, like the pearl inside the shell, smooth and hard. People think nursing is about compassion, but it isn't. It's about practicality. Nurses don't blubber at the sight of blood or faint at broken limbs. They deal with them, calmly and methodically. The practical application of skills.

She picked up her handbag and took the bus to the Lims' neighbourhood. She had studied maps, bus routes and the series of pictures Martin had brought back with him. She walked down a road with restaurants and shops, most closed now at this early hour, to the first junction and turned left. This street was quieter and stretched away into a snaking sprawl of terraced houses. Another turn, at the second corner, right this time, and she was surrounded by a mixture of houses and light industrial work units. There was nothing very attractive about the area but even here Singapore was leafy, with rows of lofty trees and shrubs softening the hard urban edge.

This street was called Lorong Makam: Tomb Lane. She'd grimaced at the name. The houses and units were closed up, vegetation sprouting from cracks, bleached Chinese characters emerging here and there from the grime. At its culmination, Lorong Makam formed a short T. In the middle of the cross bar was a pavement which led to a pedestrian bridge over the wide storm drain beyond. On either side of the T were four houses. To the right the houses were abandoned and crumbling, paint peeling, leaves gathered in drifts inside the gates. To the left were numbers 43 and 44, inhabited, but looking no better than the other two. The Lims lived in number 44. There was a 'For Sale or Rent' sign above the gate. These two houses stood opposite a disused factory. She read the fading lettering across the top of the building. Wai Wai Prawn Cracker Co. Ltd. She had examined it yesterday morning, quickly, wandering around with a map in hand, appearing lost. She needn't have worried. The area was deserted. The factory was locked and empty, just as Martin had said. Martin's plan had begun exactly at the moment he'd seen how close this factory was to the Lims' house. It was like a sign from the Almighty.

Maria knew that number 43 was the home of a man called Neo for he had been interviewed by the newspapers during the trial. When asked if he knew about the terrible things going on inside his neighbour's house, he simply said that, even had he known he would not have told the police. 'Not my business,' he said.

Running along one side of the factory, the end of the cul-de-sac and one side of the Lim house, there was a culvert which fed the storm drain, lined with trees, and beyond the trees was an alley way which traced the backs of low buildings. It was isolated. Maria felt Flora's awful isolation, imprisoned here with these monsters.

Now though, Maria saw what Martin had. The isolation was their friend. She did not stop to examine the houses, did not allow her feelings to overwhelm her, but went onto the bridge and crossed to the other side of the storm drain into the small park beyond. Seated on a bench behind the rim of the tall trees, she was invisible.

Martin had taken a lot of photos from here. She sat and took a bottle of water from her bag.

The houses backed on to the storm drain. They both had high walls concealing the lower part of the buildings. Only the upper storey was visible. Sitting here now, she felt tears rise. Had Flora thought of this leafy park as she lay dying in agonising pain? Perhaps these trees were all of the outside world Flora saw for the final six months of her life. Maria felt the pity of it like a knife in her guts. She understood why Martin had taken so many photographs.

Maria intended to get inside the house. It was part of the plan of course but she needed to see for herself the prison in which such tortures were inflicted. She needed to see it with her own eyes and not in the dreams which had haunted her for months.

She and Flora had been like sisters, for Maria's mother had raised Flora after the death of her own sister. They had held hands on the way to school, they had skipped and played together. They'd braided each other's hair and talked about boys and felt lonely apart. And Martin was her brother too, for he was always in the house though he lived with his father. When Flora's father had remarried six years later, his two children went to live with him and his new wife, but they all lived nearby. The new wife was a decent woman but Flora's father simply wore women out and, within two years, she had left him.

Flora and Martin endured his bitter tempers and foul language. They escaped to Maria's family but by then Maria's father, too, was sick. As soon as possible Martin got out. He ran off to Manila. When Flora was sixteen she got out too. Two years later she came here. It was a fatal mistake.

Dawn was creeping up and it was almost pleasant in the deep shade of the rain trees. An old man came by, hobbling along, followed by a young Indonesian maid. She looked no more than fifteen. The nappies of the young and the nappies of the old, the house, the cooking, the car, work, work, work. *Why you want to eat? Greedy! Why you need rest? Lazy! Why you alive?*

In the Philippines, Maria had talked to other women who had been maids here, in Hong Kong, in Saudi Arabia. She desperately needed to understand how sweet, lovely Flora had been ground into dust. So many of their tales, especially in the other countries, were a litany of horror. Abused in every possible way: imprisoned, raped and beaten, their bodies shattered by starvation and violence, their minds by a torrent of words which spilt like filthy slime over them day in, day out.

The Lim children were not here. When Cyril went to prison, Pearl had taken her children to her aunt in Penang. Pearl and Stella's livelihood was a small hair and nail salon. Maria smiled at this thought. Skinny Stella and Fat Pearl: the Laurel and Hardy of the beauty world.

Some in the *kopitiam* on the corner were happy to talk to Martin, who posed as a foreign reporter. During the trial it was the constant talk of the neighbourhood. Pearl and Stella Lim were ashamed and didn't want the children to know, the *Chicken Rice* woman said. Ashamed of the prison sentence, Maria mused, not of murdering a young girl. When Lim got out, the *Roti Prata* stall owner said, the whole family was getting out of Singapore permanently.

It was six o'clock. She rose and walked along the edge of the storm drain, keeping amongst the trees until she came to the end of the park. Here another little bridge led to the small street on the opposite side of the culvert. She crossed and walked up the back alley. The units had been small businesses, places that made fish sauce, paper decorations and incense. The flickering sunlight dappling the ground was in pretty disproportion to its flaking, sagging surroundings.

Where the bushes were dense she slipped across the culvert and saw the door. She took the key and turned the lock. Martin had cut off the old one and put on his own, equally aged, one. She slipped quickly through and shot across the bolt she knew was inside the door.

She took her torch. It was powerful and she swept it around the dark space. She walked surely to the front of the building. Martin had drawn her a map and she knew every step.

When the sentence had been handed down, they had known what they had to do. Martin, a steward with Philippine Airlines, was often in Singapore. Three months ago he had come and checked out the warehouse. It was still empty.

Martin had asked about the area at the *kopitiam*. Urban redevelopment, they said. Two years from now the last of the houses would return to the state and the area would be razed.

She went into the room opposite number 44. The grimy window gave a perfect view of the house and now a filtered light was beginning to seep through the dirt. She turned off the big torch and turned on her pencil light. A cardboard box stood in the corner. Maria quickly ran through its contents. Martin had been thorough, everything was there. There was an old chair and three bottles of water. The factory creaked. Martin had put a slide lock on the door of this room. It was creepy, he said, to have the door open behind you into such a huge black space. He was right. She slid the lock across and felt safe. She sat down and looked at the house across the road.

Chapter 3

She and Martin had had time on their side. Time for Maria to complete her nursing qualification and get experience in a hospital. Time for her to apply to the UK and be accepted. On the last weekend of the month, if Martin was in Manila, they made the trip to their home town, to the cemetery where Flora was buried. The brutality of her death had been television news and Philippine Airlines had flown her home for free and delivered her to the Manila funeral home. They had asked to see her. Maria was used to corpses but this was the hardest thing she'd ever done. Her lovely cousin was a wraith, her poor bruised body covered in scars, her bones protruding under her skin. They touched the puckered burnt skin on her cheek and neck and the scars of cigarette burns on her hands. Lim had thrown boiling water over her as a punishment for making the bath too hot for his toddler and put out cigarette butts on her hands for any reason at all.

The horror of this had run like a cinema reel inside their heads and they had cried and cried over her body. They cried for her pain and loneliness and for their own feelings of guilt. Martin was filled with remorse for letting her go to Singapore. Maria was ashamed that they had let six months go by without wondering why she had not written or called.

217

Maria's mother had prayed at the church and preached fortitude and forgiveness but she had not seen Flora's body. Forgiveness. The concept was ludicrous. To forgive, they had to clean their hearts of the hatred and obsession which lived there. Flora's agonies filled their waking thoughts and their sleeping dreams. Scalding water, suppurating wounds, burning flesh, despised and used, then the heart-stopping, life-ending, violent impact of a boot to her tiny frame; these were the images which overwhelmed them. When all the cockroaches are dead, Martin said, then we will forgive them and find peace.

Lim had escaped a murder charge through the eloquence of his counsel. Involuntary manslaughter. For the systematic and sadistic destruction of a young girl, these acts were deemed to be the 'unlawful killing of a human being *without malice aforethought*'.

Maria finished her bottle of water, put it in her bag and mopped her brow. It was hot, humid and airless inside the factory. When her two years in London were up, she would go to Canada. With her skills and abilities, the world, crying out for nurses, was her oyster. She was sick of the heat. She wanted big, open, cold places, white winters, the clean purity of snow.

The door at number 44 opened. Skinny Stella came out with a shopping basket over her arm. 'Off to market, is it?' thought Maria. 'A nice little celebratory dinner, perhaps?' Stella was almost past the gate of number 43 when she stopped. A man came out and they began to talk. Maria rose and went to the window. The neighbour, Neo, was about seventy-five, short, fat and bald. Martin had discovered he was divorced and lived alone. He was unpopular in the neighbourhood. His only friends were the Lims. Could he have known about the mistreatment of the maid, Martin had asked. Few were willing to venture a guess but one, an old man, a cobbler, who plied his trade on the street corner, said he'd known Neo for years. He'd told Martin that Neo boasted he got his house cleaned for free. That meant that Flora was cleaning both houses. That meant that Neo knew about the abuse.

Stella moved off and Neo went back inside his house. Ten minutes later he came out. He turned the corner towards the park. A truckful of men came by and cleaned the street. Maria smiled. Even in this wreck of a neighbourhood, Singapore's streets were cleaner than some of the best streets in Manila. Maria ticked the times against Martin's notes. He knew when the rubbish was collected, when the streets were cleaned, every regular activity of the area. Stella came back forty minutes later. Neo had not returned. For one hour Pearl and Cyril were alone in the house. On the whole people, Maria knew, were creatures of habit. Stella went to the wet market early. Neo went off for whatever he did. It wasn't important today. She would get to him tomorrow.

She waited. Another empty bottle of water went into her bag. She needed to pee and went to the corner of the room where Martin had dug a hole in the crumbling floor. She crouched and finished quickly. The shovel stood to one side and she piled earth into the hole. This primitive earth toilet would be filled in when she was done and the broken concrete replaced. It was probably unnecessary with what they had planned but it paid to be careful and they both liked attention to detail.

The day was up now and shadowy sunlight fell into the room. She stretched and resumed her vigil on the chair just in time to see the gate of Neo's house closing. She noted the time but was annoyed she hadn't seen him return. It was ten o'clock.

There was no movement inside number 44. Maria grew sleepy. The heat was intense, the roof creaked and cracked as the sun rose higher. Her head nodded. Then she heard a small squeak and looked up. Neo walked to the gate of the Lim house and went inside. He was carrying a plastic bag. Maria couldn't see what it was but it looked heavy. Drink. Probably. To welcome home his murdering friend.

There was no point in watching any more. She would come back tonight. The Lims and Neo were settling in for a celebratory lunch and a drinking session in their charnel house. Enjoy it, she thought, for it might well be your last.

Chapter 4

Two days later she waited in the park. She was dressed sombrely with a dark headscarf to cover her hair. Exactly on time Neo turned the corner and crossed the storm drain. She had followed him yesterday and, as expected, he set off diagonally across the park. He looked neither left nor right and walked with a rapid shuffling gait, as if stiff-hipped.

On the corner of the street opposite the park there were shops, small offices and a hawker centre. She waited until Neo had greeted many of the occupants of the tables and settled himself at one under a slow-moving fan. An old man came up with a glass of milky coffee and some toast. They chatted for a few minutes, then Neo began to eat.

He was known here. She wanted Neo to die in a public place. She didn't want him mouldering in his house for months. She didn't want police sniffing around Lorong Makam. He had to be the first to go and his body found quickly.

She skirted round the back of the hawker centre. It was exactly as Martin had told her. All the buildings in this area were old and ramshackle. The hawker centre had one set of toilets accessed from the back of the building where cars and rubbish bins parked indiscriminately. Her heart was beating out of her chest. She had felt so sure, was so sure of what needed to be done, but now it was here and her hands were trembling.

She ducked into the women's toilets and shut the stall. She took deep breaths and calmed herself. She heard movement and the clanking of a bucket. A woman came and peed noisily in the stall next door, then moved out, screaming something loudly in Chinese. Maria swallowed, her throat felt dry, but she was sweating. Classic symptoms of nervous anxiety. She knew it and fought to bring herself under control. When she felt calmer she left the toilet and went down the short corridor to the hawker centre. Neo was wolfing down toast. For an old man, he had a voracious appetite. He'd known every foul act of Cyril Lim, probably heard Flora's screams. She'd cleaned his house covered in bruises and half-terrified. Maria was certain that he had probably even abused her himself, called her a lazy whore, pushed or struck her, the small thrill of his pathetic existence to see her cringe. She felt the iron re-enter her soul and fear evaporate instantly.

She bought a can of iced tea, sat down near the back door and opened *The New Paper*. No one paid her the slightest attention. A bowl of noodles arrived at Neo's table and she groaned inwardly. She was ready and the delay annoyed her. Come on, she said under her breath. She popped the top of the can and drank half the tea.

Just as she thought she would have to endure a lengthy slurping session, he rose and turned and walked directly towards her. She kept her head down. Neo went out the back door. She waited but no one else moved. She rose and felt a surge of adrenaline as she stepped into the alleyway, looking right and left. It was deserted. She opened the door and went into the toilet. He was standing against a urinal, one hand on the wall, his head down, watching his piss.

She went up to him and took his neck firmly in her left hand. With the thumb of her right she pumped three times on the vagus nerve. As expected, Neo quivered ... and slumped. She had practised this manoeuvre so many times it was automatic. She let him fall to the floor. This over-stimulation of the vagus would induce almost instant fainting as the heart slowed.

She felt his pulse. It was very faint. This vagus pressure alone should have killed him at his age, causing immediate erratic heart rhythms. She pinched the carotid sinus and felt the breath seep out of him. She smelt the bowel go. He lay dead in his shit, his dick hanging out.

She pulled open the door and looked quickly around. She walked rapidly away and turned the corner of the building. The entire event had taken no more than forty seconds. Within thirty more she was back in the park, heading away from the scene. She willed her heart to calm down and sat on a bench, breathing, holding her shaking hands. Then she felt a rush, an amazing heady rush of excitement, like fingers of fire were racing along her spine and out of her head.

She had killed him. He was Neo-more. She laughed and got up. She felt filled with energy and knew it was dangerous. She went fast to the end of the park and then slowed down, turned and walked back towards the hawker centre. She heard the sound of the ambulance coming closer and waited. It stopped and a sheet-covered body was wheeled out. She walked away.

That evening she returned and went into the prawn factory. She watched number 44 for two hours. She could see lights inside the house but very little movement. Then, at around eight o'clock, they all came out. They stopped in front of number 43 and rang the bell. Clearly, they didn't know.

They set off and turned the corner towards the park. Maria was quite certain they were going to the hawker centre. She left the factory and locked the door and moved quickly along the culvert and into the park. She could make them out moving from light to light. She was right. Perhaps they were searching for Neo or perhaps they were just going to eat. Either way, they would find out.

She went back and stood in front of number 44. Here Flora had drawn her last breath. Her spirit had been snuffed out here, as indifferently as if she was nothing. All afternoon she had rewound Neo's killing inside her head and every time it was mixed up with Flora's burnt and beaten corpse. She wanted to get inside the house and tried the gate but it was locked. She would have to wait.

She made her way back to the hawker centre. They were there, eating and talking rapidly amongst themselves. Few people paid them any mind. If anyone knew who Cyril Lim was and what he had done, they kept it to themselves.

She was suddenly sideswiped by exhaustion and felt her legs

weaken. She was stressed. The last four days had taken their toll and she needed to stop. Everything was going according to plan. Tomorrow she would eat and sleep and then the real work would begin.

Chapter 5

Maria woke with a blinding headache. She had taken sleeping pills and it always made her groggy but she could not have faced a night without oblivion. She took two paracetamol and a long cool shower.

After breakfast she called Martin on her cell phone. They had agreed not to speak until after Neo was finished. He wanted to know all the details and she thought she didn't want to talk about it but actually she did. Now she was calm, it was over and she was proud how quickly and efficiently she had despatched him. Neo had been the really hard part, the public part. From now on everything would take place inside the killers' house.

They talked some more. Martin's voice was reassuring. They were in this together. He would be there as agreed. Stick to the plan.

It was nice to take time away from her thoughts. She wandered along Orchard Road looking at the shops, stopping for a meal in a road filled with elegant shophouses. The women ebbed and flowed around her with their Gucci bags and Chanel dresses. Their day would be spent shopping, lunching with friends, going to the spa, whilst their maids washed their dirty clothes, cleaned their toilets and watched over their children.

She had no trouble sleeping that night.

Inside the prawn factory she checked her watch. Nine o'clock.

Stella Lim was talking to a middle-aged man outside number 43. Maria was not sure who this was. She and Martin had allowed several days for unexpected events and this was one of them. A relative of Neo's? Or a house agent?

She had something of an answer half an hour later. A van turned up. The man greeted the three workmen in the van and together they went inside the house. For the next three hours, they removed clothes and furniture, the remnants of Neo's pathetic life. Then the man locked the house, put a fat padlock on the gates and drove away.

Maria left the building and made her way to a hawker centre well away from Lorong Makam. She shook her head. Unpredictability was disagreeable. She decided to start today. Delay was no longer an option.

She called Martin and explained the situation. They talked for a few minutes and when she hung up, she rose and walked back towards the house.

She went round to the factory door the long way and let herself inside. She switched on the big torch and walked to the food preparation area in the centre of the building. It was probably in her imagination but it still smelled vaguely of prawn paste. The industrial grinders stood silent but she could see Martin had cleaned and oiled two of them and hooked them up to the petrol generator. He'd chosen a top-of-the-range Honda which could run for 12.5 hours on one tank of fuel. Two extra petrol canisters stood nearby however, just in case. The pit was dug, nice and deep, each grinder linked to it by tubing, to carry away the blood. Lights were linked up to the generator, too. He'd been meticulous. The three years since the trial had been well spent. Little by little, every trip to Singapore had allowed them to put together another element in the plan.

The old cold storage room nearby was ready. The plastic sheeting and their plastic body suits were folded alongside the surgical knives, waiting, on the shelves. Martin had dug another hole here, to take the dissection blood which would seep into the thirsty ground. Her job was the elegant and efficient separation of the body parts, making them small enough for the grinders. The heads would be smashed with the sledgehammer. Martin would do that. She'd studied dissection techniques carefully, had been permitted to sit in on the student doctors' corpse sessions. During this whole preparation, she'd thought seriously about why she hadn't become a doctor. She would have been a brilliant surgeon.

Martin would grind the remains into the wheel barrow and release them slowly into the drain outside the side door. Now, in the monsoon season, it rained massively every day. With two machines he'd calculated five to seven hours of solid work. If the rain obliged these three would be carried away to the sea, food for fishes, every trace of them gone. He would get his plane and return to Manila as usual.

If family members in Penang came hunting or the police turned up, there would simply be nothing to find.

There was a steel staircase leading to the upper floor and she tested it. It felt secure and she went up and looked out of the window, down onto the street. From here she could see into the abandoned front courtyard of 43. Why hadn't she thought of this before?

She went out of this room and into the next. This window looked down on 44. She had a clear view into the front courtyard of the Lim house and into the upper windows of the house.

She could see him. He was sitting on a chair with a newspaper spread out on a table. His bony back was to her. He was wearing a vest and baggy shorts. He sat cross-legged on the chair the way many Chinese sat. He had a mug of tea and drank from it from time to time. She stood and looked down at him. This man was the murderer of her cousin, her lifelong friend. Sitting calmly in his courtyard drinking tea.

He suddenly looked up and around, towards the factory and she backed rapidly away from the window. The grime was thick but the sun was slanting into this room. When next she peeped he was gone. Had he seen her? She felt her heart beating in her throat. Had she ruined their plan? Everything depended on them having no suspicions about her.

Then he came out of the house, out of the gate. She almost cried out. Was he coming here? But she let out a sigh when he went up to 43 and stared into the front yard. She waited until he returned to his house.

She felt sticky. It was hot inside the factory. She left by the side door, locking it carefully and walked quickly to the park. There she sat a while before taking out her mirror and some wipes, cleaning her face of sweat. She redid her make-up and ran a comb through her hair.

She rose and straightened her skirt. She turned the corner and rang the bell of number 44.

Chapter 6

A light came on in the courtyard and the front door opened.

Stella Lim came down the two steps and peered at the gate. She barked something loudly in Chinese.

'Hello,' Maria said. 'Do you speak English? I'm here about renting the house.'

Stella whined something towards the interior of the house and Pearl appeared on the door step. She came to the gate, wiping her hands. Cooking smells wafted from the open doorway.

'What you want?' Pearl said in guttural English.

'Good evening. I want to talk about renting your house.'

Pearl peered at her suspiciously. Maria smiled reassuringly. 'Cash in full,' she said. 'No agent fees. Can I talk to you about it?'

Pearl didn't move, then Cyril appeared in the doorway. He pushed Pearl aside and came down the steps to the gate.

'What do you want?' he said. He spoke good English. She remembered he was some sort of tour guide. Despite being face to face with Flora's murderer, Maria felt calm.

'I was just saying, I am interested in renting this house. For two years. It's for rent, isn't it?'

Cyril looked up at the 'For Sale or Rent' sign as if he was seeing it for the first time.

'Yes, but you have to talk to the agent.'

Stupid, stupid man. She wanted to reach through the bars and grab his skinny neck and kill him right there and then. She smiled and then looked grave.

'I was just saying I have cash. No need to pay an agent. I don't want to waste time. I saw the ad in the paper. I'll pay what you want and can give you six months in advance.

What they wanted for the goods on offer was ridiculous but, since she wasn't going to pay it, so the price was irrelevant.

Pearl, who had understood, said something quickly to her husband. Maria didn't understand the words but she understood the urgent tone of greed. Maria decided to push it.

'Look, if you're not interested, I'll take my cash elsewhere.'

She stood a moment longer and then turned. She heard the key turn in the lock of the gate. And then she walked into the house of death.

Cyril Lim went in front of her and Pearl, behind. In the hall, under the harsh neon light, the three of them stood and looked at her.

Maria looked around the hall. It was gloomy and grimy. Dust and cobwebs everywhere, and the furniture looked greasy. A flash of the misery of Flora's existence in this grim house passed through her mind.

'I'm a nurse. Two colleagues and I are staying in Singapore for two years on a working contract at the hospital not far from here. We need a place to live. This is what we can afford.'

Pearl nodded. 'We don' fix up,' she said, pointing to the house.

'No, not necessary,' Maria said.

Pearl said something to Cyril and Stella . Cyril shrugged. He looked tired, worn out. Stella smiled nervously.

'Do you want to look around?' Cyril said. Maria nodded. Yes, indeed I do, she thought.

She went into the living room which led off the kitchen. There was a table and three chairs, an ancient sofa and a television. It was on but the sound was down. The house was filthy. The floor had obviously not been swept in months. There was food lying around the kitchen. Pearl had turned off the gas under the frying pan. Cyril went back to the sofa and sat down. She heard the sound of the television go up as she followed Pearl. They went up the stairs. Maria was careful to touch nothing, keeping both hands on her bag to be sure she didn't forget and unconsciously hold on to the stair rail. There were three small bedrooms up here. Pearl and Cyril in one, she guessed, Stella in the other and the third was filled with stuff.

Downstairs, they went through to the backyard which was nothing more than earth covered in dirty loose tiles. The toilet and bathroom were off the yard to one side. Next to the toilet was a tiny room with a small window.

Maria stopped. This had been Flora's room, she knew it. It was small and dark and damp, like a tomb. It wasn't fit for any living thing. She felt sorrow seep into her bones.

She followed Pearl back to the living room. Cyril didn't turn down the TV.

'It needs a clean,' she said. 'Don't you have a maid?'

Stella and Pearl exchanged a quick glance. Maria saw it. Cyril didn't move, but something in his stillness told her instantly that she had made a mistake. She should not have mentioned a maid. It had just come blurting out. She wanted to see something, guilt, remorse, anything.

'No,' said Pearl. 'Maid is thief and lazy. No good.'

Maria nodded. She felt sweat break out on her neck and silently cursed herself.

'Well,' she said. 'Nothing that can't be fixed. The roof is sound?'

Cyril looked up at her, his eyes expressionless.

'The roof's fine. Take it or leave it.'

Maria felt his hostility. Despite his skinny frame and sunken chest, he had an air of malevolence. He was unsettling and it took all her willpower not to wipe her face or show her anxiety.

Pearl glanced at her husband, a quick movement of her eyes, up, down. Maria knew that the roof was probably not fine. It didn't matter.

'OK. Please call the agent tomorrow and get the sign removed, explain you've changed your mind. My cousin is a lawyer here in Singapore. His money is helping us and he will draw up all the paperwork free of charge.'

Pearl looked at Cyril like a little dog. She saw dollar signs and was desperate to get out. It occurred to Maria that, with a husband in gaol for such a disgusting crime, her life had been very difficult round here: pointed out, gossiped about, her children far away. Maybe the beauty salon lost customers. Poor thing, she thought with a remorseless lack of pity.

Cyril said nothing for a moment. Pearl's face started to get angry. She barked something sharp at him.

'I'll come back at six tomorrow,' Maria said. 'If the sign is still up I will look elsewhere. Otherwise I'll call my cousin and we can be ready to go immediately.'

Cyril seemed to make up his mind. He waved his hand.

'Six.'

Maria nodded and turned to go. She was at the doorstep when

she realised Cyril was behind her, with the gate key.

'I know your accent. You're a Filipina, right?' he said, opening the gate. Maria felt a repulsion at his proximity and a trickle of alarm. She moved through the gate quickly onto the street. Outside she felt a degree of safety. Her disgust of him rose.

She managed to look into his face. 'Yes,' she said. 'Why?'

He shook his head silently. Maria thought she detected a shadow move across his face but in the half-light, she couldn't tell if she'd imagined it.

He locked the gate and she walked down the street. As she turned the corner she looked quickly back. He was standing at the gate staring at her and, despite her bravado, she felt a shudder go through her.

Chapter 7

Maria was filled with foreboding. She was sure now that she and Martin had underestimated Cyril Lim. She should have picked up the package on her last visit. This return to the factory was not in the plan and she had cursed herself.

It was ten in the morning but dark, rain falling steadily but quietly. Maria pushed into the bushes of the culvert. She was about to cross when, from the corner of her eye, she detected movement and melted back into hiding. Cyril Lim turned the corner and stood staring along the culvert. The water was gurgling and splashing in the drain but she put her hand over her mouth to stifle any sound.

Cyril put his foot onto the small path which flanked the culvert and traced the factory wall. Suddenly lightning flashed across the sky, a wind sprang up and the heavens opened. A tropical rain began to fall, strong and blinding. Maria was drenched in seconds. Yet Lim did not retreat. His shadowy figure moved along the path. When he got to the padlocked door, he put out a hand and shook the lock. He was standing, his bony back to hers, not more than six steps away. They were both shrouded by the violent force and deafening din of the rain. She feared him. In a blinding flash, she realised this one important fact: despite his skinny frame he was an object of fear, for he could cause injury and death with an unemotional and relentless determination. She quietly moved back, further into the depth of the bushes. He was suspicious, this much she knew. Which meant that their plans were in jeopardy.

He shook the lock again and from the bush her rain-soaked face stared through the branches and leaves at the indistinct shape of his back. She desperately wished Martin was here. She felt her resolution flow out of her like the water streaming down her body. Then suddenly he turned and she froze on the spot, her eyes staring into his. He had seen her, she was sure, and panic brought bile into her throat. But he moved away, back down the culvert, back towards his house.

Maria fell to her knees, her breath heaving. She watched him disappear like a ghost into the heavy rain. She waited a minute more, then gathered her courage and stepped across the culvert and put the key to the lock. Her hand was shaking so hard the key would not go in. She looked down at the lock and up, along the culvert, convinced that any minute, he would step out of the rain and take her by the throat. Tears of panic joined the streaming rain on her face and as the key engaged the lock, she stifled a groan of relief, went inside and threw across the bolt.

He had seen the padlock. If he came back again he would know. This thought hit her the instant she was inside. She looked at the dripping object in her hand. All the ground floor windows were barred. She pulled out her pencil torch, ran to the front of the building and looked outside. The deluge even blotted out the houses across the street. The rain might keep him inside for the moment but she knew, absolutely, when it stopped he would be back.

She went to the box in the corner, pulled out the package and slipped it into her bag. Then she grabbed the big torch and began a tour of the outer walls of the building. The rain was pounding on the roof. It was deafening. She could see no other way of getting into the building. Martin had done all this before. She should have stuck to the plan.

She heard the rain lessen and her brain went into hyperspeed. Get out, get out. She cursed herself. Half of her had wanted to see them again. Maybe that was why she'd forgotten the package. She'd wanted to watch them, to see them on their last day, like God watches mortals before the hour of their death, like humans watch cockroaches scurrying before squashing them.

She ran to the door and put her hand on the bolt. The rain was still falling but less so now. She hesitated. What if he was on the other side of the door? She was instantly filled with fearful indecision. She flashed the light around and walked quickly to a metal stairway leading upstairs. She raced to the side of the building and looked down. The view was limited. Without opening the window she could not see directly below. The sun suddenly pierced the clouds and she let out a cry of anguish.

She ran downstairs. There was no time to lose. She pulled back the bolt silently and took a deep breath. If he was on the other side she would beat his brains out with the torch and pull him into the building. She found her courage and opened the door quickly. There was no one there and she put her head out and glanced along the culvert. In an instant she had thrown on the padlock and disappeared into the bushes. She ran as fast as she could away from the factory and didn't stop, wet and mud-splashed, until she saw the main street ahead. She realised she was still gripping the torch like a cudgel; she slowed down and dropped it into her bag.

Chapter 8

Martin was furious with her. At her hotel she'd called him, her hands still shaking, her voice anguished. Then he calmed down and so did she. His flight would arrive at 15.30. He would pose as the lawyer and they would go together. They had planned it carefully. He was staying the usual stopover time of one night, flying back on the 18.30 flight the next day. Nothing unusual, nothing out of the ordinary.

She showered. She checked her bag twice. Everything was ready. She went into the street and ate something soupy with rice, checking her watch every few minutes. Finally, she decided to go. Martin would meet her in the park at 17.45.

The rain had departed and the afternoon was dewy fresh, a light wind blowing, the sun casting long shadows under the trees. She walked quickly down Lorong Makam and glanced at the house as she passed onto the bridge. The 'For Sale or Rent' sign was gone.

She sat on a bench in the park and stared at the back of the houses. It was 17.15. She rose and began to pace along the edge of the trees. Some children with their maid came screaming down the path and made for the playground a few minutes away. 17.45 came and went. As the hands of her watch crept towards six o'clock, Maria rose. Where was he?

She looked into her bag again. The three injection pens were prepared. The etorphine had been brought in by Martin on one of his flights. It was easy. The veterinary drug was so powerful, only the tiniest amounts were required. A drop on human skin would kill instantly.

'Maria.'

She turned and cried out in relief. She fell into his arms. He smoothed her hair and waited.

'Martin, thank God.' Martin released her. He took her hand.

'It's time, Maria. Where the offence is, let the great axe fall.'

Chapter 9

The house was quiet. It felt empty. Martin and Maria exchanged a glance. Martin went to the door and rang the bell. Nothing happened. Then the front door opened slowly and Stella looked outside. When she recognised Maria, she came towards the gate, standing silently, motionless.

Maria was amazed at Martin's reaction. He looked at Stella.

'Well. Are you proceeding with this matter or shall we go?'

He was forceful, aloof, lawyerish. He looked at his watch and pursed his lips. Pearl appeared on the doorstep.

'Have to wait my husband. My husband say wait him come *lah*,' she said. Martin looked over Stella to Pearl.

'Mrs Lim, is it? Are we proceeding?'

Martin took an envelope from his pocket and waved it at her. His voice took an angry tone. Maria realised he knew exactly what he was doing. He had watched these women more than her. He knew them. He knew they were weak, that they would do what a man ordered. That they had stood watching as Flora was beaten and murdered. He hated them even more than she did.

'Are you wasting my time?'

When Pearl hesitated, he put the envelope back into his pocket and turned. He took Maria's arm and began to walk away. At the sound of the key in the lock he smiled grimly.

'OK, OK. Come. Wait my husband.'

Martin and Maria glanced at each other. They turned back. The gate was open. Stella closed it carefully, put the key in her pocket and went ahead with Pearl. The instant the front door closed, Maria took one syringe into her hand. She was no longer nervous. This was the clinical part and it was easy. Stella was trailing Pearl. Maria plunged the needle into her back and pushed. Martin lowered her deftly to the floor. Within a few seconds, Maria had put the second needle into Pearl and her body slumped to the floor.

These disgusting women were gone. She had not the slightest feeling for them.

'We should move the bodies now,' Martin said. Maria looked at Martin.

'What about Cyril?'

'We'll get him later. The turd.'

'No,' Maria said and her voice filled with alarm. 'Don't underestimate him. You haven't seen him close up. He's smarter than you think.'

Martin shrugged, took the key from Stella's pocket, opened the gate and peered out into the street. He came back and draped Stella's skinny limp body over his shoulder. Maria raced ahead, along the culvert and opened the lock, pushing in the door. Martin rolled Stella inside. It took no more than a minute. Pearl was heavy. They had to carry her, armpits and feet, swung between them. Maria kept darting glances all around. It wasn't until Pearl was inside the factory that she stopped to breathe in relief.

She was about to speak when they both heard it. A noise. Someone was inside the factory! The sound of movement came to them from the vast black depths.

Maria looked at Martin. She opened her hands, indicating that her bag was not with her. He shook his head. She had left the bag with the final syringe inside the house. She made a plunger motion with her hand and shook her head. He understood. He motioned her to go, cracked open the door and peered outside. Maria hesitated. She didn't want to leave him. They were both certain that it was Cyril inside the factory. He pushed her outside and closed the door quietly.

Maria had never run so fast in her life. It was getting dark. She stopped and flattened herself against the wall. Something was wrong. She was certain she'd shut the gate after taking Pearl outside, and now it stood half open. Maybe she'd made a mistake. The mind played tricks. She ran the scene back in her head but before she could come to any conclusion, suddenly a light went on in the courtyard and, before she could move, Cyril Lim appeared in the gateway. She saw her bag in one of his hands. In the other was the unused syringe. There was no time to think of anything sensible.

From the darkness she shot out a hand and grabbed his wrist. He dropped the bag and syringe to the ground. He grabbed Maria's arm and pulled her into the courtyard. He was much stronger than he looked. The back of his fist landed hard against the side of her head. She felt an explosion of pain in her ear and cheek, and fell to the earth with a loud cry.

He stood over her. 'Where's my wife? Who the fuck *are* you?' He was screaming.

Her bag was lying by the gate. Her head was ringing from the blow. She tried to get up but her neck felt wobbly. She could see the syringe lying just out of her reach.

Cyril came close and stared down at her. 'Who the fuck are you?'

She saw his foot go back. He was going to kick her in the ribs. She flinched. She was going to die like Flora. No! The word screamed inside her head. She scrambled and pulled towards the syringe. As her fingers clutched it, she saw Cyril's leg go back, his knee bend and heard the roar of his anger. She rolled into a ball and closed her eyes. But his foot never reached her.

'You fucking monster,' Martin said.

Maria opened her eyes and saw Cyril sprawled on the ground. She watched as Martin quickly pulled Cyril to his feet. Martin was young and strong. Cyril was like a rag in his hands. Martin pulled back his fist and struck Cyril in the stomach. Two heavy body punches. He dropped to the floor and groaned, blood coming from his mouth.

Martin came to her and helped her up.

'You all right?'

Maria made a quick medical examination of herself. 'OK. Big bruise and swelling tomorrow but nothing broken. If he'd landed his kick … thank God you came.'

'The noise in the factory? It was goddamn owls. A lot of the windows upstairs are broken.'

They both stood and looked at Cyril. He was wiping his mouth and staring up at them. Martin went forward, grabbed Cyril under the armpits and dragged him into the house. Maria locked the front gate, picked up her bag, put the syringe inside and followed, shutting the door.

Cyril had got to a sitting position, his back to the wall.

'Who are you? Why?' His voice was rasping.

Martin took a step forward and slapped his face hard.

'You stupid dumb fuck. Who do you think we are? You killed Flora, our sister.'

Cyril held his face and stared at Martin and Maria.

'Accident. It was an accident. I paid. I went to prison. I'm sorry, I'm sorry.'

'Accident. You piece of shit,' Martin yelled at him. 'Torture, murder? Shut the fuck up,' Martin pulled back his fist again. Cyril cowered. Maria put out her hand to Martin's.

Martin lowered his fist and stared at Cyril.

'Shall we torture him, Maria? Like he tortured Flora? A couple of hours. Crack his bones. Get something sharp and hot to fry his skin.'

240

Cyril let out a load groan.

'No, please. Please.'

Maria looked down at him. 'Why, Cyril? Why did you treat her that way? She was just a little girl.'

She felt a sob in her throat.

Cyril shook his head. This was the question she wanted answered.

'She was here. I didn't mean to kill her.'

Maria nodded. Of course, it was as simple as that. Day by day, her powerlessness, her availability for degradation were there, too tempting to pass up in his sick brain.

Maria took the surgical gloves from her bag and handed one set to Martin. They put them on carefully. Cyril's eyes opened wide. Then Maria took the syringe from her bag. Cyril flinched and let out a cry.

'Pearl is dead, Stella is dead. It's quick. Too quick really.'

Maria looked at Martin.

'No more. Let's finish it.'

Martin nodded. Cyril let out a high-pitched scream and began to scramble along the floor. Martin went up to him and placed his foot on his back, holding him in place. Cyril's legs and arms were flailing. He looked exactly like what he was. A squashed cockroach. Maria plunged the needle into his spine and he stopped moving.

Chapter 10

The disposal went according to plan. They worked through the night. The monsoon was obliging and poured down for hours,

241

flushing the remains down the culvert and into the violently raging drain. It was enjoyable, the clinical removal of limbs and organs, and so easy. She particularly relished the cutting up of their sick, pathetic brains. Once she'd got the hang of it on stringy Stella, Pearl and Cyril were quick. When the light began to glow, it was done.

They washed the bloody plastic sheets and their suits, cut them up into smaller pieces and put them into bags, washed and tied up the instruments for disposal, flushed the pits and holes with rainwater, filled them in and replaced the concrete slabs. The petrol canisters were emptied down an old drain and left by the door. The generator was sacrificed, pulled apart and packed into smaller plastic bags. The wheelbarrow was cleaned and left in a far corner of the building. The grinders were sluiced with rainwater, then sprinkled with earth and left to resume their rusty state. Everything was laid ready inside the door. Over the next few days, Maria's job was to quietly dispose of every incriminating item in the factory.

They left the factory and walked to the house. They were both stinking hot and in need of coffee and food but there was one more thing to do. They got out their fresh clothes and shampoo and both took a shower in the dirty bathroom, careful to flush away all traces of their passage. They wiped down the shower, poured bleach down the drain and packed their dirty goods in the sports bag. Then they put on fresh gloves and filled a fresh bag with some of the clothes from each bedroom. They found the Lims' paperwork, their identity cards and passports. They found whatever money there was, not much, two cash cards and family photos. These went into the sports bag too.

Maria took the holy water Martin had brought from the

church where Flora was buried. Together they sprinkled it in her small room, the kitchen, the bedrooms, everywhere. To cleanse her spirit from every corner of this foul house. Then they went to the courtyard where the lofty branches of the trees floated against the morning sky. The rain had cleansed the world and the rays of the sun began to filter through the leaves. Maria and Martin sank to their knees and put their hands together in the Nunc Dimittis.

'Lord, now let your servant depart in peace, according to your word;

For my eyes have seen the salvation which you have prepared for all peoples.'

Martin locked the gate and they walked quickly away. On the main street, Martin gave the key to Maria.

'Don't go back. This is in case you need a place to hide. But don't go back, Maria. Three days and you leave.'

Maria kissed Martin and they hugged. He hailed a taxi, threw the two bags on the seat and was gone. Maria knew Martin would dispose of everything in Manila.

Epilogue

Getting rid of the stuff had been tiring and boring but had gone without a hitch. Twice a day she took a bag of plastic and bits of the generator and distributed them into dumpsters here and there. Random and unconnected bus stop rubbish bins were a favourite for the smaller surgical instruments which she'd crushed with the sledgehammer into unrecognizable metal. When she was done with the sledgehammer, she slipped into one of the disused industrial

243

units and dropped it and the plastic canisters into a dark corner. The saw was a bit of a problem. In the end she decided it was fitting to drop it into one of the big reservoirs, along with the petrol tank of the generator. The kitchen chopper, cleaned with bleach, she simply left by the back door of the hawker centre which Neo and the Lims had frequented. The idea of food being prepared with it appealed to her.

She gazed down as the plane swept along the south coast of Singapore, watching until it faded into blue haze. She touched the yellowing bruise on her cheek which was beginning to hurt. She opened her bag to get the tube of anaesthetic ointment and her fingers felt metal. She took out the key to the gate of the house on Tomb Lane. She'd never really looked at it before. It was old-fashioned, and the wide head and slender body had something of the look of a cross. It was fanciful, she knew, but it pleased her to think it.

'Hail, Flora, full of grace, the Lord is with Thee,' she said silently. She put the key back into the inner pocket and closed the zip.

When the stewardess came, she smiled and ordered a Bloody Mary.

Singapore-based DAWN FARHAM is the author of three historical novels set in Singapore, *The Red Thread*, *The Shallow Seas* and *The Hills of Singapore*, published by Monsoon Books, and an Asian-based children's book, *Fan Goes to Sea*, published by Beanstalk Press, Kuala Lumpur. She is working on a crime fiction series set in Western Australia as well as several screenplays, for which she has received grants from the Singapore Film Commission. Website: *www.dawnfarnham.com*.

The First Time

Carolyn Camoens

The aroma of lamb biryani crept up the stairs and lingered with the scent of cardamom, cloves and chillies, making the house feel warm even though the air-conditioning had chilled the house to near arctic temperatures.

The laughter and clink of glasses had died down, but the music continued to serenade them. When she thought back to that night, she remembered how the kitchen bore the evidence of the evening's activities—and its descent from civility. In a corner, soup bowls were stacked neatly on a tower of side plates, spoons resting in the bowl at the top of the pile. In the sink, dinner plates and cutlery lay where they had been dumped. The turn the evening had taken by dessert was clear, as the crystal glasses lay callously strewn over dinner dishes, the delicate stem of one snapped where it had borne the brunt of an empty bottle of champagne that had also been tossed into the sink. On the white counter, rings of red wine, from glasses that had been filled with the urgency of greed and impatience.

The kitchen light went out and darkness veiled the chaos that would greet them in the morning. In the living room, a similar sort of disorder—glasses everywhere and bowls of *muruku* and *papadum* softening after hours of languishing in the open.

From upstairs, she heard the music stop and, soon after, the sound of the living room door closing. He only did that on nights like this, when he wanted to deny the aftermath of the evening. Otherwise, he preferred to leave the door open. He believed that an open living room door was a constant sign that a home and the family who lived there welcomed guests. Good impressions meant the world to him, even when there was no one around to impress. Illusions were the order of the day.

The sliver of light beneath the bedroom door dimmed slightly as he flicked a switch on the staircase landing.

She ran her fingers through her hair, pulled the locks back into a ponytail and then changed her mind and shook them loose again. Tugging gently on the belt of her worn terry cloth robe, she undid the knot and shrugged out of it. The small pink flowers in the pattern were beginning to lose their colour and the sleeves were now a bit short for her. She relished the thought of crawling under the covers, anticipating the dreams she'd enjoy that night.

Lying still, she waited for the warmth to fill her bed. She breathed deeply, taking in the rosemary, but also the cigarettes he smoked and the aftershave he wore too much of. Together the smells formed a slightly heady mix that she breathed in, wondering if all men wore the same scent. She would, over time, come to develop an elimination process based on the memory of this scent.

Thinking back on the evening, she recalled the chatter and cheer. She later understood that they were actors and this was what they did best. They put on a play: a demonstration of unity so convincing they had everyone fooled. Sometimes, they even fooled themselves a little.

She had often wondered why they put themselves through the charade. Later, she reasoned that they liked losing themselves in their own fantasy of bliss, even if it was just for an evening. In the morning though, the sun would throw light on reality: dirty dishes, broken glass and shattered dreams.

She heard a click, and the corridor light was extinguished. She turned on her side and closed her eyes. All was still in the house that a mere hour ago was heaving with the energy of drunken revelry, licentiousness and the crude, hurried flirtation that happens as a party draws to its close.

He did not falter—neither from all the drink nor from hesitation. He knew what he was doing when he turned the door knob and entered her room.

She didn't hear him come in, even though she had not been asleep for very long. His weight on the edge of her bed woke her and she turned as he reached out and touched her hair.

Facing him, blinking to focus, she felt him stroke her forehead, pushing the hair from her face. Then he bent down and kissed her just above the bridge of her nose. Brandy and cigars—another illusion among many the evening had presented. Those luxuries were strictly reserved for performance nights, but the audience would never know from his generosity. That was part of his clever guise of abundance.

He stroked her hairline, occasionally twirling a soft lock around his fingers. She looked into his eyes and when, for the first time, she saw right through him, she knew. He had looked at her many times before, stroked her face and hair too, but something was different now.

Suddenly, the warmth of the bed she had sought earlier became too stifling and she started to breathe a little harder. She could feel the heat rise from her skin, lifting the strawberry scent of the soap she used into the air.

Then it happened. Holding her face with one hand, he rested his weight on the other and leaned down and kissed her lips ... softly first, then passionately. She closed her eyes. It was instinctive, like everything else that was to follow. It seemed like her senses began to shut down, and it occurred to her that she now understood how silence could be deafening.

He stroked her neck, her shoulders and the top of her arm, all the while kissing her. Then he pulled the duvet back. She lay still as his hands roamed over her body. The skin on his hands was dry and calloused, scratching her soft skin. Then he put his hands under her small arms and lifted her, whispering to her to sit up. When she did, he undid the small teddy bear-shaped buttons on her pyjama top. She heard him say she was beautiful as his lips brushed her ears. Then he sat back and looked at her for a moment before touching her. She jolted, partly from the iciness of his finger against her nipple, but mostly from the growing realisation of what was happening.

He stroked her and kissed her and gently lay her down again. Beneath a veil of cold on her skin, she burned with a fever she had never known. As he reached down and touched the edge of the cotton knickers, light-headedness overcame her and her head seemed to float in her pillow cloud. They slipped off too easily and then everything was fragmented; fingers, strokes, touches.

As she felt his hand pry her legs apart, her head fell to the right and she opened her eyes for the first time in what seemed like an eternity. Past the flicker of the candle flame and out the window, her eyes strained to focus on the branch of a tree she climbed as a child.

Once, she had reached out the window and tried to pluck a mango straight off the tree. She remembered inching forward, standing on the very tips of her toes. She didn't want that mango. Not that badly. She just didn't know anyone else who could reach out of their bedroom window and pluck a mango off their very own tree. And she had to have that experience. But it continued to elude her. The mangoes always grew on the other side of the tree.

She later recalled feeling the same way that night—as the episode unfolded. It was like she was standing on the tips of her toes, trying not to fall over, reaching out for something wonderful that was just beyond her grasp.

He was panting as he moved inside her, making the sound he makes when, occasionally, the casserole was just right. It was a moan, which didn't properly describe either pain or pleasure.

The feeling that had started in her stomach was now lumped in her throat and escaped suddenly with a gasp. But that didn't surprise her half as much as the tears that ran freely down her cheeks.

She felt cheated by her body as waves of pleasure pushed past the pain to flow through her. And feeling drunk and dizzy, she tried to concentrate on behaving as she thought she should in the situation, but the situation was without precedent, and her emotions refused to be fettered.

Worse, in that most private of places, a feeling took seed and started to grow. She knew she was on the brink of something explosive, and desperately tried to stifle it. But it manifested itself like a spirit that had possessed her and completely taken over. Just beneath the pleasure, a thick layer of fear, disgust and incomprehension rose to the surface and erupted in a pained but muted sob, which teetered dangerously on the edge of nausea.

She glanced at him briefly. His eyes were closed. She quickly looked upwards and away, focusing on the luminous stars on her ceiling. He had put them there so she would always sleep under a blanket of stars. She blinked through the tears, trying desperately to focus on the stars—but they wouldn't shine for her, not that night. Her head began to spin wildly and just as she started to raise her hands to his chest, he jumped to his feet.

She didn't hear him leave, just as she hadn't heard him come in. She turned back on her side, pulling the blanket up and around her. That was the first time.

She spent the next few minutes making sure her world hadn't really caved in around her. She looked up. The ceiling was still there, luminous stars and all. The walls hadn't exploded and she wondered how that could be in the wake of the terrible thing that had just happened within them. The mango tree stood firm just outside the window, where it had always been. Even the moon was in its place. The world was mocking her it seemed, telling her that her pain meant nothing in the grand scheme of things. She might have been knocked off the axis of her own existence, but everything else remained unshaken, unmoved even. Was this what it meant to be inconsequential?

The question would haunt her all her years. Life would always be to her a party she had not been invited to. But for now, she closed her eyes to lock the world out and retreat into her dreams.

Sleep came quickly, and when she would wake in the morning, she wouldn't remember the details. But she could never forget the sound of her mother's footsteps walking towards her door, pausing briefly just outside it—long enough, she was sure, to hear the moans and sobs—and then walking away again. She was only twelve when she learnt about betrayal.

And it would take her thirty years to find the voice with which to shatter all the carefully assembled illusions of their life. Some would call her selfish for doing so. She would wonder about the ones who remained silent. Were they hiding similar scars? Or did they just understand that it was her truth and she had every right to reclaim a part of herself stolen all those years ago.

CAROLYN CAMOENS is a full-time PR consultant and part-time radio presenter. In addition to writing in her professional capacity, she has also written for film and theatre. Her short story *The First Time* was part of the programme for the Singapore Writers' Festival 2009. Its publication in this anthology marks a milestone for her as a writer.

Unnatural Causes

Richard Lord

What you should really know right up top about the private eye business is that you probably know nothing about it. All those cheap novels, those classic films you've seen about private eyes ... forget it. OK, I'm hooked on them myself, but they provide about as much useful information on this business as *Cinderella* gives you about the shoe industry.

I say all this because I myself happen to be a private eye. And let me confess something here that I never would have confessed to a client: I myself really know so little about the business. And I had been doing it quite successfully for fourteen years. But the last few months of my career taught me as much as the previous fourteen years. Then again, six months ago, I didn't know how little I knew. As superficially successful as I was.

Actually, it's not too hard to be successful as a private eye in Singapore if you're smart as hell, got a pretty sharp eye and a bit of street smarts. That's check, check, check for me; not that I like to brag all that much. But it's hard not to when you're as clever as I am.

Truth is, being a private eye in Singapore is nowhere near as difficult or as dangerous as it is in many places. The level and scope of crime is much milder here, which makes detective work in the Lion City a more easy-going affair.

A good example: one steady source of income for us is what I sometimes call 'the club-scrub detail'. What it is, I have these ongoing contracts with a number of clubs, bars and restaurants. The owners of these places get worried that their employees are cheating them by skimming some of the cream off the top. So we go in there for the scrub once a month, sometimes more often if an owner is suddenly worried there's a big skimming operation going on.

What we do is we go in and sit at the bar near the cash register. Our people will order a drink, then pay for it. Then we casually glance over at the cash register as the purchase is being rung up and see if the employee is skimming.

Here's how the skim works: you order a beer that costs, let's say, $12. You then give the person at the bar $20. He or she rings it up, then gives you, the customer, $8 back. So where's the crime? Simple: the amount the employee actually rings up is not $12, but let's say $6. That means that the employee will pocket the $6 difference and the employer will have no idea that he's been cheated. The customer gets all the change due him back, so he's not upset or complaining. In fact, the vast majority of customers have no idea what just went down, as they weren't watching. But it's our job to watch, and then to report the employee for cheating. In fact, we watch as closely as we can, trying to determine whether the employee is doing the same thing with all the customers that evening. Which he probably is.

The really clever employees will keep a little notepad next to the cash register where they jot down the amount skimmed on each purchase. That way, they can add it up easily and see how much they can lighten the cash register before they end their shift.

But we try to stop that before it gets that far. We'll call or SMS the owner or manager right there at the bar or in the toilet. The owner then makes a surprise appearance and confronts the cheating employee. Or the manager will do it. The only trouble with the latter arrangement is that the manager is often in on the embezzling, taking his cut for allowing the employee to pull it off. Sometimes the manager even initiates the whole operation. That's something else we try to determine.

As you may have noticed, I use the term 'we' a lot there. The reason is that I usually assign my full-time assistant or one of our freelancers to do this work. I take my cut as owner of the firm and give the spy the rest of the fees we earned. I save myself for the more complicated, and more interesting, assignments.

In fact, our biggest revenue-spinner for years has been spying on adulterous spouses. To be blunt, we'd be out of business if it wasn't for sexual jealousy. I think every private detective agency in the Lion City would be.

Lust, I would argue, is the number one renewable resource in Singapore. Especially lust for someone you're not married to. There seems to be a lot of cheating going on—or at least people who think they're being cheated on.

You'd think this source of income would dry up at some point. I mean, what are the permutations of adultery in a medium-sized city like Singapore? Yet every week, we have new clients finding their way to our office, or repeat customers, all with slight variations on the same sad tale: their wives or their husbands are cheating on them. Or at least, they're pretty sure they're cheating. I shake my head, assume a very sympathetic look, etched in shared pain, and start jotting down calculations of how much I should charge and stand to make from this patch of misery.

* * *

I can divide my whole career, my whole life really, into two parts: before Glenda came on the scene and after she came on the scene.

Let me make this introduction to Glenda brief: She was Chinese, was relatively tall for a Chinese lady, and when I say she was gorgeous, I am looking at six strokes of the cane for aggravated understatement.

When I first laid eyes on her there in my office, I swallowed hard. Swallowed so hard, I started choking a little. I excused myself with a hand gesture while she smiled sympathetically.

She then asked if she could sit down. 'Of course,' I replied. 'Sure. Anywhere.' As there was only one other chair in my office other than the one I was sitting in, that was not the most cool of suggestions. But this babe had really knocked me off my stride. The fact that such a woman had come to me, I was starting to think that maybe there might really be a God ... though he was something of an absentee landlord in these parts.

She introduced herself, then smiled again, looked down all demure like and said, 'I've been speaking to a few people, and I've been told that you are very possibly the best private detective in Singapore.'

I nodded politely, then replied, 'I think we're in the realm of the very possible on that one.'

'Good,' she answered. 'Because I need the very best.'

'I'll try to measure up to my reputation,' I averred. (I love that word.)

She sighed and looked away. Playing my part perfectly, I started getting my deeply concerned look ready. I was in the pre-deep concern stage, when she turned back and threw me a pained smile. My own face shifted into Concern 2.0.

'It's my husband,' she said, a hairline crack in her voice. 'What he's been doing to me.'

I am an expert at this. I've done it so many times, I should take out a franchise on it. I leaned forward, elbows plunked on the desk and put on the look of deep, total concern. 'No!' I said. 'A woman like you, and your husband's not treating you like the best thing that could ever happen to him?'

'Far from it; far, far from it.'

'What a fool,' I said, with just the right blend of disbelief and indignation. But this time, for maybe the first time in years, I kind of meant what I was saying.

'He's been cheating on me.'

'No way.'

A sad nod. 'He curses me when I confront him about it. He belittles me in front of our friends and his family. He stops my credit cards out of spite, no other reason.'

'This sounds … despicable.'

'And sometimes he even …' A choke came into her voice as her fantastic eyes started watering.

I leaned forward a few inches more. My voice was drenched in high tide concern. 'He resorts to … intense physical persuasion?'

'Very intense. I've … got bruises in places you can't imagine.'

I've got a very vivid imagination with regard to such things; that's one of the advantages of being a private eye. But I didn't want to contradict her at this point. It's good to let a new client think at the start that you don't know as much as you really do. It gives you another edge.

Let the client tell her story, that's one of the first rules you learn in this game. I nodded.

'He beats me. And not just with his fists. He uses … objects.'

At this point, she started crying. This happens a lot in my business. In fact, I'm surprised there's no severe water damage in that spot where the client's chair sits. Usually I sit there in my seat and try to calm them down; I'll pull out a bottle of mildly drinkable Scotch and pour them a big gulp. But with Glenda, I decided to be really noble. I jumped up and made my around the desk (bumping my knee badly as I made the turn) to where she sat. I was ready to put my arms around her and comfort her ardently. But she raised a hand and told me it was alright. I winced slightly and limped back to my seat.

'So that's why you came here. You want me to …' I wasn't sure if she wanted me to get proof of his philandering or his manhandling. Either one would get her a signed-and-sealed divorce with no trouble. The two things together, she'd probably be looking at two-thirds of everything this bastard had, including his balls. And I would get my own juicy taste on part of that amount. (Though I'd pass on his balls.) I was waiting for her to tell me what she wanted, my Terms of Agreement within a few fingernails of my reach. And then she hit me with a bombshell.

She nodded as if this next sentence was the most obvious thing in the world. 'I want you to kill him for me.'

This broke my composure. For maybe five seconds. Then I decided that this must be, like, a metaphor for picking the bastard clean. I smiled; I figured I was looking at a sizeable fee on this case.

'And by "kill him", you mean ...'

Her look suddenly got mean. 'I want him dead. I want to stand over his grave, look at that thick carpet of fresh dirt and spit down on him.' She paused for a moment, then sobrely intoned, 'He has no right to be alive. I want you to kill him for me. Either yourself or one of your agents.'

I couldn't make any sound for the next moments. I gurgled a bit, then started getting some words out. 'Mrs ... Lee. I don't think you understand the nature of my business. I'm involved in private investigation. I can get you all the incriminating evidence you want about his husband of yours. But this thing, this ... killing people is just not one of the services I offer.'

She had a very disappointed look at this revelation. It was full of hurt really. It almost broke my heart. She looked up. 'Can you recommend someone else at least?'

'Mrs Lee, this is Singapore. We are very civilised here. We are mostly law-abiding people. We have very strict laws here against killing people—even abusive spouses. And I don't see those laws being changed anytime soon. I'm sorry. I really wish I could help you, but ...'

'I understand,' she said as she eased herself out of her chair in a seductive manner. 'I guess I was being unrealistic in my expectations.' I nodded. I felt like I was watching ecstasy about to slip out of my office—and my life. She turned, but then she turned around again. 'Let me give you my card anyway. If you find some way that you can help me, just give me a call. The number on the back. That's a second phone, and I use a SIM card on that one.'

I smiled in admiration. 'Can't be traced.'

'Can't be traced. Well, thank you, Mr Lozario. I appreciate all your concern and helpful information here. Maybe the next time I need your help, it will be with some service you can provide.'

'I would certainly hope so.'

She turned again and this time walked straight to the door and out of my life. I savoured every step, staring at her shoulder blade-length hair, her sloping back, her hips, her ass, her legs, her ass again. I stopped there, but she was out the door a second later.

After she was gone, I started to ask myself if that whole episode had really happened, the way that I just recounted it. Was she such a vision of loveliness, was she that alluring in her manner, did she really ask me to kill her husband for her? I decided that it made no difference whether it happened or not; it was a wondrous, maybe even magical, episode that I needed to fill in the empty spaces in my life.

* * *

I had been divorced for eight years at the time that Glenda walked into my office. And except for some extremely awkward episodes with prostitutes in Geylang, I hadn't had much sex during that time.

Come to think of it, I didn't have much sex in the last two years of my six-year marriage. So when I was lying in bed that night, thinking of Glenda, I ... well, let's just say that I became very grateful for the solace of my own right palm. I became grateful four times, waking up a number of times with visions of that gorgeous woman scrambling my senses.

I tried throwing myself into my work for the next three days, so I wouldn't even think about what had happened that day. Of course, the more I didn't think about it, the more I couldn't stop thinking about it. Friday morning, I decided I would just give Glenda a quick call, see how she was getting along with her problem. I was thinking of asking if we could maybe meet for coffee and explore other possibilities for dealing with that problem.

And then the phone rang and, amazingly, it was Glenda on the line. I couldn't believe it, and I decided that I had been a little unfair in my judgement of God and his dispensing of grace. I gave her a big 'hello'.

'Have you had time to consider what I asked you about on Tuesday?'

'I ... have been giving it some thought.'

'Maybe we should get together and see what's possible.'

'I think that's a very good idea. When are you free?'

'My husband is off on a "business trip" this weekend. I don't think he's going to be too lonely on this trip.'

'I see.'

'So I thought maybe we could meet for a drink this evening, discuss the whole matter, from start to finish.'

'I think that's an excellent idea. When and where?'

We made arrangements to meet on another part of the island, a corner where people who go places don't go very often. After one drink, she suggested we go back to my place and continue our discussion. I did not raise any substantial objections and tried my hardest not to speed that much as I drove back to my condo complex. When I got there, the guard, who I have done a number of serious favours for, waved me in and didn't even cast a glance at who was sitting next to me. That's another advantage of being a private eye.

OK, I admit that I don't have a lot of major experience in sexual encounters, but that first evening with Glenda was fantastic to say the least. Not only was she three times as gorgeous without her expensive clothing, but she was amazing in bed, a gold-medal Olympian as far as I'm concerned. And I was myself at the peak of my performance, which I attribute mainly to her.

Afterwards, we lay there, staring out at the next pastel-tinted building, stroking palms. My breathing was just getting back to normal when she sighed, turned and nuzzled her face into my chest. I immediately realised this had to be one of the peak moments of my earthly existence. Then she started speaking, her face still on my chest, nibbling lightly at the hair.

'Do you think you might be able to help me get rid of my husband? It would be so much easier for us to get together like this if he were out of the picture.'

'I'm sure it would be.'

'I don't know how these things are done, but I'm sure it's a lot easier than it sounds. Especially for someone like you, who is so clever ... and works in a related field.' At this point, she had started moving down from my chest, past my slightly protruding gut, and began another form of persuasion. I breathed deeply and closed my eyes. I knew that I had just taken on a new client.

The next morning—late the next morning, I should point out—we sat at my small kitchen table sipping at our instant coffees and discussing how we should proceed with killing her monster of a husband. I did a rundown of the many pitfalls with her, the mistakes often made before and after a crime, the clues criminals inadvertently leave behind.

'But you know all these things. You're a master of the field. You're the best. That's why I came to you in the first place. And, I have to admit, I'm so glad I did; for many reasons.' I nodded and told her that I would work out a plan.

She had a lot of things to do that day, but asked if she could drop by later. I of course told her I would cancel all my other appointments and would gladly entertain her later. I spent much of the evening hours watching TV, but she arrived shortly before midnight. And it was another night of high ecstasy. She and I were clearly partners now.

Her husband returned Sunday evening, so she didn't come over. On Tuesday, she came to the office and dropped off a helpful packet with photos, maps, etc. to help me track her husband. I smiled. Usually I just follow a cheating spouse and shoot them with my phone camera. This time, I was thinking, I might have to shoot him with a revolver. And that was starting to worry me.

I also have this standard contract which I sign with new clients after filling out the specific brief the client wants me to handle. This time, of course, I dispensed with that part of the deal. I would just have to trust her.

On Thursday evening, I got down to the fieldwork on this case. Glenda told me that her husband was meeting a business client that evening, supposedly, but she was sure he was actually out there doing the dirty on her.

As I already mentioned, I do have one full-time assistant on the payroll along with several freelancers, two of them fairly reliable. They are near essential in tracking a suspect. I say that in all sincerity. But on this job, I couldn't use any of them; I just couldn't risk them finding it oh so convenient that a guy we were trailing suddenly ends up comfortably dead. As difficult, and dangerous, as it is to go solo on a tracking exercise, I had to do it.

I eased my Audi into a narrow corner not far from his Merc in the park house and waited for him to come out and head off to his assignation. Which he did after only a short time, for which I was grateful. Self-employed cheating spouses generally do make the easiest targets; they've got more control of their time and are far more punctual.

So Mr Wee headed off, took the Mount Pleasant Flyover, hit the PIE, then turned around after a short stretch and headed back to where he had got on the PIE. At the end of all this, he ended up about ten streets from the park house where he'd started from.

From this, I deduced one of two things: either he suspected his wife had put a tail on him or he was heading off somewhere else, then got a call telling him to change his plans. My seventh sense told me it was the former, and I had to be really careful here not to show any shadow. One false move from me and he would start acting like a boy scout on a celibacy pledge.

I parked on the other side of the small street, about fifty metres from him, then watched as he climbed out and bounced off to a fancy bar. I then noted time and place in my palm-sized notebook. That done, I flipped the switch on my car stereo to start playing my audio book where I'd left off. The book? A Stephen Leather classic. I love those books.

I thought I might be able to rip through several chapters on this watch (to say nothing of bloating my fee), but my prey was evidently a fast operator. He and his lady friend emerged exactly twenty-three minutes later, obviously enjoying some joke one of them had just delivered as they strolled over to the Merc. Wee played the gentleman, holding the door for her, helping her all the way in, then leaning over to whisper something. He waddled around to the other side of the car and climbed in. He didn't have to unlock the door, which suggested that she'd done it for him; this was more than a business acquaintance.

I watched as the white Merc pulled out, then slowly pulled out myself and took after them. They drove to a condo in Upper Bukit Timah, which is where he turned in. I knew I couldn't follow them into the complex, so I pulled into a side street and parked there. I then came back, armed with another audio book, and took my sentry post against the wall of a building almost directly across from the front gate of the condo.

All I needed to confirm Glenda's suspicions was for him to be there more than a few minutes. He was there for one hour, 17 minutes from the time he drove in. He clearly was not just dropping her off and wishing her a pleasant evening. They had spent the intervening period in a room up there. Discussing the vagaries of the stock market over cranberry juice, no doubt.

But then I reminded myself this case was completely different. On this one, I didn't have to prove infidelity, piling up evidence that would stand up in a divorce court. Glenda had all she needed about the guy. What I was doing now was seeing how he operated, to get an idea of his movements and then to see how I could 'intervene'.

The more difficult part of this case was how we were going to close it. I knew we couldn't kill him in any obvious manner. If he ended up clearly murdered, suspicion would fall immediately on Glenda. She'd have to go through long periods of police interrogation, court appearances, all that crap. Though she was an admirably hard bitch, I didn't know if she could withstand a heavy police grilling. Also, the insurance companies might balk on paying out, maybe draw things out in court even longer.

No, we had to make this truly look like an accident, or death by natural causes. Luckily, Mr Wee was old enough to suddenly keel over without causing people to hoist their eyebrows too high. We just had to find the way to make it all look unsuspicious.

Over the next two weeks, I tracked Stanley Wee frequently, figuring out where he went, how he did things. I also discussed his health with Glenda, usually while in bed. I wanted to see what conditions he might have, what sort of sudden illness he might be prone to. If Wee was going to pop off just like that, it had to be from something his doctor had warned him about. And then, I had to find a way to help him pop off from that condition.

Which is why I found myself doing all sorts of research. I burrowed through more arcane reading material than in that last semester before I dropped out of law school. I had to find a good, believable accident that we could stage or some fatal health blip that we could arrange.

If I had been this determined when I was at uni, I probably would have finished, taken my degree in law and become a lawyer. And then I'd probably be defending some fool like me, I told myself in an aside.

I did a lot of the research at this Internet café across from Raffles City. I didn't want to take any chance of the authorities being able to connect the dots between me, that research and the sudden departure of Stanley Wee.

But even in the cocoon of anonymity that those Internet cafés promise, I had to be careful. This is Singapore after all, and I suspect that a flashing light goes off somewhere if you go in and google 'Ways to kill someone and make it look like an accident'. So I went through all sorts of twists and leaps to find what I wanted. Some of my research I did at the National Library. A few times, I would spend two hours at the café and the next three hours in the stacks of the Nat.

I'd quickly scratched the all too obvious solutions, like making hubby a hit-and-run victim as he crossed the street. These are the sort of deaths that arrive gift-wrapped at the door of police with a tag reading 'Highly suspicious'. But the first one I did scribble down as a possibility was a variation on another old standard: the tumble down the steps.

The way I had it, we would grease up some steps, have him do a Humpty Dumpty, then use a syringe to shoot some alcohol down his gullet. Later, we'd clean off the greased step. This would not be my first choice, but I thought it was nice as an option, a possible back up. Still, I needed to come up with some better options.

One afternoon while I was doing my library detail and really tired, about to call it a day, suddenly a short paragraph pretty much leaped off the page at me. I read it a second time, then a third, and other threads of possibilities started coming together in a grand weave. Here was the perfect solution: it brought together a great way to stage a fake fatal accident *and* a plausible method for making it look like a natural, health-related death.

Now I just needed to assemble the various elements to make it totally possible. And I found that easier to do than I thought it would be.

Let me say I was proud as hell of myself for coming up with this plan and contacted Glenda almost immediately. I said I had something important I had to show her. She suggested we hold off for a few days, until her husband flew off to Taiwan on a business trip. Then she wouldn't have to worry about contacting him or being home by any specific time. I started getting horny just hearing her mention that last bit.

Three days later, at 10.16 in the morning, she called. We arranged to meet near my place. About nine hours later, she climbed into my car and we went back to my apartment.

She looked so fucking irresistible that evening. She had on a dark blue dress with a white, frilly collar. She was made up beautifully. I started telling her about all my research and my practical assembly of the goods, but halfway through my Tuesday doings, she suddenly stretched her hand out and put it to my lips. 'I want you,' she whispered. 'I've been wanting you so bad these last few days. Let's make love. We can talk about all these other things later. They'll wait.'

She didn't get a big fight with me on that proposal. A minute later, we were in the bedroom, two minutes after that in the bed, naked. And it was fantastic. I felt like I was the luckiest stiff on the planet. Yes, pun intended.

A half an hour later, we were back in the kitchen nook having coffee and going over what I was sure was a brilliant plan. I brought out my jacket, pulled out a shadow-blue handkerchief, unfolded it and carefully spread it out on the table between the coffee cups and the sugar bowl.

'What's this?' she asked, not unexpectedly.

'It's the instrument we use to wipe up this whole matter.'

She kept staring down at it, as if there was something there in the cloth itself she was missing. 'What? You're going to strangle him with that? Or stuff it down his throat and choke him to death?'

'Nothing so difficult.' I filled the pregnant pause with a big grin. 'But we also need this to finish the matter.' I had pulled out a small green vial and placed that next to the handkerchief.

'And this is ...?'

'A very potent chemical compound. It's called ... well, I need a pronunciation guide just to come up with an approximation. The only thing we really need to know is that when Stanley inhales it for just maybe ten seconds, he will go into something resembling a coronary or a seizure. Something not at all unlikely for a guy of his age and ruthless disregard for his own wellbeing. Now the seizure itself would not necessarily be fatal, but we will see to it that he has it while close to a heavy piece of furniture.'

'Like one of those horrendous, macho desks he has in his office.'

I nodded. 'Precisely. He will then fall backwards, hit his head hard against said piece of macho furniture and it's all over. Stanley rolls out the final credits, and you are free of him forever. Death will have done you part. And it's all natural causes.'

Glenda sat up straight and gave me this big, high-beamed smile. 'We're really going to be able to do this, aren't we? We're really going to get rid of him?'

This made me stop for just a moment and reconsider. The last week and a half, it had all been a kind of game, like those video games kids play. Now I had to face up to the fact that what I was planning was a murder. A murder. I was really going to be accomplice to a most serious crime, ending the life of another human being. Accomplice, hell; I was going to be the main perpetrator.

'We are going to do it, aren't we?' She then slid her leg all the way under the table and ran her foot up my leg, from the ankle to the knee. She then ran it back down again, stroking the leg in a wonderful near-masturbatory manner. And she accompanied this with a pleading look, like a child asking whether she was going to get that very special Christmas present this year. I couldn't say no.

I couldn't say yes either, so I just nodded. I then looked more deeply into those alluring eyes than I'd ever done before and nodded again, resolutely. The eyes led the rest of her face in regaining the smile. 'Thank god! I'm going to be rid of him. I think I may just fall in love with you!'

I didn't need to hear that, but it sort of sealed the deal.

I smirked proudly: this fall-and-head-slam against the furniture seemed like a perfect arrangement, especially as Glenda had once explained that her husband's taste in furniture ran towards strong, heavy desks and tables.

'And where did you get the chemical?' she asked as she shifted her chair and grabbed me around the elbow.

'A chemist I know from another case. He works for one of these big pharmaceutical places. Very smart guy. And I did him a really big favour once.'

'What? You discovered his wife was cheating on him?'

I paused and swallowed. 'No. I *didn't* discover that he was cheating on *her*, even though I caught him in the act.' She gave a frown of confusion. 'I decided to let him off with a warning.' I shrugged. 'He was a nice guy. I didn't think it was right to serve up his genitals on a plate, especially since his wife was part of the problem.'

I thought Glenda would be annoyed to hear this; you know, female solidarity and all that crap. Instead, she gave me this nice, warm smile. It probably proved to her that I had a feel for moral ambiguity and sometimes placed something else above duty and money.

Anyway, back to dispatching Stanley Wee. Now we just had to fall back into watchful waiting. We had to spring a couple of traps and see which one the rat went to first. But somehow, I had to meet up with him at his place of real business, then overpower him, force the handkerchief soaked with chemical compound against his mouth and nose, then slam his head hard against the desk. And it had to be done right. No forensics team would buy the tale that he had slipped once, tried to get up, slipped and slammed his head a second, and then maybe a third time.

I finally got in touch with Wee's office (from an untraceable landline phone) and arranged a meeting for three evenings later. He set it up for his second office, the one at the edge of Chinatown. Perfect spot for a murder, I thought. I was starting to feel really good about this project.

A half an hour before our scheduled meeting, I was parked on Club Street, keeping an eye on Mr Wee, who was in a bar building up some vigour for our assignation. Clouds were pulling in from the east and it looked like a nasty rain coming. Not before the murder, I was hoping, as it's a pain in the butt tailing someone in a heavy rain. OK, we had that appointment, but that didn't mean he would show up.

I was sitting there too nervous to even put on my audio book. I again checked to see that the vial was secure in its box, up straight, stopper in tight. I reached over, folded and unfolded the handkerchief for about the fifth time that evening.

Staring out my window, I started cursing Wee for not coming out and heading back to his office a little bit early. I wanted to get on with this. I had to admit … I was scared about what I was about to do, terrified really. I mean, I was bigger than Wee, stronger than him and about twenty years younger than him. But things can always go wrong. You never know with these older, flabby types. He might go into panic, start flailing wildly, and land a lucky jab to the ribs. Or poke to the balls. Sometimes that flab can pack a lot of force. I had to be careful *and* good.

Then it struck me: as scared as I was about anything going the least bit wrong, I felt so … so incredibly alive. And that's when it truly sank in: The money, the sex with Glenda, all that was great … but the hook that sank deep in my soul and pulled me in, made me love this assignment, was that fantastic charge I got from it.

Before Glenda, my work had become one long stream of chronic boredom, relieved by some laughs and amusement. I was truly burnt out before she entered my life. The fact that she was the most gorgeous women I'd ever met just made everything that much better, that much easier. But it was the return of the thrill, the thrill I got in the first months, maybe the first year of my career as a private eye. That was now back; back stronger than I'd ever remembered it, in fact.

Sitting there, I finally grasped this quintessential truth: I was going through with this insane mandate because it made me again know what it meant to be alive and to love what I was doing, and to know how long I had missed those feelings.

When I peeked quickly into the rearview mirror, I saw that there was this jowl-to-jowl smile slapped on my face. But then I noticed something else, and I was slapped back to reality. I had been so hopped up by this adrenaline surge lately that I had let my usual caution slip. And that was a foolish thing to do, especially as I was pursuing this case solo. It struck me that I'd been ignoring one of the prime rules of private detectives: I hadn't been watching my own back.

I hauled out my pocket mirror and started looking down the street in the other direction, behind me. And that's when I saw a very familiar scowl-grey Honda parked on the other side of the street, about four cars down. I peered harder into the sideview and I knew I was right: it was Damien Ong, my main competitor, but somebody who was so way behind me in skills, expertise and experience. So what the hell was he doing in an obvious stakeout on the same street as me?

I looked closer, as close as I could. This was really a great coincidence: Singapore's two best private eyes on two different cases on the same night, on the same street. And then the painfully obvious hit me over the head: this wasn't two different cases. We were both there at the same time because our cases were intimately connected.

It was one of two possibilities at play here: either Glenda had hired Ong too, because she didn't quite trust me to do the job right … or Ong was there trailing me. I was leaning towards the former explanation, as that was the easiest to live with. But I needed to get a better idea what was going on here.

I first reached up and loosened my car light so that it wouldn't flick on when I opened the door. Then I slipped down in the seat, slid over to the other side, opened the passenger's door and slowly crawled out. I closed the door behind me and, still crouched down low, started making my way back down the street. When I was about twenty metres behind Ong, but on the other side, I scurried across the street to his side. As I started to make my way back up, luck gave me another big pucker: I saw Ong slide over to the passenger side of his car and start looking intently at something on the other side of the street. I knew immediately what his problem was: he couldn't see his prey—i.e., me—any longer.

I had carefully made my way to the car in back of his when Ong, obviously concerned, suddenly opened the door and slipped out. He took a few sneak-steps in the direction of my car and started twisting his neck, trying to see what had happened to me without being all too obvious.

He was so absorbed with finding his missing target that he didn't notice someone slipping up behind him until I was there right in back of him. I loved that moment, and every second of the next few minutes to follow.

I tapped him on the shoulder. 'Excuse me, sir, can I be of some help? You look like you've lost something.' He spun around with a look of absolute shock on his face. I returned that look with a big, triumphant smile. 'Hi, Damien. How's tricks?'

He looked and at first sounded like he'd just swallowed a small animal. After he got over the initial shock, he tried to cover up everything. 'Hey, Robert, what do you know! What a coincidence seeing you here.'

'You think?' I said. He pushed out a smile that hung limply to one side. Now I knew that I was absolutely right. This was no fucking coincidence. He was there on the same track as I was or he was tracking me. I still leaned towards the first theory and was suddenly as pissed off as I could be: he knew that I was out tracking Stanley Wee, but that bitch Glenda never let me know that there were two of us on this case.

He then threw out a few lame explanations about why he was there, but I couldn't even listen to what he was saying because I knew it was all lies. The one thing I was sure of was that tonight's big finale was postponed indefinitely. I suddenly stopped his babble by telling him I had to go see a sick friend, then turned, trotted back to my car and took off.

* * *

When I turned the corner, I saw a dark KIA swing out of a parking spot and speed up till it was about a car's length behind me. I knew this was one of Ong's assistants, but I also knew that he used incompetents so as to save money. A quick U-turn at a traffic light about to turn red, then a quick swing down a side street and I was all alone again. Ong's scout was probably sitting back at that light with his dick up his ass.

I drove straight to Glenda's office because I knew that's where she'd be. (Yeah, she had her own office in Bukit Timah, though she didn't conduct any business there except trying to look busy.) On the way, I phoned and asked her to stay there so as to dispel all later suspicions. She promised me she would. I told her I'd call her as soon as I had some big news.

When I got to her office and knocked on the door, she was there. 'Just a minute,' she called out. She probably thought it was the police or some medical personnel come to tell her that her husband had had a terrible accident. When she opened the door and saw me, she looked stunned. I pushed my way in and strode over to her desk. I plopped my ass on the shiny top and folded my arms tightly. Meanwhile, she closed the door and rushed over to me. But seeing my crossed arms and cross expression, she stopped about a foot away.

'What is it, darling? What happened?'

I think that was the first time she ever called me 'darling', but far from making me feel good, it only pissed me off more. 'Mrs Lee, I would like to know just what the hell is going on here. And I want to know exactly what game you're playing.'

She looked baffled, so I explained about seeing Ong and

confronting him, and being tailed by one of his associates, and ... I said something nasty, which I now regret.

Her look quickly passed from baffled to shocked. She swore she'd never heard of this guy Damien Ong and certainly had never hired him to do any work for her. I stared at her for about ten seconds, then realised she was telling the truth. Plus, it suddenly registered how shocked she was to see me there at the door. If Ong had also been working this case for her, he would certainly have phoned her to say I had suddenly shot off without waiting for her hubby to emerge and was probably on my way back to her.

This was bad. This was worse than the first possibility. After apologising, I explained what this meant: that Ong was trailing *me* because somebody wanted me followed. She then asked if it was possible that anyone I knew would set Damien on me. I answered with a sour nod.

'You mean, my husband then?'

'He's the only one who makes sense here, isn't it?' She clenched her gorgeous lips and, after a few moments, nodded. I then went through the ramifications of all this. The primary one was that our programme to get rid of Stanley had to be put on indefinite hold. She was not at all happy to hear that.

'So when do you think you can do it?'

I gave an enormous shrug, then looked at her sympathetically. 'Not for a long time anyway. Maybe ever. But look, we probably have enough to hold up in a divorce court; I think you should just settle for getting out through the divorce loop and pulling in a nice windfall from that.'

She shook her head, angrily. 'No, I want you to get rid of him entirely. I want you to do what you promised to do.'

'Glenda, what are you not understanding here? He has me tailed. That means I probably wouldn't even be able to get close enough to pull off that nice, neat murder we planned. And even if I could kill the bastard, they would know it was me. I would hang. And you would too, probably.'

I then offered to give back most of the retainer she'd paid me, after deducting additional expenses and a little bit for the time I'd spent. If nothing else, she had gained some valuable information: that her husband was a fairly clever bastard and he knew how to protect himself.

Her immediate response? 'You're a failure. I knew I shouldn't have trusted you. I probably should have gone to this guy Damien Ong right from the start. Then I'd most likely be free of Stanley right now.'

I started to point out all the holes in that theory, but she turned her back to me and asked me to leave.

'Glenda, look: maybe there's still some way we can—'

She wouldn't even turn around. 'Please go now,' she repeated. 'I need to be alone for awhile.'

I'm well aware that there are times you just can't reason with clients, and this was certainly one of them. I nodded and walked out. She never once turned to see me as I left. I felt like waffled shit. To make things even worse, it had started raining during my visit.

Back in my car, I decided the safest thing was to drive straight home and get thoroughly drunk. I'd try to call her sometime the next morning and see how she was feeling. Maybe she could get over her disappointment a little quicker than I suspected it would take.

After I'd driven a few streets away from her office, my mobile started ringing. It had stopped by the time I managed to pull over and see who was calling. I felt really lifted when I read an unidentified number and realised it came from Glenda. Maybe it was just a sudden surge of pique back there and now she was ready to try to work things out reasonably.

I called her back, but there was no answer. So I decided the best thing to do was to drive back and see what she wanted. Hopefully, she would still be there.

When I reached her door, I gave a knock. There was no answer, so I knocked again and called out, 'Glenda, are you still there? Come on, it's Robert.'

At that, the door opened slowly. But it wasn't Glenda who opened it. Glenda was lying flat on the floor, her legs splayed, her head flush against the heavy desk. I bolted towards her. As I did, the door slapped closed behind me.

I spun around, my hand ready to grab a heavy paperweight sitting on top of the desk which I had once admired on a previous visit; only now did I realise the basis for my admiration.

It was Damien Ong there. I should have known, right? He looked at me sympathetically, which I did not really appreciate. 'Don't leave too many fingerprints,' he cautioned. 'It's made to look like a perfect accident, but you never know how the Singapore police will respond. They can be damned clever, as we know.'

I was now clutching the paperweight, getting a sense of its shape and its heft. I decided I should smash his face in with it. But I did want to ask him a few questions while he could still speak.

'You did this? You're responsible for this?'

'No, I didn't do it. And you know who's responsible for it.'

'The same bastard who was paying you to tail me?'

He nodded, then added, with just the right subtle twist of irony, 'The bereaved widower.'

Hearing that word 'widower', it suddenly sunk it: she was not just injured, unconscious … she was dead. They'd killed her.

'How did he do it?'

Ong took a few cautious steps in my direction. 'He hired two experts in the field. A business associate of his up in KL recommended them. The two apes are themselves on their way back to Malaysia right now.'

'I hope they get front-ended on the expressway.'

He nodded. 'I wouldn't shed any tears.'

I spun around harshly. 'Hey, don't think that you're some innocent bystander on this. You've got your own claw dipped into the blood here.'

'You look at it a certain way, all of us do.' He then stared at me in a way he would have never have dared to before.

Just then, I heard this irritating sound coming from Damien. OK, I often hear lots of irritating sounds coming from him, but this was something I never heard before. He reached into his coat pocket and pulled out a mobile phone. Its ringtone was one of those obnoxious, taunting laughs. I winced. Actually, I wanted to strangle the thing.

Without even looking at the display, he said, 'It's for you.'

'For me?' He nodded and held out the phone.

I took it and clicked it on. I wasn't going to say anything until

I knew what this was all about. As I nestled the phone against my ear, a raspy voice came on. 'Hello, Mr Lozario. I'd ask "How are you this evening", but I don't think it a good question right now.' I didn't need any introduction; I knew after the first few words that I was finally hearing the voice of Mr Stanley Wee.

I asked him why he was calling me. He said we still had a few things to straighten out before we could put everything to rest. 'We've all got enough here to put us in prison for a long time. Maybe even send us to the hangman's noose. I don't think you would want to go to the police now and tell them how you and my wife came to know each other so well.'

'So you think you'll get away with this thing, not pay at all?'

'Well, that's the whole point here, isn't it? It's what you were planning on. Besides, let's be honest here: you of all people who are still with us know that what I did could just be seen as self-defence. The deceased was trying to kill me; I just did what I had to do to save myself.'

'You could have just reported us to the police and stopped it right there.'

'Oh, but what would be the fun in that? Come on, Mr Lozario, you've got to appreciate the element of sport in all this.' I winced, realising that what he was talking about was akin to that adrenaline rush I got from the project.

'Anyway, I'm sure it would be best for all of us involved if we just leave things as they are—a terrible accident claims the life of a somewhat young and so beautiful woman. Any refinement on that could just sink us all.' He paused for a moment, and I swear I could hear a supercilious smile on his face. 'Don't you agree?'

I can't remember when I had ever felt like such a shit. 'Yeah. Yeah, I agree.'

'Splendid. By the way, in a few days, your friend Damien will drop by your office with a little something from me. A nice little sum of money.'

'Keep your money. I didn't do anything for *you*.'

'Oh, let's call it a finder's fee then. You helped us find Glenda this evening so that we could finish everything off quickly and cleanly. And, in a certain way, you helped me find the solution to my problem. Anyway, you did save me a lot of money, Mr Lozario. I don't even want to think what a divorce from that bloodsucker would have cost me. I just want to express my gratitude. And I always express best with money. Good evening, Mr Lozario.'

And right there, he hung up. I gritted my teeth. Just from having that three-minute conversation with Wee, I felt like I needed to climb into the shower and stay there for about a week to get all the slime off me.

I also found myself getting nauseous from the sight of Glenda lying there. I was just getting comfortable feeling very sorry for myself when the phone rang again. 'This one's for me,' Damien said, and held out his hand. I handed him the thing as if it were a radioactive turd.

'Yeah. That's right. Yeah, he ... seems to be fine with all that. I know. Of course, of course; I know. Yes. Right after I hang up here.' He hung up, then held up the phone.

'Got to trash this thing. Totally. No trace it ever existed.' He shook his head. 'It's only been used a few days, maybe four or five calls, and I've got to destroy it. And that was planned right from the start. The same with that phone he just called us on. But look at his thing: top of the line model. You know how much one of these things costs? To use four or five times, then trash?' He shook his head and gave that rodent-like laugh he has. 'Some people in this world just have too much money.'

I shook my head. 'Can't buy them happiness.'

'Maybe not. But it can flush away a lot of misery.' He put the phone back into his pocket. 'Anyway, that's a world you and me will never squeeze into. Or ever really understand.'

I smirked and started to think that's what makes me a much better detective than Damien Ong. I could understand that world. But then I stopped ... and wondered if I really could. Maybe that's why Damien had topped me this time: he understood what he couldn't understand.'

I turned to look back at Glenda. This time, I noticed that one of her shoes was off, the heal broken loose. A few inches away there was this long, shiny cylindrical object. I bent down to check it out.

'It's her mascara. Don't touch it, it's clean at the moment.' I rose and gave him a weary scowl. 'So there you've got it: a gorgeous women slips on her own make-up stick, hits her head on her designer desk and kills herself.' Here he took a sniff of the chilled air. 'Oh, the horrible irony of it all.'

I stared, wondering where this O-level washout had suddenly managed to pick up a sense of irony. Reading the same books I did?

I turned back and started to move towards her again. I wanted to touch her once more while there was still a little bit of warm there. Damien grabbed my arm and tugged. 'Come on, Robert. You can't do anything more for her. And the longer we stay here, the bigger the chance we'll get caught at the scene. It's over; he won.'

He tugged again and this time, I let him pull me away. But just after I stepped outside, I turned once more and took another look. She seemed to be rested, almost contented. I felt sad, sick and useless.

Wearing a glove, Damien pulled the door shut. I breathed deeply a few times, and then we started down the corridor to the stairs. (There was a CCTV camera facing the lifts downstairs.) We said nothing to each other all the way down to the ground floor. Then he turned to me. 'Sorry it had to end this way. I swear I had no idea he was going to kill her till he called and told me she was finished. I handled this like just another pre-divorce thing.'

I nodded, not really believing him. 'So when did you start tailing me, Ong?'

'She stayed the night at your place. About a month ago. I don't know if that was the first time, but it was the first time I was watching you.'

'You must be getting much better. I had no idea you were on me.' He shrugged, a smug little smile on his face. Right at the side door of the building, he spoke again.

'Did you have feelings for her?'

I stared out straight; his was not the face I wanted to see just then. 'Having feelings for a client violates the second rule of being a private detective.'

'You know it.'

We stepped out of the building and started walking down the street. He walked me all the way to my car, though his was around the corner, in the other direction. Just as we got to my car, he spoke again.

'What's the first?'

He'd caught me off guard. 'First what?'

'First rule of the private detective?'

'Never think you really know too much about this business. Never.'

I nodded, pushed him aside gently, and climbed into my car. He waved goodbye as I started to drive off and I gave him a limp wave in return.

As I drove through the slick, calm streets of Bukit Timah, fighting back what some sentimentalists might see as tears, I told myself it was all just a part of the job. You never win, you never lose in this field. You just do what the clients want you to do and hope that you can still wake up half-sane the next morning. And the whole thing defies understanding.

I guess you could say private investigation's a metaphor for life. You do it because you don't want to spend too long dwelling on the alternatives. We all get to those soon enough. Quite soon enough.

RICHARD LORD is the author or co-author of eighteen published books, both fiction and nonfiction. He has published ten short stories in different anthologies and edited more than a dozen books, including anthologies, novels and memoirs. Also a playwright, Lord has seen a dozen of his plays and over fifty sketches professionally produced.

Copyright Notices

Explore Singapore Nonfiction

The following nonfiction titles, all published by Monsoon Books, are set in Singapore.

- *Country Madness: An English Country Diary of a Singaporean Psychiatrist* by Ong Yong Lock
- *Gone Troppo* by Stu Lloyd
- *In the Footsteps of Stamford Raffles* by Nigel Barley
- *Indiscreet Memories: 1901 Singapore through the eyes of a colonial Englishman* by Edwin A. Brown
- *Invisible Trade* (I & II) by Gerrie Lim
- *Pairing Wine with Asian Food* by Edwin Soon
- *Rice Wine & Dancing Girls: The real-life drama of a roving cinema manager in Fifties Malaysia & Singapore* by Wong Seng Chow
- *Singapore Girl: A true story of sex, drugs and love on the wild side in 1970s Bugis Street* by James Eckardt
- *Sold for Silver: An autobiography of a girl sold into slavery in Southeast Asia* by Janet Lim
- *Stif-fried and not Shaken: A nostalgic trip down Singapore's memory lane* by Terry Tan
- *The Boat: Singapore Escape—Cannibalism at Sea* by Walter Gibson
- *The Golden Chersonese: A 19th-century Englishwoman's travels in Singapore and the Malay Peninsula* by Isabella Bird
- *The Great Singapore Quiz*
- *You'll Die in Singapore: The true account of one of the most amazing POW escapes in WWII* by Charles McCormac

Explore Singapore Fiction

The following fiction titles, all published by Monsoon Books, are set in Singapore.

- *And the Rain my Drink* by Han Suyin
- *Best of Singapore Erotica* by LQ Pan & Richard Lord (eds)
- *Best of Southeast Asian Erotica* by Richard Lord (ed)
- *Locked Out* by Alison Lester
- *Love and Lust in Singapore* by Goodwin, Tewari & Hoye (eds)
- *Malayan Life of Ferdach O'Haney* by Frederick Lees
- *Paranormal Singapore* (Vols. 1, 2 & 3) by Andrew Lim
- *Rogue Raider* by Nigel Barley
- *Singapore Sling Shot* by Andrew Grant
- *Straits & Narrow* by Grace McClurg
- *The Hills of Singapore* by Dawn Farnham
- *The Lies That Build A Marriage* by Suchen Christine Lim
- *The Red Thread* by Dawn Farnham
- *The Rose of Singapore* by Peter Neville
- *The Shallow Seas* by Dawn Farnham

Monsoon Books titles are available from leading highstreet and online retailers worldwide as well as from *www.monsoonbooks.com.sg*.